Dead Heat

Other novels by William Murray:

TIP ON A DEAD CRAB
THE HARD KNOCKER'S LUCK
WHEN THE FAT MAN SINGS
THE KING OF THE NIGHTCAP
THE GETAWAY BLUES
I'M GETTING KILLED RIGHT HERE
WE'RE OFF TO SEE THE KILLER
NOW YOU SEE HER, NOW YOU DON'T
THE SWEET RIDE
MALIBU
THE KILLING TOUCH
THE AMERICANO
THE DREAM GIRLS
THE MOUTH OF THE WOLF
BEST SELLER
A FINE ITALIAN HAND

Nonfiction works by William Murray:

ITALY: *The Fatal Gift*
THE LAST ITALIAN: *Portrait of a People*
CITY OF THE SOUL: *A Walk in Rome*
JANET, MY MOTHER, AND ME
THE WRONG HORSE: *An Odyssey Through the*
  American Racing Scene
THE RIGHT HORSE: *How to Win More, Lose Less,*
  and Have a Great Time at the Racetrack
HORSE FEVER
THE SELF-STARTING WHEEL

William Murray

Dead Heat

Lexington, Kentucky

ECLIPSE PRESS

Library of Congress Control Number: 2005920848

ISBN-10: 1-58150-131-5
ISBN-13: 978-1-58150-131-5

Printed in the United States of America
First Edition: 2005

Distributed to the trade by
National Book Network
4720-A Boston Way, Lanham, MD 20706
1.800.462.6420

A Division of
Blood-Horse Publications
Publishers Since 1916

"Nothing is forever, not even horses."

—*The Wrong Horse*

PROLOGUE

It was very dark that night, with no moon and with wind-blown clouds obscuring the stars. It was chilly, too, and she shivered as she moved, alone and barefoot. She crept around the side of the house, trying not to make a sound. When she arrived below the lighted bedroom window, she lingered just long enough to listen to what was going on inside, behind the drawn Venetian blinds. She tried to look, but could see very little through the slats. The sounds, however, left no doubt about what was happening. She felt as if someone had grabbed her gut and twisted very hard. She could barely breathe. She backed away in horror, then turned and stumbled blindly through the shrubbery and the trees, running away from her life.

***

The sound of helicopters hovering overhead and skimming the shoreline alerted the village something was going on, that and the sirens of the police cars and the ambulances, the roar of car engines, the crunch of tires on dirt roads. Down by the lakeshore a group mostly of men, some in uniform, stood and watched as the divers worked, searching mainly along the shoreline. It was less than two hours before one of them emerged, carrying the body in his arms. Only the paramedics moved toward it. Everyone else stood and watched. Alone, his face a pale mask of grief, a tall, gray-haired man stood apart. Some of the spectators glanced at him, but no one said anything. There was nothing to say, really. It was clearly too late.

CHAPTER 1

Bones was leaning up against the wall of Jake Fontana's tack room when the girl showed up. She stood there waiting for them to notice her. The trainer was sitting at his desk but had his back turned to her because he was looking at the chart pinned to the wall behind him. He still had two horses to gallop that morning and another to work, Gamblin Man, the old gelding he almost always took out last. "Jake, you got a visitor," Bones said. Jake swung around and saw her standing in the doorway.

"Mr. Fontana?" she said. "I heard you were looking for help. Steve Bullion sent me over."

She was five-six or -seven, lean, graceful, dressed in worn jeans, scuffed brown boots, a plaid shirt, and her skin had the glow of someone used to the outdoors. A nice-looking kid, the trainer thought, but with something a little off about her, maybe in her green eyes or the set of her mouth. It was hard to tell how old she was.

"Yeah, I'm looking for someone," Jake said. "What can you do?"

"Just about anything there is to do around horses," she said. "I can groom 'em, walk 'em, ride 'em, you name it. And I've got my jock's license."

"That so? From where?"

"I started back in Utah and Nevada and Wyoming riding the fair circuits," she said. "Then I moved to the Bay Area, rode and worked up north."

"Win any races?" Bones asked.

"A few in Elko, Nevada, a couple at Santa Rosa and Stockton. It's hard to get mounts, especially down here, I know that. Still got my bug, though."

"My name's Sal," Bones said. "Sal Righetti." He stuck his hand out, and she shook it, a nice firm grip. "Some people around here call me Bones, but let's stick with Sal."

"Bones?"

"Don't ask," Jake said. "Okay, I don't need a race rider. I could use an exercise boy, sure enough. Just to gallop the horses, maybe breeze 'em, too."

"I can do that," she said. "I'm real good at that. Horses like me."

"How long have you been out here?"

"About a week. I'm trying to get started. I'll do just about anything."

"What happened up north?"

"Some personal problems. Besides they say Southern California's good in the winter," she said with very serious eyes while flashing a quick smile and nice even teeth.

"It can rain," Jake said.

"I guess I know that." She looked at him intently. "I'd sure like to work for you, if you'll give me the chance."

The trainer put his hands flat on the desktop and heaved himself upright. "Damn knee," he said. "Come on, I'll introduce you to Eduardo. What's your name?"

"Jill. Jill Aspen."

"Eduardo's pretty much in charge back here. If he says you're okay, you're in." He grinned at her, then limped around the desk and out into the shed row. He moved like a crippled old plater with a couple of bowed tendons. "I'm going to get this fixed," he said, "when I get the time."

"It's bad?"

"Could be worse. Torn something or other, but I can't do much about it now. Not in the middle of the meet."

"Anyway, you ain't running," Bones said. "Your horses are. You could be a goddamn gazelle and what good would it do you?"

"Always a kind word from Bones, right?"

Eduardo saw them coming, stepped out of the stall he'd been working in, and came shuffling toward them, rub rags in hand.

"Okay, Jill, this here's Eduardo," Jake said. The Mexican nodded, stuck out his hand, and Jill shook it. Her grip surprised him. "Jill's looking for work, Eduardo. I think we can use her, right?"

"*Sí, señor,*" the Mexican said. "Hector not coming back, and Pablo, his wife is very sick."

The trainer turned to the girl. "Eduardo'll tell you what to do." He glanced back at the groom. "Everything all right, Eduardo?"

"Yes, boss. Just two to go. And the Old Man."

"I got Leo to work him," the trainer said. He looked at the girl. "Want to get up on a horse?"

"Sure thing." Another of those quick, mirthless smiles.

"Pablo usually gallops for me, but he weighs a hundred and thirty these days and, anyway, he isn't here. What's your weight?"

"A hundred twelve right now, but I can make a hundred eight easy."

"That's good. Go with Eduardo and I'll see you at the track. The mare needs to go a mile and a half nice and easy. She's two months away, and I'm just getting some of the fat off her. She's real lazy, and she won't give you any trouble. Leo can take the two-year-old out. He's a handful. Remember now, nice and easy."

***

The early morning mist lay heavy on Santa Anita racetrack, blurring the outlines of the San Gabriel Mountains and cloaking the scene in a cool gray. Bones and Fontana leaned against the rail at Clockers Corner, cups of hot coffee warming their hands from the morning chill. There was a slight breeze, a hint of rain to come, according to the TV weatherman earlier that morning. Fontana wasn't so sure. He sniffed the air. It didn't have the feel of rain, he thought, only winter cold. Maybe it would peter out, pass them by. He had five of his charges coming up to a race, and he didn't like to work his horses on wet tracks. So far this winter he'd been lucky; the rains had held off.

Eduardo showed up. "All done, boss," he said. "That girl, she look okay on the horse."

"Leo come by?"

"Yeah. He look like shit, so I put him on the Old Man first."

"One of these days he isn't going to make it."

"Still boozing, huh?" Bones said. "Nobody wants to handle his book anymore. He's going to blow his career."

"Most of his life Leo's been a day late and a dollar short," Jake said. "It's too bad; he's got good hands."

"So did Horowitz."

"Who's that?"

"A piano player. He's dead."

"Jesus, Bones."

A few minutes later the mare came by, Jill Aspen sitting easily in the saddle, the reins in one hand, the other patting the mare's neck reassuringly. "She's nice to ride," she said, as she passed the outer rail where the two men stood.

"Remember now," Jake said, "nice and easy."

The girl clucked, and the mare moved out into the middle of the track, and then broke into an easy gallop. Jill stood high in the stirrups, leaning forward, moving as one with the mare, nice and easy, the way Jake had planned it. They swung around the clubhouse turn, with horses working hard and fast along the inside, others cantering or walking back along the outside. Steam rose from the sweat on the necks and flanks of the two dozen or so Thoroughbreds on the track.

The trainer took a deep breath and sighed. It was the time of day he liked best at the racetrack, the morning chores almost done, the feel and the sound of the horses out there in the open the way he thought God had intended them to be, even though he was equally sure God had nothing to do with it.

Bones looked for the girl and spotted her moving easily along the backstretch, still leaning over the mare's neck, the two of them in a conspiracy of skill and quiet dedication. "She looks good, Jake," he said.

"Yeah, she can ride all right," the trainer said, "but whether she can ride a green two-year-old or a tough old rogue, well, hell, that remains to be seen."

"I got to get back, boss," Eduardo said. "Two still to go." He walked away toward the gap.

Leo Di Stefano came by on the Old Man, which is what they called Gamblin Man around the stable. The horse was seven now, his glory days behind him, but he didn't know it. He still ran like a conquering fool and headed for the winner's circle after every race whether or not he'd actually won, which he often did. He was a money machine, made of old oak or hickory, hardly ever failing to bring in a check—sixty-eight lifetime starts, twenty-two wins—now relegated to the claiming ranks but still winning his share. Jake could have tried to run him cheap, maybe won even more races with him, but he kept him in against slightly better stock because he didn't want to lose him. You're not supposed to be sentimental in racing; you're not supposed to fall in love with your horses because they come and they go; they flash like comets across your sky and disappear just as quickly. But Jake Fontana had made a career of falling in love—with horses, with his wife, with the few men in his life he admired and who mattered to him. Which was why he and Bones were friends. They both thought most people were shit, not worth the cost of the dynamite it would take to blow them up. They both came from the same background and had similar values: You find the few good people you can trust and hang on to them.

"Jesus Christ, Leo, you look like shit," Fontana said, as the jockey rode up to him on the Old Man. "You sure do beat on yourself."

Leo Di Stefano's eyes, small red beacons in his ravaged face, stared back at him in the morning light. "I'm okay," he mumbled. "I got a cold last week, and I can't get over it."

"One of those eighty-proof colds of yours," the trainer said. "Why don't you stop beating on yourself? You could still win some races."

"I'm trying."

"Okay, look, I want you to breeze him a half-mile in about forty-eight, no faster. Any hint of soreness, you pull him up, right? You got that?"

The jockey nodded and rode off, the Old Man, his legs wrapped up tight as a mummy's, moving a bit stiffly under him. Jake was wondering how much longer he could hold the horse together. Five, six more races? A dozen? Not likely. More like two or three, but maybe he'd be okay. The horse kept fooling everybody. You wished you had a dozen like him. You could pay off your stable bills every month on time.

They watched Leo angle the horse out into the middle of the track, moving him easily along until he could let him go at the half-mile pole and let him run a bit. The two men took their last sips of coffee, tossed the paper cups into the trash basket behind them, and headed back to the rail to watch the girl gallop past on the mare. She looked good out there, thoroughly professional.

Steve Bullion came up beside them. He was short, stocky, with dark, greasy-looking hair combed straight back and a pawnbroker's smile on his face. "That girl come over to see you?" he asked.

"Yeah," Jake said. "I put her up on Abernathy's mare. She's out there now. She can ride. Thanks for sending her over."

"I heard you could use some help."

"Yeah, I'm short-handed. I can use her, all right. What do you know about her?"

"Not much. She was riding on the fair circuits, got a few mounts, doing all right, I guess. Moved to the Bay Area, then got into some kind of trouble and decided to get out."

"Do you know what kind of trouble?"

"I'm not sure. Personal, I guess. She was with some jock's agent for a while, I heard, then they split. After that she showed up at Bay Meadows and then went to work on the Furman place for a while."

"Paul Furman? Heritage Farm?" Bones asked.

"Yeah. After that she came down here. Lou Smith called me about her, said she could ride, groom, would do just about anything around the racetrack. I didn't have room for her."

"Hell, Steve, you got about forty horses."

"Yeah, but everybody wants to work for me. It's because I win so many races."

"Sure it is," Bones said. "It's also your charming personality."

"I almost took her on. She'd look real good on my sheets."

"You probably don't get laid a lot. Too much grease on the pillows."

"Fuck you, Bones," Bullion said. "Oh, yeah. There were rumors about her, Lou told me. She banged a couple of guys."

"Big fucking deal," Bones said. "If she were a guy, who'd give a shit?"

"You're right. But there's something else. You remember about Furman's kid drowning?"

"Yeah, what about it? She had something to do with that?"

"I don't know. Lou didn't either, or he wasn't talking. Anyway, he likes her, says she worked for him before going to Heritage and was a straight arrow."

"That's good enough for me," Jake said. "Lou's a good horseman."

"I guess." Bullion moved away from them toward the gap. "Got to get back now. If I'm not on top of them, they fuck everything up."

"That was a nice win in the San Antonio last week, Steve."

"Yeah, it was. That colt is a running fool with a brain the size of a pea, which just about matches the jockey's."

"You took Leo off him."

"I had to. That guy's in no shape to ride these days."

"All he did was win for you," Bones said.

"You can't trust him anymore. I can't risk it. He shows up in the morning looking like death warmed over. My owners won't sit still for him."

"Yeah," Jake said, "I know."

"I'll see you, Jake." He ignored Bones and shambled away toward his barn and his string of winners.

"What's his secret?" Bones asked. "He's that good? Or is he using a little moose juice?"

"No, he's good," Jake said. "Those Arabs knew what they were doing when they hired him. They leave him alone, and he wins races for them."

Fontana started his stopwatch just as Leo got the Old Man to run, a little stiff-legged at first, then looking better, stretching out those heavily bandaged legs and straining against the bit. Keeping a tight hold on him, Leo moved the Old Man slightly out from the rail and gave him his head until he hit the finish line. Fontana glanced at his watch as Leo stood up and pulled hard to bring the Old Man to a slow gallop. "Forty-eight and two, perfect," he said, "just what he needed."

The jockey looked like a plague victim, but obviously he could still ride; he could handle this old pro. "Maybe he'll come through this latest binge," the trainer said. "At least, I know the Old Man will run for him." The race was five days away, $32,000 claimers going six and a half furlongs, horses the Old Man had once horrified but that would now give him all he could handle and maybe a little more than that.

The girl came past on the mare. "She is lazy," she called out, "but she's nice to ride."

"Take her back to the barn and walk her for an hour," Fontana said. "Eduardo'll tell you what to do."

Bones turned his back to the track, leaned his bulk up against the rail and tried to will the sun to break through the cold mist. "I'm going back to the barn," Jake said. "You coming?"

"Nah, I'm going to wait for the programs to show up, then go home and do a little handicapping. Maybe I can hit another pick six."

"You still living on that money?"

"A hundred and thirty-eight grand can carry you quite a while," Bones said, letting the thought of the money warm him. "As long as I don't go crazy and buy a horse from you."

"You'll probably blow most of it back, Bones."

"No way, pal. Most of it's in a safety deposit box at Wells Fargo. I'm playing these days with the few thou I took out. When it's gone, I'll go back to work."

"You could handle Leo's book, if he sobers up."

"That kind of crazy I'm not."

Jake grinned. "You could hotwalk for me again."

"I'm afraid of horses, you know that. Big dumb beasts with brains the size of Ping Pong balls and teeth that can tear your arm off."

"You must have bluffed everybody back in Jersey, killer."

"Don't kid yourself. I was the best. Tony Ears will tell you. But it was a lousy way to live. Tony I could deal with, he was always straight with me, but the rest of the Family, forget it. Now, betting on horses, that's something else. It's clean, it's beautiful, and when the numbers all add up it's Christmas, right? If my luck turns bad, find me a good jock and I'll make him a star."

"You're on your own there," Jake said, with a small wave as he walked away. Just then the sun broke through the clouds and Bones began to feel real lucky.

CHAPTER 2

Bones hadn't worked in months, not since his last client, Tim Fortas, had gone down leaving the starting gate on the Del Mar turf course and broken his back in two places. He was still in rehab, but he was never going to ride again. He was lucky to be alive and not paralyzed; the accident, one of a dozen or so in his career, had woken him up. Tim had just turned forty-two and had saved most of his money as a successful journeyman jock. He planned to go back to his native Maryland to spend his retirement years eating softshell crabs and drinking good draft beer. Not a bad plan. As for Bones, he was in no hurry to handle anyone else's book. The roster of potentially available riders didn't look promising, and he wasn't going to work for the three or four temperamental assholes who were always looking to drop their current agents for anybody who could put them on live mounts. Then there were the boneheads, druggies, drunks, wife-beaters, cheap hustlers—jockeys like Leo Di Stefano—who would give any horse the arm to cash a bet.

Besides, he was winning at the windows. Ever since the second week of the Santa Anita meet, he'd been cashing tickets in bunches and not on favorites either. Every day, just about, he left the track with rolls of hundred-dollar bills bulging in his pockets. It couldn't last forever, as every horseplayer knew, but he was going to enjoy the run as long as it lasted—longshots, exactas, doubles, trifectas, pick threes, bang, bang, bang. The horses were running for him like little trained pigs. The streak had culminated two weeks earlier in a pick six on a carryover day that had enriched him to the tune of $138,000, after withholding taxes, on an investment of only $140. Who needed the stock market or that numbers game they call the lottery? With the horses, if you knew what you were doing, you stood a chance, because you weren't playing against the house but against your fellow players. If it weren't for the 15 to 25 percent takeout from every dollar wagered, it was a game the pros like Bones could beat consistently. In fact, he was doing it and having a hell of a good time, because what was better in life than watching a horse race? Women? No. He'd been married once, and it was like running for the finish line carrying 140 pounds of lead on your back. He liked women, all right, but as a sort of hobby. Candlelight, flowers, small gifts, a good dinner somewhere with the right wine, then in, out, and home in time to study the *Racing Form*.

He'd come a long way in this game. Once he'd managed to get himself out of the enforcement business in New Jersey and decided to stick to the horses, he'd turned his whole life around. He'd begun by keeping a low profile. He stored his operating capital in a shoebox under his bed in a series of cheap motels. He didn't want anybody from the old days to come looking for him, even though he'd gotten out clean, no loose ends, no unpaid debts. But with the Family you could never be sure. They couldn't believe it when he'd told Tony "Ears" Capestro, his capo, that he was leaving. No one else had ever done that and not wound up underground in the Jersey marshes. He'd had some uncashed chips from having once bailed Tony Ears out of a small jam, and he played them. Tony backed him, and they'd thrown him a farewell bash, with go-go dancers, a naked broad coming up out of a cake, the whole bit. It had been fun, but he was out and gone the next morning. And he didn't miss the old gang one bit. He hoped they didn't miss him, but he was careful. He slept with one eye open, always, and a piece under his bed.

He'd fallen in love with the horses early. His father had been a bookie hooked on his own racket. He'd made money on football, basketball, hockey, every other sport, but he blew his winnings on the ponies. Bones had watched his mother become bitter and remote because of his father's gambling. So he went to the track whenever he could on his own, read the *Racing Form* every night, and studied hard. He learned how and when to bet and, more importantly, when to lay off. He even tried to straighten out his old man, but his father had never seen a favorite he didn't like, the lower the odds the better. It was hopeless. After his father shot himself and his mother moved in with her sister and her husband up near Albany, that's when Bones had gone to work for the Family. It had been tough at first, but the horses kept him sane. He fell in love with a few of them—John Henry, Seattle Slew, Affirmed, Secretariat, Sunday Silence—but he never let sentiment get in the way of reality. You bet in this game with a cold heart, a sharp eye on the numbers, and your impulses in check.

Luckily, Bones had no record, so eventually, after months of hanging around the backside walking hots for Jake and others, he'd been able to get his agent's license. He'd handled some good jockeys as well as some bums. The bums you get rid of; the good ones you work hard for. He and Tim hadn't been pals exactly, but they'd respected one another, and these past few years Bones had never wanted more than one client. With two you had to work too hard and conflicts of interest arose. When Tim went down for keeps, Bones had decided to take a break. Just betting, clocking the horses, hanging around the backside, that's all he thought he needed out of life at the time.

At the track, as elsewhere in life, you learn who the good people are and you hang around with them. That's how he'd gotten close to Jake Fontana. He'd met him when he'd gone to work in the barn area, and they'd begun trading jokes and stories. Then, when Bones began to handle Tim's book, Jake put the jock up on some of his live mounts, even though in those days Leo had been his principal rider. Leo had been sober most of the time then.

Bones had often tried to figure out why Jake liked him. Maybe it was because their people had all come from around Naples. The blood sings to you. When he wasn't out hustling or handicapping, Bones liked to hang around Fontana's barn. He'd gotten to meet Jake's wife, Maria; they'd all gone out to dinner together a few times before Maria got too sick. She'd been a little afraid of Bones when she found out how he'd gotten his nickname, but she got over it. Bones could make her laugh, and he thought she had a great sense of humor.

What Bones liked most about Jake was the way the trainer ran his operation. He had this calm, efficient way around his horses, which mostly were low-level allowance or claiming animals that always ran up to their potential. Jake wouldn't run a sore horse or one with major problems, and he was no good at bullshitting owners. He told them the truth, which kept his operation small. His string never included more than ten or twelve animals, which meant he could pay close attention to every one of them. He'd had a few good horses in his career, but not lately; none of his owners would spend the money to buy one for him. The big bucks went to the Bullions, the Bafferts, the Frankels, the Zitos, the glamour boys on the scene. Good trainers most of them, sure, but with the added ability to convince the moneybags to toss the loot their way. It didn't bother Jake much. He loved what he was doing. The only thing that had darkened his life was Maria's death. He'd taken that very hard and some days had trouble coping with it. Sometimes, when he least expected it, darkness would envelop him like a shroud. He and Bones had talked about it, but Bones had always tried to kid him out of it. "My mother once told me I should be more religious," Bones said to him one morning, "get in touch with Jesus. So I told her, 'Hey, Mom, look at the fix that poor clown got himself into.' She stopped talking to me after that."

***

Two days after Jill Aspen went to work for Fontana, Bones showed up at the barn again, mainly just to enjoy the usual early-morning routine. He found the trainer in his tack room on the phone with his principal owner, Rich Abernathy. "He's ready to go any day," Fontana was telling Abernathy. "I'll put Leo up on him." The owner must have protested, because Fontana added, "He's not drunk now, Mr. Abernathy, and he handles the Old Man as well as anyone … Yeah,

I'll see you at the races." And he hung up.

"I see you got a horse running today," Bones said.

"In the fifth," the trainer said. "Princely, that four-year-old, eight-race maiden."

"I'm glad I don't own him."

"It's a partnership," Jake said. "They split the finances four ways, so they can't get hurt too much. And this sucker may like a mile better than sprinting."

"You telling me to bet on him?"

"No, but then I'm not a betting man."

"He's a bum."

"Like Charlie Whittingham, the wisest trainer I ever knew, once said, you never knock a horse until he's dead," Jake said. "You just never know."

"Yeah, you do."

"John Henry, Stymie, Seabiscuit?"

Bones laughed. "Okay, maybe once every ten years or so."

They went out to the track to watch Leo work one of Fontana's two-year-olds, a high-strung, wild-eyed dark brown colt called High Jinks. The jockey's face was faintly green when he came back. "This sumbitch is a handful," he said, "but he can run. You're going to need to put blinkers on him. He's looking around all over the place."

"Yeah? Well, we'll see. I caught him in thirty-six and one."

"He could've gone ten lengths faster, but he's fuckin' nuts. You ought to cut him."

"Too soon for that, Leo. He's by In Excess. And he could settle down."

The jockey shrugged. "I'd cut all these crazy sumbitches," he said. "He could kill somebody out there. I hope it ain't me." He rode off back toward the barn, the colt tossing his head about against the rider's tight hold.

They followed him. When they got there, the jockey had already dismounted and handed the reins over to Eduardo. "You'll have to walk him yourself, Eduardo," the trainer said.

Jill Aspen stepped out from the stall she'd been mucking. "I'll walk him for you," she said. "I'm done here."

Jake hesitated. "What makes you think you can handle this colt? He's a tough one."

"I've seen worse," she said. "Let me try."

"I'll see you at the races," Leo called out, heading for the parking lot.

Eduardo unsaddled the two-year-old. Meanwhile, the girl had been talking softly and steadily to the animal, one hand firmly on his halter, the other patting him gently, caressingly on the neck. "Junior, you're just a mess," she said. "How can you be like that? Everybody here's your friend; everybody loves you, don't you know that?" On and on the river of words flowed, washing over the colt's bruised soul like a warm wave. Still talking, still cajoling, Jill now began to walk the colt in a circle outside between the barns, falling into line between two older animals from the next stable over also cooling out. She never stopped talking to the colt, one hand on his neck, until she had him as docile as a big trained dog. Fontana watched her at work until, totally convinced, he retreated back to his tack room to call his owners. It was a chore he disliked, but he was conscientious about it. Unlike some trainers, he felt he owed it to them. They paid him their money; he delivered information and, he hoped, enough winners to keep them happy.

While Jake was on the phone, Bones walked down the trainer's shed row and looked at the horses. They were all comfortably settled in, with clean straw in their stalls and their feed bins full. Only at the stall with Princely was the feed bin empty, but the colt seemed indifferent; he stood placidly in place like an old commuter waiting for a bus.

When Bones got back to the tack room, the girl was standing in the entrance looking at the trainer. "I want this colt," she said.

"High Jinks? I don't know. We'll see," Jake answered.

"I can handle him easy. And I'd like to work as many horses as you'll let me," she said. "It's what I do best. I'd like to ride for you."

24

"Race ride?"

"Yeah."

"Well, we'll see. That's a ways down the road. You sure handled the colt nicely, but ride him … "

"He's okay," she said quickly. "He's just like a little boy, that's all. Not a mean bone in him."

"Yeah, you got that right. You talked to Phil, my accountant, about getting on the payroll?"

"Sure did. You pay good."

"I try to keep the good help. Sometimes it works. Where you living?"

"I'm still in that motel, but I'm looking for a place. Maybe I'll get a room on the backside."

"I wouldn't advise it," Jake said. "Not for a woman alone."

"I'll find something."

"Eduardo has your number, right?"

"Sure. You need me at the races today?"

"No. We only have the one maiden going. See you in the morning."

"You bet." She waved good-bye, then walked away.

She moved gracefully, like a trained athlete. Bones liked the look of her in motion and felt a twinge of desire. "Pretty girl," he said to Fontana.

"Listen, Bones, I'm fifty-two years old," the trainer said. "I don't need that kind of trouble. She's an employee, that's all."

Bones smiled. "Yours, not mine," he said.

Jake sighed. "I thought you and Bingo …"

"Hey, Jake, you know me—they come and they go."

"Don't mess with this girl, Bones. I think she's been through some bad times. You understand me?"

"Yeah, I do. Don't worry about it."

CHAPTER 3

The sun had broken through by the time Bones headed for the saddling paddock that afternoon, where Eduardo and Fontana were busy around Princely. To his surprise Jill was also there, patting the horse's neck and keeping him relaxed while Jake tied his tongue down. It made the horse look goofy, his tongue now sticking out of the side of his mouth, but the animal had a habit of slipping his tongue over the bit so that it became difficult for the rider to control him. "Hello, Jill," Bones said. "What brings you here?"

"I figured I could help, what with Mr. Fontana's being short-handed and all."

The trainer heaved the saddle up on the maiden's back, tightened the cinch, then gave it a firm tug to make sure it wouldn't slip. Eduardo took the colt out of his stall and began to walk him around the inside area just to keep him calm and moving. Fontana eyed the horse carefully for any sign of soreness.

"He looks good," Jill said. "Can he run?"

"Some. Not much, but some. He picks up pieces of checks."

"He always works okay," Bones said.

"Yeah, he works just fine, but that's in the morning. He's a typical morning glory. Once the real racing starts he doesn't have the heart for it."

"So you figure he might like the mile better than the sprints you've been running him in?" Bones asked.

Fontana shrugged. "Well, like I said, he can run some, but he hasn't much speed out of the gate. What I don't know is whether he can go a distance. His daddy was a sprinter, though his dam won a stakes at a mile. I guess we'll find out."

As they followed the horses out toward the paddock, Bones spot-ted Princely's owners, four sharp-looking men from some dot-com whose stock had plunged when the bubble burst. They had offered to get Jake involved to the tune of a few hundred shares, but luckily he'd declined. "All I know is horses," he'd told them. "I have a few T-bills and an IRA and that's about it. I'm not about to shoot craps in the stock market." They had laughed at him, but then their stock had gone from ninety-six to a fraction over twelve and nobody was laugh-ing much anymore. Still, they'd been good sports about it, never grip-ing about their losses. The only thing was, Jake had been hoping to talk them into another horse or two, but that didn't seem likely now.

"If I could just get this common son of a gun of theirs to win a race, at least it would make them happy," he said to Bones. And who knew what might happen. Stock markets had a way of going up and down for no discernible reason, at least to Jake.

The trainer introduced Jill and Bones to the owners. They barely glanced at Bones but reacted very appreciatively to Jill. They were all in their mid-thirties, unmarried, partygoers, good-time guys, and they all liked her looks. One of them winked at Fontana and pulled him aside. "Where'd you find her?" he asked. "She's a doll."

"She showed up one morning looking for work," the trainer said. "That's all I know, really."

"No boyfriend?"

"Charlie, you're on your own. I'm not running a dating service."

The other three men had moved close to Jill and began kidding around with her, probing in their boyish ways to find out if she might be available. The girl kept a smile on her face, but her eyes were cold and soon they gave up. "I don't think we're making much of an impression," Charlie said. The trainer shrugged and turned away from him. Jill joined Eduardo to help him walk the colt around the ring.

"So, Jake, what about him today?" Charlie asked.

"He'll run better than last time," the trainer said. "I think the distance will suit him better, and we drew a good post down on the inside. He isn't going to get carried wide on the first turn."

The jockeys appeared from under the stands, looking like Disney gnomes in their bright silks. Leo Di Stefano, in the glowing orange and green colors of their stable, came trotting up to them, the last of the riders to reach the paddock. His swarthy features looked less drawn than they had two days earlier, but his eyes still looked like tiny road maps. He shook hands all around and turned to Fontana. "You know about this colt, Leo," Fontana said. "He hasn't got a lot of speed, so don't go wide with him. He ought to lay three, four lengths off the pace and make a move at the three-eighths pole. Keep him on the outside when he starts his run because he'll hang on you if he gets too much dirt in his face."

The jockey nodded and Fontana gave him a leg up into the saddle when the paddock judge called out, "Riders up!" Jill and Eduardo stood off to one side as the horses headed out toward the track, while the dot-com plungers struck out for the grandstand.

"We're two rows back, just beyond the sixteenth pole, Jill," Jake called out to the girl. "In case you want a seat."

"I'll watch it from the rail," she said.

"I guess she doesn't need those four studs hitting on her," Bones said to Jake. He recalled the coldness in her eyes and it made him wonder again about her. Maybe she did have a boyfriend somewhere. Maybe she didn't like men. She was good to look at, though, even if she wasn't available. Bones had been on the scene for a long time— he wasn't coming off an untimely death like Jake—and he was still in his forties. In his prime, he figured.

He followed Jill down to the rail, about fifty feet to the left of the finish line. "Mind if I watch it with you?" he asked.

"Plenty of room," she said. They leaned against the rail, waiting for the starting gate to open.

The race went off without incident, with Fontana's colt breaking alertly and then tucking in along the inside around the clubhouse turn, just as Jake had instructed Leo to do. The horse moved up along the backside, then made a nice run on the turn for home, swinging out into the middle of the track for a clear shot. But again, as in all his previous races, he hung in the stretch, finishing third, four lengths behind the wire-to-wire winner.

Jill and Bones joined Eduardo out on the track as the horses came back. Princely hadn't even worked up a sweat and seemed still full of run. Leo vaulted down from the horse's back, peeled off the saddle, and headed for the weigh-in scales as Fontana showed up and fell in step with him. "He spit it out, boss," the jockey said. "He don't like to push himself none."

"I could see that, Leo. Thanks for the good ride."

"How about blinkers?" Jill suggested.

Fontana turned to look at her. "What makes you think they'd help?"

"He was looking around all the way down the stretch," she said. "They might help him keep his mind on business. He could have won this race easy."

"Yeah, maybe."

"I'm sorry. I don't mean to shoot my mouth off."

Jake smiled. "I might have thought of that myself, if I'd given it another week or two. I'm a little slow on the uptake sometimes. Or maybe I just think he's as common as they come."

The girl shrugged. "Like I've heard you say over and over, never knock a horse until he's dead."

Fontana laughed. "That'll cheer my owners up," he said.

They walked back together into the stands, where the trainer went off to talk to his owners. Bones fished his *Racing Form* out of his pocket as he headed back to his box to see if he could ferret out a winner or two, then looked up to find Jill gone. He didn't see her again that afternoon.

***

Rich Abernathy was sitting at his usual table overlooking the finish line and the winner's circle. He had folded his losing tickets in half and made a small pyramid of them in the center of the table. "Sit down, Jake," he said, as the trainer limped toward him after talking

30

to Princely's disappointed owners. "I can't cash a ticket. Too bad that bum of yours can't run. He looked like a winner at the head of the stretch."

Fontana sighed and sat down heavily into the chair opposite Abernathy. "I may put blinkers on him next time," he said. "They might help some."

"Try putting a rocket up his ass," the owner said. "That would really help. Anyway, the only smart move I've made all day is not betting on him."

"I just stopped by to tell you that your two-year-old worked real good and that Gamblin Man runs on Wednesday. The two-year-old is still green, but he'll be ready to roll by Del Mar. He has a ton of speed. Leo had a stranglehold on him and he still worked thirty-six and one."

"Let's hope he stays sound."

"Yeah, that's always the problem. But that old plater of yours will bring you a check on Wednesday, and you can bet on him, too. The race should come up pretty soft for him."

"If it doesn't rain."

"Hell, he loves a wet track. He hasn't run on one for two years, but the last time he caught one he won by ten."

Abernathy's dark eyes lit up with greed. "Shit, I'd forgotten. That was a long time ago, and the race doesn't even show anymore in the *Form*. You know any rain gods I can pray to?"

"Anyway, just thought I'd bring you up to date." Fontana started to get up, heaving himself up off the table with both hands to favor his bum knee. "By the way, Bullion's horse in the feature should run well."

"Steve tell you that?"

"No, but I saw him on the track three days ago. The clockers caught the blowout in thirty-five, but I caught him a second faster, and you know Steve, he doesn't work his horses all that fast. He looked good."

Abernathy's habitually dour expression remained unchanged. "He's the favorite," he said. "He won't pay much."

"Maybe two to one."

"Yeah? Well, a winner's a winner. Thanks for the push." The train-er started to move away from the table. "Hey, by the way, who's the girl with you?"

"Her name's Jill Aspen. I took her on a few days ago as a groom and exercise rider. Bullion sent her over."

"She's hot. You got good taste. She looks familiar, too. I've seen her somewhere."

"She rode some on the fair circuits, then worked up north."

"Yeah? Maybe that's where I saw her. But there's something else about her. I'll think of it."

"She also worked for Furman at Heritage."

"That may be it. Doing what?"

"Working with the yearlings and two-year-olds, mostly, I guess. She seems like a nice kid and she's good around horses. How good a rider she is I just don't know yet, but I figure I'll find out someday."

"How are you doing, by the way?" Abernathy's dark gaze now focused on the trainer's face.

"Okay. I'm feeling good. Just this damn knee of mine."

"Did you go and see Ed Barrow?"

"Yeah, thanks for sending me to him. I like the guy. He's a diseased horseplayer."

"The worst. But a great doctor."

"He gave me some pills to help me sleep. If I remember to take them."

"You can trust him. He's pretty conservative."

"The dreams have pretty much stopped."

"Glad to hear it. You weren't looking too good."

"I'll see you, Rich."

"Yeah. You know, I was really sorry about Maria. I still think about her."

"I think about her all the time. That's how it started, I guess."

"Listen to Barrow. He knows what he's doing. He took care of my daughter after her suicide attempt, kept on top of the case every day for over a year, never lost sight of her all the time she was in the psycho ward. He'll do the same for you."

"Yeah, thanks. But I'm not going to any psycho ward."

The bugler blew the call to the post and Abernathy reached for his *Racing Form*. Two races to go on the day's card, his last two chances to get out, maybe even turn himself into a winner. Bullion's horse was going off at 8-5 or less. It would take a five-hundred-dollar wager on him to win just to get even, but Rich Abernathy never thought twice about making that kind of bet. He had a first name that exactly matched his circumstances in life.

When Bullion's horse won easily, it not only bailed Abernathy out but also enriched Bones, who had him hooked up in a twenty-dollar exacta that put more than three hundred dollars in his pocket. "I'm sorry, Bones, I forgot to tell you about him," Jake said the next morning when they met at Clockers Corner.

"Forget about it," Bones answered. "I came up with him on my own. I know about Bullion. I can read him and his horses like the guy who figured out the Rosetta Stone."

"The what?"

"An old rock. Don't worry about it, Jake. The thing is, they're still running for me like—"

"Yeah, little trained pigs."

"You got it."

CHAPTER 4

"**W**here the hell is Leo?" Jake asked, not really expecting a satisfactory answer but merely expressing his frustration. "Hasn't anybody tried to find him?"

"Nobody seen or heard nothing, boss," Eduardo said. "I ask around, but I get no answer."

"He's probably holed up somewhere," Bones said, "inside a bottle."

"This'll be the end of him," the trainer said. "If I don't put him up on my horses, who the hell is going to?"

Eduardo didn't answer; he simply stood in the doorway of the tack room and waited for his employer to make a decision. Gamblin Man was scheduled to go in the fourth that afternoon, and now somebody else would have to ride him. Leo Di Stefano was on a binge, having dropped out of sight for the third time since the meet started, and this time Eduardo and Bones both knew that Fontana would not be around for him when he did resurface. Not that it mattered; the stewards would probably suspend him for at least six months and force him into rehab somewhere. They'd done it to him before, and for a while it had helped to keep him sober, but now they'd probably throw the book at him. Drugs and alcohol, the two biggest hazards riders and stable-hands faced these days.

"Jake, can I talk to you for a minute?"

Jill had come up behind Eduardo to peer over his shoulder. He quickly stepped aside for her. "Boss, I take care of the filly," the Mexican said, "and the two-year-old; otherwise, we ready to go here."

"Okay," Jake said, "we'll talk later."

Eduardo scurried away to wind up his chores; he wanted to have no part in what he knew Jake and the girl would be discussing. The trainer now looked at her. He also knew what she was going to say, but he wasn't at all sure how he would answer. He waited for her to speak, hoping she wouldn't ask him for the impossible.

"I can ride the Old Man for you," she said.

"What makes you think so?"

"You know I can. You've seen me ride every one of your horses in the past four days and you've seen me work the two-year-old. What makes you think I can't handle an old pro like the Old Man?"

"I don't know, Jill. Working a horse is one thing; race riding is another. You know that."

"I rode twenty-three races last year," she said. "I won three of 'em and I picked up checks in seven of 'em. They weren't favorites neither. One was a fifty-one-to-one shot. And then there's all them races I won in the bushes. You think I still can't ride good enough?"

"I didn't say that, Jill."

"Then all I'm doing is asking you to give me a chance. You couldn't start me off on a better horse than the Old Man. He could run around the track with a monkey on his back."

"He won't put out his best for a weak rider," the trainer said. "You have to let him know who's up there. These old geldings get pretty smart in their dotage."

She smiled, a quick flash of those green eyes, a backward shake of her dark cropped hair. "He'll know on the way to the post who is up on him, I promise you that," she said.

Fontana leaned back in his chair and sighed. "How am I going to explain putting an inexperienced apprentice like you up on this horse to his owner?"

She laughed. "You said he was a gambler."

"But not a fool."

"If you put her up on this horse, it'll double the odds on him," Bones said, tilting his chair back against the wall and clasping his hands behind his head. "Abernathy likes to cash tickets. Plus the track is wet from the rain last night."

"They sealed it after the races yesterday," the trainer said, "and they're calling it fast."

"So what?" Jill said. "It's wet-fast, just what the Old Man wants, you said. So let me ride him."

"With the last-minute rider change we won't even get your apprentice weight allowance on him."

"Does it matter? I'm down to a hundred and eight."

"He's got to carry a hundred and twenty pounds. That's twelve pounds of lead, all dead weight."

She didn't answer; she just stood there and looked at him. The trainer shut his eyes briefly and thought it over. What did he have to lose? "If you fuck up the ride, Abernathy'll be all over me," he finally said.

Bones leaned forward in his chair and stretched. "So what?" he said. "He'll get over it. He's a pain in the ass, like most owners, but he's a loyal one at least. If she wins, Jake, Abernathy will cash a huge ticket."

"He'll want to take us all out to dinner at one of those fancy restaurants of his," Jake said. "I hate them, but we'd have to go." He shut his eyes and shook his head. "All right," he added at last.

"No kidding? You mean it?" She looked dazed with unexpected happiness, like a small child suddenly presented with a longed-for toy.

"Yeah, you got the mount."

"Well, all right," she said. "I'll ride the hair off him."

"Just don't fall off, that's all I ask. Go home and get some rest. I'll see you at the receiving barn." She turned to leave. "By the way, where are you living these days?"

"I'm still at that motel in Monrovia. I can't afford an apartment right now because they all want a month up front and a deposit. But I've got to find a place sometime soon."

"You can move in with me."

She looked suddenly wary. "I don't think so, Jake."

"I've got a room with a bathroom and a hot plate and a sink over the garage. You can live there for a while."

"How much?"

"It's free. No one's using it. My wife, Maria, fixed it up to accommodate guests. How do you feel about dogs?"

"How should I feel? I love dogs."

"I've got three of them, noisy mutts. They have the run of the place."

"No problem. This is nice of you, Jake."

"I'd have thought of it sooner, only I had to make sure you'd work out."

"And now you are."

"Well, I don't know about you as a rider, but we'll find that out soon enough." After the girl had gone, Jake sat at his desk and looked at Bones, who was drumming his fingers idly on the arms of his chair. "Shit, what am I going to tell Abernathy?" he asked.

"Nothing," Bones said, "not until the last minute. They'll announce that Di Stefano's off all his mounts and he'll hear it then."

Jake grunted, got up, and together he and Bones walked out into the trainer's shed row. A warm sun was beating down over the barn area. In the background Old Baldy, the San Gabriel Mountains' highest peak, loomed over the green infield and the old art-deco grandstand, which the track's new owner had disfigured but not quite destroyed with a clumsy-looking elevator tower that split it into two sections. Another act of disrespect for tradition, Bones had once called it, and Jake had agreed with him.

"I suppose you're still winning," the trainer said, stretching in the sunlight and watching Princely still being cooled out from his morning gallop. The new groom, a thin young Chilean named Tommaso, seemed capable enough and eager to please.

"Yeah, I'm still on a tear."

"I better find you a horse to buy before you blow all that money back through the windows."

"No chance, Jake," Bones said. "I trust horses more than people, but that ain't saying much."

"I'll see you in the walking ring," the trainer said, as Bones waved good-bye and headed for the parking lot.

***

Two nights earlier Bones had taken Jill out to dinner. He'd told himself he wanted to get to know her better, but he wasn't quite sure why. He was curious about her and attracted to her, but he wasn't even sure she liked men. It had been a Monday, the first of the two days the track was dark. At first she had hesitated, until he'd said, "Hey, kid, I'm not dangerous. I won't lay a finger on you, I promise."

"So why do they call you Bones?" she asked.

"I used to break 'em now and then," he confessed, "but that's all in my past. Now I'm just an unemployed jock's agent and full-time horseplayer. I'd just like to talk to you. I know a lot about this game and maybe I could be of some help, you know what I mean? And my real name is Sal, short for Salvatore. So call me that, I'd prefer it."

"Okay, Sal," she said. "I trust you, I guess. Mr. Fontana likes you."

"We're buddies, even if he does have bad taste in friends."

He picked her up at her motel, a dismal-looking dump on the outskirts of Monrovia, about four miles from the stable gate at the track. She was waiting for him out front, dressed unglamorously in scuffed loafers, jeans, a black open-collar shirt, and a red windbreaker. She'd put on a trace of lipstick and small gold hoops dangled from her earlobes. "Where do you feel like eating?" he asked her.

"I don't care," she said. "I do have to watch my weight, if I'm going to have any mounts while I have my bug. They don't give nothin' away on this circuit. Especially as I'm a girl."

They drove into downtown Pasadena and found a small French restaurant that looked at least passable. It was dark, with a pool of round tables under white tablecloths crammed between a bar and a row of booths. There were only two other couples in the place and the hostess settled them into one of the booths. Jill refused a hard drink, so Bones ordered a bottle of modestly priced Australian Shiraz. "This I like," Jill said, after taking a cautious first sip. "But I don't know anything about wine. Where I come from people drink a lot of bad stuff."

The bad stuff applied to her personal life as well. Her father had

owned a hardware store in a small town in the Texas Panhandle near
Amarillo, she told Bones, but he had died when she was eleven. Her
mother had quickly remarried, this time to a traveling meat sales-
man. When he was home, the two of them drank themselves into
oblivion every night. They fell into debt, lost her mother's house to a
bank foreclosure, then began to drift from one small Texas town to
another, her stepfather finding work wherever he could, mostly as a
handyman and day laborer. Her mother's older brother, Uncle
Robert, had tried to come to their rescue by buying a small ranch for
them outside of Prescott, Arizona, where they attempted to raise cat-
tle. "Then, when I was fourteen, it got real bad," Jill said. Her stepfather had begun beating up her mother and also knocking around Jill
and her two younger brothers from time to time.

She found refuge in horses. She'd gone to a county fair and gotten
a job after school working with a gypsy trainer who had Quarter
Horses. "That's where I learned to ride," she said. "I got real good at
wingin' and dingin', and Buddy, the trainer, put me up on his stock.
We'd go around the little fairs in Idaho and Utah and Montana, and
I'd win a lot of head-to-head races. I brought some money home and
that kept my stepdaddy off me. But one day I came home and he'd
beat up Mom so bad I called the law on him. They took him off to
jail, and I got Mom out of town to Uncle Robert. He had a business
down around Biloxi, Mississippi, and she stayed there with the boys
for a while. My stepdaddy went after her and damn if she didn't go
back to him. After that I kind of gave up on her. I was seventeen by
then. Buddy gave me a place to stay for a while, and I went on riding
for him. And then I got married. That was my biggest mistake."

Bones asked her about that, too, but at first she didn't want to talk
too much about it. "He'd been a rider; then he became a jock's agent
up in the Bay Area," she said reluctantly. "He was fifteen years older
than me. I was so damn green. I didn't know anything about anything
except horses. The main trouble was I was a girl and he couldn't get
me enough mounts, so he kind of dropped me. I got mad and we
used to fight a lot. But horses run for me, and I did manage to win a

few races on my own. So then he got mad, couldn't handle it. Shit, you know, Sal, I've won races in towns and tracks where the *Racing Form* ain't even sold. In those places it's all dust and lickety split on these little bullrings where the turns ain't even banked. Jocks ride right down to their nuts there, assuming they got any. Mostly half-mile tracks at county fairs. At Elko, Nevada, one four-day meet over Labor Day I won four races, two of 'em on broken-down nags that could hardly get around the track. Goddamn, but it was fun, though! I loved it! I loved everything about it! It's the only thing I really want to do with my life."

"And your husband?"

"We split up real quick and I got a divorce. That weekend in Elko kind of finished us off. We got into a big argument and all, and sure enough he hit me. I picked up a chair and slammed it on his head, knocked him out cold. And then I packed and got the hell out of there."

"Where is he now?"

"Dead," she said, in a voice as icy as a winter wind. "He got into drugs after we split and got shot in a police raid in Oakland."

He started to ask her something else, but she shook her head. "Come on, Sal," she said, as the waiter cleared their plates. "I'm sure you've had a better life than me. Let's talk about Bones."

"You don't want to hear too much about all that," he said, but he told her about his father the bookie and his mother moving away. "So I started running errands for a bunch of guys who had a restaurant supply business in New Jersey. They were into some other things, too."

"Like what?"

"Waste disposal, party rentals, stuff like that. They had a couple of nightclubs, too."

"You ran errands?"

"Yeah. It was a service business, you could call it. Supply and demand, you know?"

"So where does this name Bones come from?"

"Well, later, I became the guy who had to collect the late payments, you know what I mean? I mean, not everybody paid on time. I'd go talk to them. Some of them had to be persuaded a little bit."

She looked at him with those green eyes wide open now. "You mean like in the movies? Like Mafia stuff?"

He smiled. "Not really all out like that. Yeah, but it was a family, you know? It was a family business. It was like—"

"An I-talian family, right?"

"Yeah. But we weren't into drugs, killing people, nothing like that. It was mostly legit stuff. You lease equipment out; you take away garbage and stuff, then you wait to get paid. That's where I came in. I mean, when the payments didn't come in on time."

"Nothing illegal?"

"Nothing real bad. A little bookmaking. You know, over the phone, like that. But, hey, you can't stop people from gambling, now can you?"

"No, I guess not." She thought it over for a moment, then looked up at him again. "Wow, I never thought I'd be going out with a guy who breaks people's bones," she said.

"That didn't happen too often," he said. "And never on purpose. Sometimes people get violent, you know? You take a lot of abuse. So then you do what you have to do. I was good at it. I got a good reputation. People began to pay on time."

"You never got arrested or nothin'?"

"Nah. I never did anything really illegal like, you know? It was the people I was collecting from who were doing the illegal stuff, like not paying their legit bills, see?"

"What did you do? Use a baseball bat or something? Maybe karate, like that?"

"No, Jill. Mostly I just grabbed 'em around the neck and rammed them up against something hard. That usually worked."

For the first time since she'd met him she took a really close look at him. At first glance he didn't look so terrific, maybe five-ten or five-eleven, too much weight around the middle, his arms usually hidden by shirtsleeves, but there was that big bull neck that hinted at a lot of muscle hidden by the dark-blue sports coat he was wearing. "You really that strong?" she asked.

"Yeah," he said, "I am. I used to work out every day. Still do two or three times a week. I could lose some pounds now, but I like to eat, you know? And good wine, too."

"So when did you go straight?"

"A few years ago. I got tired of it. And I was really into the horses. So I came out here, got clean away, went to work walking hots for a while, even though horses scare the shit out of me. They're dangerous. I worked for Jake, then I got my agent's license, also got real good at handicapping and betting. It's a good life, Jill. There's nothing better than the horses, is there?"

"That's the way I feel," she said. "I love 'em. They never let you down, like people do. They're pure. That's all I want to do, Sal—ride, become the best."

"The second Julie Krone, huh?"

"Yeah, she's great. She's my role model. I want to be just like her. I want to win a bunch of races and ride the best horses at the best tracks. You going to help me do it?"

"Maybe. We'll see."

When they pulled up in front of her motel, she leaned over and pecked him quickly on the cheek. "This was real nice, Sal," she said. "I had a great time." Then she was out of the car and running up the stairs before he could think of anything else to say.

CHAPTER 5

Rich Abernathy came storming into the saddling area just as Jake Fontana was tightening the cinch on Gamblin Man. "What the hell do you think you're doing?" he asked.

"About what?"

"What do you mean about what? Putting this girl up on my horse, that's what I mean."

"Leo didn't show up this morning. Nobody knows where he is." The trainer gave the cinch one last hard tug, then slapped the Old Man's neck affectionately. "He's probably holed up somewhere inside a bottle of tequila."

"And out of the whole jockey colony, the best in the whole damn country, you elected to put this kid up on my horse."

"She's not a kid, Rich. And she can ride. I've watched her work my horses real close. She's good."

"Come on, Jake. Are you banging this girl or what?"

"I thought you liked to bet."

"What do you mean?"

The trainer turned to Eduardo, who was standing patiently by the horse's head. "Walk him around, Eduardo. He needs to get loose."

The groom led Gamblin Man out of his stall and walked him away. Rich Abernathy waited until they were out of earshot, then turned to confront the trainer again. "Sure I like to bet. So what?"

"Have you looked at the odds?"

The owner glanced toward the television screen mounted over the row of stalls. Gamblin Man was listed at 8-1, twice his morning line. "With this girl on him he ought to be twenty-to-one."

"And I'm telling you she can ride. You want a price on your horse, you got one. Plus he's going to love this racing surface. It's fast but wet, just the way he likes it. If Jill gets him out of the gate, he'll run like the wind."

"Big if, Jake. How do you know she can do that? A lot of races are lost in the gate."

The trainer grinned. "I don't know if she can boot and scoot, but I guess we'll find out, right?"

The owner blinked, growled something under his breath, and turned and walked toward the paddock. A few minutes later Jake followed him, with Eduardo leading Gamblin Man by his side. The tote board blinked a change in the odds, with the number on Gamblin Man showing a rise to 10-1.

Jill Aspen was the first rider to show up. She ignored Rich Abernathy's scowling face and thrust out her hand. "Don't worry, Mr. Abernathy," she said. "I'm going to ride the hair off your horse."

Reluctantly, the owner shook her hand and mumbled something. Jake Fontana put a hand on his rider's shoulder, feeling under the blue silk the firm contour of muscle and bone. "There isn't much to do about the Old Man," he said, "except let him get into the race at his own pace. He'll break well for you, he always does, and then he'll settle into stride, maybe two or three lengths off the pace. There are a couple of speedballs in here. Let 'em go, don't dingdong with them. You're drawn out in the ten hole and the extra half a furlong is going to help. Keep him outside where he won't get too much of this wet dirt in his face. If he likes this surface, he'll run good. Anyway, he's a pro; he always gives you his best. I wanted a race against an easier field, but Mr. Abernathy here doesn't want to lose him, so we run him a notch or two up above where he should be at this stage of his career." He smiled at his owner. "Isn't that right, Mr. Abernathy?"

The owner grunted. "Just don't leave him in the gate," he told his rider. "This is a sprint, not a distance race."

"I guess I know that," Jill said. "I'm going to win this race for you, Mr. Abernathy." She turned away from the owner to look at the horse, now being led around the ring by Eduardo. The sun was out and the air crisp and clean after the night's brief rain. The odds blinked again. Nine-to-one now on Gamblin Man, who hadn't won in two attempts since the end of the Del Mar meet in early September, even against horses he would have demolished in his prime.

"Don't I know you from somewhere?" Rich Abernathy suddenly asked. "From one of the sales, maybe?"

The girl looked at him. "I don't think so," she said. "I rode on the fair circuits and up north. Maybe you saw me ride."

"No, I saw you somewhere else, a party or something."

"I wouldn't know," she said. "I didn't go to a whole lot of parties."

"Must have been one of the sales."

"Maybe. I did go to a couple of those."

The paddock judge called the riders up and Jake boosted his jockey into the saddle. One more tour of the ring, then horse and rider went out through the gap to the track. "Hey, girlie, don't fall off!" some wag called out as Jill rode past him. "Get 'em to tie you on, babe!"

"Oooh, look at her!" somebody else shouted. "She's a doll! Hey, honey, you want to ride my horsey?"

Bones, who was leaning on the rail next to him, said, "Shut up, you dumb fuck!"

The girl kept her eyes focused straight ahead. As they left the paddock, she leaned forward and stroked the Old Man's neck. Abernathy was looking at the odds, and Jake could see the greed in his eyes. "You better be right about her," the owner said.

"Hey, I'm not always right," Jake answered, "but I'll tell you one thing, this kid can ride some."

Bones lingered for a moment at the rail, allowing the crowd to thin out around him, then headed for his box. He was wondering how much he was going to bet on the horse himself.

***

By the time Bones got back to his seat in the grandstand above the finish line, the horses had already paraded past the stands for the

first time. Then they turned and came by a second time at a leisurely canter or a trot toward the starting gate across the infield at the
head of the backstretch. Gamblin Man was the only one of the
entries unaccompanied by an outrider. The old gelding, his neck
bowed and head hanging low, was moving steadily, purposefully on
his own toward the gate, Jill standing lightly upright in the stirrups,
a firm hold on the reins.

As Bones sat there, eyeing the scene through his binoculars,
Moonshine Barkley, the racetrack cynic, flopped into the seat next to
him. "I was going to bet on Fontana's horse," he said, "but then the
dumb bastard puts this girl nobody ever heard of up on the beast.
What's the matter with the guy?" It was not a question to which he
expected an answer; what he wanted from Bones was confirmation.
"So?"

"So I see a bet," Bones said, still focused on the track.

"On what?"

"On Fontana's horse."

"You've got to be kidding, right?" Moonshine said. "Who the hell is
she?"

"She rode in the Bay Area, won three races up there. Also on the
bullrings."

"Those aren't racetracks; they're the bushes. Are you telling me she
can ride here against Victor and Pat and Julie and Flores? Give me a
break!"

Bones lowered his binoculars and set them down on the counter in
front of him, then turned to look at Moonshine. He was sitting there,
the *Form* sticking out of the side pocket of his food-stained sports
coat, his program clutched in one sweaty hand, the eyes in his
drawn, anxious face radiating disbelief. He looked poised for flight,
like a small cornered animal facing a dangerous predator. "Jockeys
don't count for all that much," Bones said, "especially in sprints.
Don't you know that by now, Moonshine? And Fontana knows what
he's doing."

"The horse is in over his head anyway and you know it,"

Moonshine said. "He's seen his best days. To run good here, he'd need a jock who can sting him into putting out. It isn't going to be this girl. These smart old geldings don't run for weak riders, I don't care what you say."

"He's nine-to-one," Bones said. "He'll go off maybe even better. He should be no more than four to one. He's a terrific overlay."

"Not if he's got no chance. He could be a hundred-to-one and I wouldn't play him." Moonshine stood up. "I'm putting my money on Oxonian. He's five-to-two and he's the speed of the race."

"You want an angle?" Bones said patiently. "Sit down."

"Nah. I'm going to hook up the two speed horses," Moonshine insisted, as he left the box on his way to a betting window.

You can't save some people from themselves, Bones figured, shutting his eyes briefly to concentrate. Then he took one more look at the notes he'd made in his *Form* about the race. Two years earlier, during the winter meet at Santa Anita, it had rained a lot. Gamblin Man had drawn outside at six and a half furlongs in an allowance sprint. He'd broken well as usual, tucked in off the leaders by two, then moved at the three-eighths pole and won by six lengths. The track had been listed as wet-fast, like today. The horse had a history of sore feet, which was all that had kept him from being a stakes winner. The only time he had ever gotten that kind of wet surface was on that particular afternoon against a much tougher field. Best of all from a bettor's point of view, these statistics didn't show up in the current *Racing Form* because they dated too far back. Bones had fished them out of his notes going back three years. Gamblin Man had won only once in five starts on off-tracks, but the other races had been run in the mud or the deep slop and those he couldn't handle. This old boy wanted to hear his feet rattle on a nice cool surface. Like today's. Bones stood up and stretched, then headed for the windows.

He decided to risk a hundred on the Old Man to win, and he also hooked him in exactas to the two speed horses, in case one of them got courageous. It was now four minutes to post and the tote board showed Gamblin Man at 7-1, still well above his program odds. As

Bones waited in line, Moonshine spotted him and hurried over. "I just caught the owner's action," he said. "You want to hear it?"

"Sure."

"He only bet a hundred on his horse."

"So?"

"He usually bets at least twice that. This ain't exactly a show of confidence. You still going to bet on him?"

"Absolutely."

"What? You like grief?"

"Owners are always wrong, you know that, Moonshine."

"Okay, don't say I didn't warn you." He rushed away, ever in search of the winning angle, the last of the great cynics. Bones felt sorry for him. He was the kind of guy who, if somebody said good morning to him, he'd be looking around for the sunset. Bones had known him for years and couldn't remember him ever having a winning meet. All he had was a pension and his Social Security plus a gift for scrounging small loans, which he never paid off, from his in-laws.

Jill sat quietly on her horse as the gate crew began to load the animals drawn inside of her into their starting stalls. Gamblin Man had been through this experience so many times before that nothing about the process fazed him. He was relaxed but seemed interested, as always, in the proceedings. With his head low and his neck bowed, Jill had brought him to the gate, then pulled him up and kept him off to one side, where he'd be clear of any trouble that might develop. Little Slew, the colt in the five stall, had washed out and his eyes looked wild with fright. Jill was glad to be away from him, because in that frame of mind the colt could muck up the horses next to him out of the gate, costing them the race before it had even begun. That wasn't going to happen to the Old Man; she wasn't going to let it happen. Thank Christ she'd drawn outside, only one animal to the right of her, a plodder with no speed going off at 80-1.

As Jill sat there, she felt a surge of confidence. This honest old hard knocker was going to run his eyeballs out for her and help launch her career. Across from where she sat, the crowd in the grandstand seemed merely a blur of indistinct colors. The assistant starters loaded Little Slew into his slot, then two of the men held his head in place to keep him from spooking and rearing up until the field could be released. When it came to Gamblin Man's turn to load, he stepped calmly and willingly forward, knowing exactly what was expected of him. Jill tucked herself firmly into the stirrups, leaned low over the horse's neck, waiting for the break. To her outside the last horse, the hopeless plodder, was pushed into place.

With a great clanging roar the stall gates snapped aside and the field exploded into the open. Gamblin Man lunged into the clear, until Jill took hold of the reins and exerted just enough pressure to keep him from overexerting himself without discouraging him. To her left she saw the two speed horses already head and head in a duel for the lead. She sent Gamblin Man up alongside three pursuers, so that the four of them were now running in a tightly knit bunch directly behind the leaders. Okay so far, she thought; only she found herself wishing she weren't four wide and facing the prospect of proceeding that way around the turn. She couldn't afford to lose that much ground, but for now she was trapped. No way she could take back and hope to win.

Up ahead of her the speed horses opened up three lengths, then four. Little Slew, still wild-eyed, his head thrown back, the rider fighting to control his every step, now moved into third. He would cook himself quickly, but at what cost to everybody else? The field neared the turn. Jill could feel Gamblin Man moving under her with a great ground-eating stride that told her he loved the racing surface, his feet striking over it like the hammers of doom. She felt like shouting with joy, but all she actually did was let the reins out a notch and chirp to the old boy.

On the turn Gamblin Man swung alongside Little Slew. For a second or two they ran together, then the crazy colt lugged out, bumping Gamblin Man hard, throwing him temporarily off stride. "Get away from me, you son of a bitch!" Jill screamed. The rider on Little Slew pulled his mount back into line and began to drop back along the inside. Gamblin Man gathered himself, put his head down, and resumed his stride. But he had lost ground. Oxonian now had a length on the other speed horse and four on Gamblin Man and they were halfway around the turn. Maybe it was too late now.

Jill leaned in over the Old Man's neck and cracked him once with the whip, not hard, not savagely, just as a small reminder to him that she was up there, that she expected the world of him, that she believed and trusted in him. The horse responded, his hooves tattooing the racing surface in the ecstasy of his explosive run. In five jumps he was past the fading speed horse and at the eighth pole he was two off Oxonian.

Jill had her eyes fixed on the track ahead of her. She saw Oxonian tire and start to lug out. How far out would he go? How wide would he carry her? She couldn't risk it and pointed Gamblin Man to the inside of the leader. All horses will run outside, she knew, but some won't run inside. What did Jill know about the Old Man? He was the consummate pro, that's what she knew; he'd run his heart out anywhere for her. They came up on the inside, the jock on Oxonian pumping and slashing to get that last ounce of speed out of his mount to make it to the finish line. Jill tapped her mount one more time. "Come on, Old Man!" she shouted. Together they swept past on the inside, the Old Man's head thrust toward the wire, carrying his rider to a win by nearly half a length.

Jill immediately stood up in the stirrups and raised her right arm triumphantly. She felt as if she'd won the Kentucky Derby; it meant that much to her. "Nice going, kid!" one of the other riders called out to her, as Jill turned Gamblin Man, still full of run, back toward the winner's circle. Paolo Neruda, the jock up on Oxonian, grinned at her and gave her a thumbs-up. "I tried to keep him straight," he said, "but he was lugging out on me. You did good to go inside."

At the winner's circle Jake Fontana and Eduardo were there to greet her. The little Mexican's wrinkly face cracked into a huge grin, while the trainer merely looked relieved. "You scared the shit out of me with that inside move," he said.

"I couldn't help it," she answered. "Oxonian was lugging out real bad. I didn't know how wide he'd carry me."

"It was a good ride."

"Thanks. I thought so, too."

Eduardo led the horse and rider into the circle, where Rich Abernathy joined them, positioning himself by the horse's head next to the groom. The owner was sweating and looked slightly dazed. "Shit," he said, "look at the board." The lights blinked a payoff of $23.80 for every two-dollar winning ticket. "I should have bet a thousand. Why didn't you tell me she could ride like that?"

"I did," the trainer said. "You didn't believe me."

After the flash of the track photographer's camera, Jill vaulted from the saddle and turned to give Gamblin Man one last affectionate pat on the neck. "I love this horse," she said. "He tries so hard." She turned to shake the owner's hand. "Thanks, Mr. Abernathy, for giving me a chance to ride him."

"I had nothing to do with it," the owner said. "Thank Jake here. I thought he'd lost his mind."

Carrying her saddle, Jill walked toward the weigh-in scales. "Hey, chickie," someone called out from the crowd along the rail, "nice boat race! How else you gonna win? Goddamn jocks, fuckin' crooks!"

Moonshine Barkley caught up to Bones on the way out of the track after the eighth. "That fucking Neruda," he said, "letting that horse lug out like that. He should have won easy."

"Wrong, Moonshine," Bones said. "The horse was done under him."

"Fuck you, Bones!"

Bones seized him by the arm and pulled him in close. "Watch your mouth, Moonshine," he said. "One thing you have to learn in this game is how to lose gracefully, you know what I'm saying?"

Moonshine's face was pale; his eyes, fearful. "Hey, Bones, I didn't mean anything by it. I just lost more than I should have, that's all. No offense, honest."

Bones let him go, and Moonshine took a couple of steps back away

53

from him. "I tried to tell you, you asshole," Bones said, "but you don't listen."

"You're right, you're right," Moonshine babbled. He again fell into step beside Bones as they headed for the parking lot. "So what do you know about this girl?"

"Not much, except she can ride. That move on the inside was real nice. A lot of jocks don't like it in there, especially on cheap horses. You go down, you get hurt bad sometimes. This kid's got guts."

"Yeah, yeah, a hell of a ride," Moonshine agreed. "So how much did you win, Bones?"

"Enough. And the next time you ask me something and I tell you, you'll listen, right?"

"Right. I'm sorry. I didn't mean anything bad. I made a dumb play, that's all."

"You know what, Moonshine? You got that right."

"I'll see you, okay?" He took off on a lopsided lope across the lot through the rows of parked cars. Bones thought he looked like a wounded duck.

CHAPTER 6

She hadn't been so happy in months. Every morning she got up before sunrise to arrive at the barn at the same time as Eduardo and always a few minutes before Jake showed up, his eyes still haunted by sleep. She mucked stalls; galloped, worked, and hotwalked horses; and then went home at noon to stand under a hot shower for twenty minutes. In the afternoons of racing days, she watched from her post at the rail, studying the moves and the styles of the riders. But on two of the five nights since her winning ride on Gamblin Man she treated herself to a dinner out at an inexpensive steak house in Arcadia, just up the road about three miles from her tiny apartment. Twice Sal had invited her out, but she had put him off; she needed the time to herself, to settle quietly into her new life.

At home she rarely saw the trainer. He kept to himself, alone in his house behind the small corral where The Boston Kid, his ornery fourteen-year-old gelding, munched phlegmatically on his feed or stood lethargically in one corner of his pen under the shade of a huge eucalyptus that soared skyward, poking long leafy fingers at the sky. The dogs ran happily about the property, but they went into the house at night, safe from the marauding coyotes that raided the ranches in the foothills of the San Gabriels. "They come down from the hills every night," Fontana had told her the day she moved in. "Everyone around here has lost a dog or a cat to them, including me. They'd go after The Kid, too, if he weren't so big and mean."

"What about The Kid?" she had asked him that first late afternoon.

"He was my wife Maria's horse," the trainer explained. "A stakes winner and a whole bunch of other races, till we had to retire him at

55

eight. She wouldn't part with him, so he's been with us ever since, leading the life of Riley here. Don't get near him—he's as mean as a cougar. Only Maria knew how to handle him."

Jill had, of course, ignored the advice. No sooner had Jake gone into the house than she had approached the pen, leaned against the top railing, and begun talking softly to the horse. At first The Kid had eyed her malevolently, then ignored her, but after nearly an hour of gentle coaxing he had shambled arthritically over to her, sniffed her bare arm where it lay against the rail, then nibbled at the carrot she had thrust under his nose, as her flow of soothing conversation bathed the cranky old gelding in calm reassurance.

"Well, you sure do have the touch," Jake told her. He'd been watching her through the window, then had come outside to stand in the doorway to observe, ready also to intervene if the mean old boy decided to take a chunk out of her. The Kid had once bitten off a groom's thumb, and he had left scars on several others. Not even Jake had felt safe with him. Only Maria had, she of the dark eyes and gentle hands. The Boston Kid was a rogue, twelve-hundred pounds of mean gray muscle with eyes that seemed to glow in the dark. For Maria he'd been like a big sheepdog and he'd run like the wind. Second in the Santa Anita Derby, first in the San Felipe and the Norfolk, second in the Preakness, winner of the Travers at Saratoga, and, as an older horse, triumphant in a dozen graded contests all over the country. He'd made Jake Fontana's reputation, won him money, brought him clients. Jake could have used a few more like him, despite the gelding's evil disposition. When the horse had been retired, the trainer had wanted to donate him to one of the foundations that harbored old geldings, but no one had wanted him; his reputation as a mangler preceded him. So Jake had kept him, which was fine with Maria, who alone of all the horse's human acquaintances loved him unreservedly.

"I've never met a horse I couldn't get next to," Jill said. "They're only mean if you don't treat 'em well."

"Well, mostly you're right," Jake agreed. "Only this old boy's got

the devil in him sometimes. You don't want to take him for granted ever. You promise? Otherwise, I've got to stop you from going
near him."

"I'll be careful." She gave The Kid one last reassuring pat on the
nose, then rubbed his head up between his ears. "I'll see you, Kid.
You just take it easy. We're going to get along just fine."

On the sixth morning, when she showed up for work, she found
Eduardo alone but looking distressed. "The boss, he no come today,"
he said. "He not feeling good."

"What's he got?" she asked. "A cold? He seemed okay yesterday."

The Mexican shook his head. "Sometimes he not feel good," he
said. "He stay home one, maybe two, three days."

"What's he got?"

Eduardo shrugged, his eyes eloquent in their sadness, then he
tapped his head with one forefinger. "*La señora*, he still very sad
about *la señora*."

"When did she die?"

"Two year ago."

"And he's still sad? He must have loved her a lot."

The trainer called the barn just after eleven and spoke to Eduardo,
who filled him in on the morning's activities. Twenty minutes later
Rich Abernathy called and this time Jill took the phone, bringing him
up to date on his horses and making an excuse for Jake. The trainer's
absence did not surprise the owner, who only said, "He needs to see
a doctor. Tell him to call Ed Barrow. He can refer him to somebody,
if he has to. These attacks are getting worse. But he's a stubborn asshole. He doesn't believe in medication, even though he needs it."

"I'll tell him what you said."

"What about you? Been up on anything lately?"

"No. Except for Julie Krone, who's a Hall of Fame rider, girls don't
get hired in California."

"You can ride for me anytime, kid."

"I appreciate that. I really do."

"Remember what I told you, tell Jake to call Ed Barrow. He's a doctor I referred him to. He's also nuts in his own way, but he can help Jake. You understand me?"

"Sure do. I'll tell him."

That afternoon the track was dark, the first of the two non-racing days. Jill went home and made herself a tuna salad sandwich, then went out to have a look at The Boston Kid. The old gelding snorted a welcome and ambled over to her for his daily carrots. The dogs gamboled happily about her feet, then began chasing each other around the property. They must have just come outside because she hadn't seen them earlier, and they were full of manic energy from having been inside all night and most of the morning. They had their own door to go in and out of, but she guessed they had chosen to remain inside with their sick master until they'd heard her talking to The Kid out by the corral. She glanced toward the house and saw no sign of the trainer. She wondered what to do about him, hesitating to thrust herself into his life. But what if he was really sick and needed her?

Inside the house Jake Fontana lay on his back in the darkness of his bedroom. The sun poked slivers of light through the closed shutters, but he kept his eyes focused on the blank wall to the left of his bed, as if only the dark empty space were desirable to him. The panic attacks came every twenty minutes or so, bringing with them an overwhelming feeling of emptiness and despair. He didn't know how long they lasted, perhaps no more than a minute or so or a matter of seconds, but they swept over him like small tidal waves, stripping him of logic and desire. In between these relentless attacks, he lay there almost motionless, a prisoner in his own body, helpless to rouse himself to cognitive action. Sometimes he'd hear Maria's voice talking to him, attempting to reassure him and calm him, to keep him safely within the boundaries beyond which madness lurked. He told himself that this time, too, the attacks would stop, that he'd return as always to the rational world, but he couldn't convince himself. He lay there a prisoner to dementia, his brain a jumble of wildly contrasting images and impulses in which shadows dominated, horror reigned. His loaded gun rested in a drawer of his desk in a corner of the living room and he fought an impulse to go and get it, knowing that if he did so he'd be able to end his misery. The thought of total darkness, of oblivion, the quick blinding resonating flash that would terminate his ordeal seemed irresistible to him. Twice he'd staggered to his feet to make that move, only to fall back exhausted on his bed, forced down by the weight of the wave that engulfed him. He thought, too, that from time to time Maria not only was helping him through this ordeal, but also was calling to him to join her, like a siren from some safe haven where she was waiting for him. It was more than he could stand, this love that called back to him from beyond the grave.

"Jake, Jake, it's me. I'm sorry to bother you," Jill called out. "I just thought I'd better look in on you, see if there's anything I can do."

He turned his head toward the sound. She was standing in the doorway, her face indistinguishable in the gloom. "Maria?" he mumbled. "Maria?"

"No, it's me, Jake. It's Jill."

"Go away. I'm all right."

She hesitated, hovering there in the darkness like a ghost. "Can I get you something?"

"No, I'm okay."

"I can call a doctor, somebody."

"No, nobody. Please. I'm okay."

She was still standing there in the doorway when the next attack came, a wave that thrust him upward off the bed. He groaned and stiffened, then fell back after a few seconds as if some giant hand had grabbed him, shaken him, then dropped him like a doll on his damp sheets. He was dressed only in his shorts and his body gleamed in the dark as if he'd been soaked in oil. She hastened to his bedside and felt his brow. He seemed cool enough, but she hurried into the bathroom, found a washcloth, soaked it in cold water, and rushed back to clamp it on his forehead.

It helped. He felt suddenly reassured by her presence, the cold damp cloth seeming to calm him. But when the next attack came, he pulled her down on top of him and cried out in his anguish. She did not resist. She allowed the full crushing weight of his embrace to hold her fast, then, after a few minutes, when the wave passed and he released her, she rose quickly to her feet. "I think I better call 911," she said. "You need help."

"No, don't do that." He waved a hand about in the air. "Barrow. Call Ed Barrow. Telephone. On the desk."

While she rustled about among the papers in his living room, two of the dogs appeared at his bedside and placed cold, anxious muzzles against his ribs. He reached out to stroke them, scratch under their ears. He heard Jill's voice speaking rapidly into the phone. He tried to rally, made himself sit up, swung his legs over the side of the bed, but could go no further. When the next attack came, he fell back on his sheets and cried out again. As if from a great distance, he heard a voice calling to him. "He's coming," the voice said. "He'll be here in half an hour. Just hold on, Jake."

He remembered nothing specifically about what happened after that, except for the presence of someone who bathed his head in cold, wet cloths, who held his hand in hers, who lay beside him when the waves washed over him and his body stiffened in response. He could make out nothing of his surroundings, seeing only vague shapes, shadows on the walls, hearing only the strange voices that called to him from afar. He was alone and yet not alone. Sometimes the room seemed full of presences whose features he could not quite distinguish, whose voices he could not individualize, but who seemed to be whispering about him. And then darkness would close over him, followed by a silence so profound that he imagined death had to be exactly like that, an elimination of life from the very core of his being, an abstraction of himself. He seemed to be standing outside of himself, looking down at his own body as it lay there on the bed, helplessly inert. Not even Maria's voice could now have summoned him back to life. And he realized that all along he had yearned for death, would have welcomed it, was disappointed that in the end it had failed to claim him.

***

When Jake opened his eyes again, it was to see Ed Barrow's great beak of a nose and dark, soulful eyes looking down at him. Jake tried to speak, but the only thing that came out of his mouth was an unintelligible grunt. He cleared his throat, tried to raise himself to a sitting position. The doctor's hand on his shoulder pressed him back down to the comfort of his pillows. The trainer looked around the room but saw no trace of the girl. The shutters had been partly opened, the curtains tugged aside; a pale light filtered into the room. Outside, the dogs were barking. "I want you to take it easy," Ed Barrow said. "No quick movements. I want you to just lie there for a few minutes. I need to ask you some questions."

"What time is it?"

"Just after five. You've been out for a couple of hours or so. I gave you a shot of Valium and you went to sleep. Feeling any better?"

"I think so. Not better maybe, just more myself."

"I'm going to prescribe some drugs for you. I want you to take them. They're tranquilizers. You understand me, Jake? You can work, okay, but they'll slow you down for a while."

The trainer didn't answer, but simply looked questioningly up at the doctor. Then he groaned softly and pushed himself up against the pillows. "What the hell's wrong with me, Doc?"

"Well, you could have a brain tumor," Ed Barrow said cheerfully, as if announcing a special on a menu. "But I don't think so," he added. "We can do CAT scans and MRIs, a whole bunch of expensive tests on you featuring complicated gadgetry, but I don't think we'll find anything. You're probably having what in the good old Paleolithic days I grew up in used to be called a nervous breakdown. Dr. Freud, that terrific old phony, would have had a field day with you. He'd nail all this on the recent death of your wife and your repressed grieving and then he'd delve endlessly into your undoubtedly shitty childhood, maybe figure out you were abused somewhere back there. He'd find something and write it all up for future generations to ponder and to make himself famous, but it wouldn't do you

61

any good. You're what—fifty-two years old? You're suffering from some sort of biochemical imbalance up there behind your glassy blue eyes, something medications can control, maybe even fix. The trick is figuring out which medications. To do that, we need to get some blood tests, even though you had a physical two months ago and there was nothing wrong with you. Are you listening to me?"

Jake again didn't answer him at once. He'd felt the wave gathering to overwhelm him once more, but this time it receded. He sighed with relief.

"Another one?"

"Yeah, but it stopped. I just feel real tired suddenly, like I want to sleep forever."

"That's natural. I gave you enough Valium to put your horses to sleep, though most of them go to sleep on me every time I bet on them. How much sleep do you get a night?"

"Three, four hours."

"That's not enough. These attacks can also be caused by sleep deprivation. I want you to sleep every night at least seven hours, even if you have to take sleeping pills, understand?"

"Yeah."

"Who's that girl who called me?"

"She works for me. Jill Aspen."

"That's the one who rode for you last week?"

"Yeah. I told her to call you."

"Good thing you did. Why didn't you let me know she could ride? I'd have cashed a ticket. I haven't cashed one in three weeks."

"Sorry. I didn't know she was any good."

"It's okay. I wouldn't have believed you if you had touted me onto her. I don't trust trainers."

"And I don't trust doctors."

"I don't blame you. We're always making mistakes."

"I hope you don't make one here. I don't want any tests."

"You have to have them. If you're up to it, I want you in my office tomorrow or the day after at the latest. Otherwise, I can hospitalize you and have the tests done there."

"No hospitals, Doc. I watched Maria suffer in there. They couldn't do anything for her. They wouldn't even give her enough pain medication."

"Hospitals and doctors don't believe in pain. They think it's over-rated, and they're worried the government will think they're dealing dope and creating terminal junkies. Too bad I didn't know you then. Your wife would have left us pain-free, I guarantee it."

"Can I go to work tomorrow? I've got horses to take care of."

"Absolutely not. I want you to take it very easy for a few days. I want you to take the medications I prescribe for you. Then you come in and see me again, we do some more tests, we adjust the medications, we get you functioning again. You'll have to stay on medications, too. And you need to sleep."

"Drugs? How long?"

"Maybe forever, Jake. We have lots of medicines now, lots of new drugs for this and that, and we test them to find out if they work, not why. Especially when it comes to the brain. The brain, Jake, is like the dark side of the moon, unknown terrain. You've got an illness; let's find out how to treat it, but let's not delude ourselves we'll ever know all the answers."

"I keep seeing Maria. I keep dreaming about her. I keep hearing her voice."

"It's an aspect of your illness. It's not the cause, Jake. Your brain is in distress and it focuses on what is causing you the most pain. Obviously it's your wife. Where's the girl?"

"Out back, or maybe in her room. She lives over the garage."

"Good. She can go and get these prescriptions filled. I also want her to look in on you a couple of times during the night and tomorrow."

"She works with my foreman, Eduardo."

"Good. Then your horses will be well taken care of, too. I'll go get her." He put a hand on Jake's shoulder and awkwardly patted it, the best he could do in the comfort zone. Ed Barrow didn't trust most people, thought they were mainly unreliable and up to no good, selfish bastards full of foolish and unmerited hubris. "Most people are shit," he had once observed during a discussion with friends on human affairs. He got up to go. "You're to take it very, very easy, you understand? Any recurrence over the next couple of days and I'll have to hospitalize you. I want you to call me first thing tomorrow morning. I'll set up appointments for you this afternoon. I'm in my office by eight sharp. And you have my home number, too."

Ed Barrow went outside and found Jill standing by the corral next to the mean-looking old gray horse he distrusted profoundly, sensing in him the criminal intent of a killer. "I want you to get these filled," he said, thrusting several small white slips of paper into her hands. "They're prescriptions. He ought to be okay and a lot better tomorrow. If he has a relapse, I want you to call me at once. If you can't reach me, you call 911 and get him to Arcadia Methodist, that's the nearest hospital here, and you have them get hold of me. He's an ornery s.o.b., but I think he's had a good scare. He'll do what I tell him, at least for now."

"What's wrong with him?"

"I can't talk to you or anyone about one of my patients."

"I'll keep an eye on him."

"That's what I want you to do." Barrow gazed uneasily at the horse. "That The Boston Kid?"

"Yes."

"Hell of a horse. I cashed a few tickets on him. I knew Fontana was taking care of him, but not why."

"He's a gelding and he's got nowhere to go. He was real good to Jake and his wife. Jake ain't about to turn him over to the killers."

"That makes Jake one of the good guys. There aren't many. You been with him long?"

"No. Going on two weeks."

"What I don't want is a repeat of these attacks he's been having."

"I'll look in on him regular."

"Even if you have to stay away from the track. Got that?"

"Yeah."

"He'll go back to sleep soon. He should be out the rest of the day and night, but you never know with these cases." Barrow's cell phone rang and he fished it out of his pocket, then walked to his car as he began to talk to some patient at the other end. "There's nothing wrong with you, Mildred," he said. "You're just an old Beverly Hills broad with nothing to do but break my balls with your imaginary ailments. I want you to go back to playing bridge. Better yet, why not go shopping?"

CHAPTER 7

On the day Jake Fontana came back to work at the barn Jill won her second race in as many tries, this one on a cheap three-year-old filly running six furlongs in a $10,000 claiming race. All the filly had to offer was speed, the trainer had told her, so it was essential to break quickly out of the gate, get her to the front, and try to hold her together till the finish line. Which is exactly what Jill accomplished, busting the filly out of the two hole, opening up four lengths by the half, then managing to keep her going without overusing the whip, so that she hit the wire a head and a nose in front of the horses closing on both sides with every stride. Bones had bet two hundred on her and enjoyed the outcome, which he had never doubted even during the last few strides. The filly was claimed out of the race and led away from the winner's circle by a groom from the new owner's string, but Jake didn't seem upset to lose her. "I don't know where I'd have run her next," he told Bones as he watched her go. "She isn't much and she's got problems, mainly an ankle."

"Sweet little thing," Jill commented as they headed back toward the stands. "She'd make a nice saddle horse. Who took her?"

"Jerry Loomis," Bones said. "She'll last two or three races for that bum. Sooner or later he breaks them all down. He wouldn't know how to train a dog to piss on a hydrant, but he's got a vet who injects them everywhere. They usually win one or two for him and then fall apart."

"No comment," Jake said.

"Fucking trainers all stick together," Bones said. "Like doctors and lawyers."

The filly had belonged to Fontana's most faithful owner, Ester Gale Dinworthy, the elderly widow of an oil tycoon who had dabbled in horses for years. She kept up the tradition but never chose to own more than one horse at a time. Fontana was fond of her. "I told her the filly wasn't much when we took her last year, but Ester Gale, when she makes up her mind it stays made up. She'd seen the horse in the walking ring two weeks before we claimed her for twenty-five thousand and I couldn't talk her out of it."

"Man, twenty-five thousand?" Jill said. "That filly ain't even bred that well and that's a lot of money for her."

"Not for Ester Gale," Jake said. "She's loaded, but she won't spend enough for a really good horse. And she's stubborn as a mule when it comes to getting what she wants when she wants it. She falls in love with all her horses. Not a good idea."

"You don't believe that, do you, Jake?" Jill said.

"Yeah, I do," he answered. "Trouble is, I can't always help myself. Maria always said nothing was worth doing if it wasn't for love. Now I have to go to the Turf Club and talk to Ester Gale about buying another horse. Come on, Bones, maybe I can get you to go in with her."

"You never know when to quit, do you? Go in on a horse with that crazy old broad?"

As they neared the tunnel under the stands, Jill turned to the trainer and asked, "You feeling okay?"

"I could use a little more energy in the mornings," he said, "but yeah—I'm all right." As Jill headed for the jockeys' room, he took her arm. "Good ride, kid. You know what you're doing out there. You don't need to come back to the barn tonight. Go on home. Treat yourself to a good dinner somewhere. You're getting too skinny. What are you now?"

"A hundred seven."

"Too thin. Maybe I ought to take you out to dinner tonight. Will you let me?"

She looked up at him unsmilingly, suddenly wary, but then she nodded her head. "Okay. An early dinner."

"I'll be home by five-thirty, straight from the barn. I'll knock on your door."

The two men left her and walked into the Turf Club, where Rich Abernathy grabbed Jake's arm as they skirted his table. "You're making me rich with that girl rider of yours," the owner said. "That horse should have paid no better than seven bucks and I got twice that on her. You going to keep using her?"

"Looks like I ought to, doesn't it?"

"You might put me ahead for the meet if you do. By the way, I think I know where I first saw her."

"Where was that?"

"At Barrett's, the fall sale last year. She was with Paul Furman and his Heritage Farm people. They sold a bunch of yearlings. I think she worked for him and there were rumors about her and Furman."

"What kind of rumors?" Bones asked.

Abernathy shrugged. "The usual kind, that she was involved with him. After Furman's kid died, she dropped temporarily out of sight."

"The girl drowned, right?"

"That was the story. Troubled teenager. But nobody's quite sure how it happened or why."

"They suspected Jill had something to do with it?"

"I never did find out. It was all over the news up there and there were big stories in the local papers, mostly in the Bay Area, but I didn't read them. There was a lot of talk. What happens around guys like Furman is always news, I guess." He smiled at Jake. "Anyway, keep riding her. I'm making money. How's the two-year-old?"

"He'll be ready definitely by Del Mar, maybe before," Jake said. "He's working good. He's fast and Jill's got him calmed down some, though he's still pretty green."

"Fast horses and faster women, that's what I like."

They left Rich Abernathy to count his winnings and went to talk to Ester Gale Dinworthy, who was sitting at her usual table a few yards beyond the finish line. She was dressed in a spangled billowing purple cape with a triple strand of pearls around her neck. "Giacomo, do sit down," she exclaimed, as they approached. "We must discuss this situation. I'm very distressed at losing my little girl."

"Mrs. Dinworthy, this is a friend of mine, Mr. Righetti," Jake said. "Do you mind if he joins us?"

"Not at all. Charmed, I'm sure," she said, holding out a jeweled hand as if she expected Bones to kiss it.

Instead he squeezed it gently. "Equally charmed," he assured her.

"Do sit down," she said, turning to Jake as the two men sank into chairs facing her. "How did this happen?"

The trainer sighed. "There was nowhere else to run her, Mrs. Dinworthy," he explained. "Believe me, you're well rid of her. She has a suspicious-looking front ankle and I don't know how many races she has left in her. Even at her best she's not much."

"Oh, you brutal horsemen, you can't see beyond your noses," Ester Gale Dinworthy declared, with a deprecating sniff. "She's such a pretty little thing. And now that we've lost her, what are you going to do about it?"

"I presume you'll be looking for another horse. How about a nice, not too expensive three-year-old?"

"Are there any?"

"This is the time of year to look around for one, before they sort themselves out after they start running. The idea is to get one we can improve. Mr. Righetti here might be willing to come in with us."

"Just as long as you're in charge, Giacomo," she said, "and the horse runs in my colors."

"No problem," Bones said, looking at Jake and wondering how the trainer quietly had managed to con him into buying a piece of this loony dame's horse. Maybe Jake knew Bones better than he knew himself; the passion never dies, the lure of owning even a small piece of a Thoroughbred is irresistible to the people in the game.

So for the next half-hour they talked horses. Jake was determined to make his client invest in a young horse with some potential, but Ester Gale Dinworthy would not commit herself to any animal she hadn't looked at herself, a condition that pretty much tied the trainer's hands. He could have worked a deal with some big string like Steve Bullion's to buy one of their less well-regarded young horses, with the idea of being able to improve the animal, turn him from a potential into a sound investment. But having to involve Ester Gale Dinworthy in the proceedings would lead to a jacking up of the sales price and she had always set herself stringent limits; she wouldn't spend more than $40,000 or $50,000 for a horse, hardly enough to get anyone into the game in these days of overpriced sales still dominated by Arab money. "I'll put in up to twenty-five grand," Bones heard himself say. "If you'll let Jake here make the deal. That way we could get ourselves a decent horse."

"Indeed," Ester Gale Dinworthy said. "Well, I suppose I ought to let you try, Giacomo. You do look out for me and I appreciate it. It's simply that I have to like what I'm doing. Isn't that the purpose of life?"

"I wish you'd call me Jake," the trainer said. "I've never even been to Italy."

"It's one of my purposes in life to get you there," she informed him. "Italy is one of the most remarkable countries in the world. And you even married an Italian girl. Where was Maria from?"

"Her family came from Naples, like mine."

"That great gorgeous whore of a city," Ester Gale Dinworthy said. "I know it well. I had a cousin who was consul in Naples. The times we had there! Of course the Neapolitans are insane and completely untrustworthy, but also brilliant and charming. Maria had all their good qualities and, I assume, none of their bad ones. Your family came from there, too?"

"Nearby. Around Caserta."

"Another remarkable city, with a magnificent palazzo. The Bourbons, you know, were a much maligned monarchy. Some members of the family were a bit corrupt and some were useless, but on the whole an admirable aristocracy. Perhaps I should send you to Italy to buy a horse for me there. Would you like that?"

Jake laughed. "I think I'd do a bad job of it," he said. "I don't know anyone in the horse business there. Do they have racing in Naples?"

"Oh, yes, and also in Rome, Milan, Florence, Pisa, Turin, and many other cities. I should send you on a grand tour. You'd get an education, connect to your Italian roots and bring us back another Ribot."

"And who would take care of my other horses and clients?"

"Oh, don't be tiresome, Giacomo. Anyone could handle your interests in your absence; I'm sure, even Eduardo."

"He doesn't know how to talk to clients," Jake said, "even in Spanish. Now, if I could persuade you to invest half a million or so and buy some really well-bred, potentially good horses, I wouldn't need any other clients and you could send me to Italy."

"A price way beyond my means," she said. "I'll have to find some other way to reconnect you to your roots. Meanwhile, go out and find me a nice horse and arrange it so I can sneak a look at it before you commit. By the way, who is this young woman you've engaged to ride for you?"

"She works for me. She's a good horsewoman."

"Very commendable of you, Giacomo," Ester Gale Dinworthy pronounced. "It's shocking to think that so few women are employed as jockeys and trainers in this backward state, which is only slightly less boorish than Texas. You're taking a strong stand. I approve. Oh, and by the way," she added, as the men started to leave, "you will make sure that my darling little filly is well taken care of by these sinister people who had the audacity to take her from me?"

"I'll try, Mrs. Dinworthy," Jake said, knowing well that nothing he could do or say would have any effect on Jerry Loomis and his vet's magic needles; the filly was, in effect, doomed. He and Bones hurried away before Ester Gale Dinworthy could pursue that painful topic any further.

***

"I don't think I thanked you enough for what you did for me last week," Jake Fontana said, his eyes still haunted by the memory of his breakdown. "It was damn nice of you."

"What did you think I'd do, Jake?" Jill asked. "Let you lie there?"

"Still, I want you to know how much I appreciate it."

"You've gone through stuff like that before?"

"Yeah, a couple of times since Maria's death," he told her, "but never as bad as the other day. If you hadn't come along, I might have tried to shoot myself. God knows I thought about it."

They were having dinner in a small Italian family restaurant in downtown Pasadena called I Monti, where Jake and Maria had gone frequently. It had the usual red-and-white checkered tablecloths and candles and bad landscapes on the walls, but the food was excellent, with the accent on veal dishes and risottos; the owners came from the Piedmont. This was the first time since Maria's death he had gone there. He'd told Jill that and she had immediately suggested somewhere else, but he had insisted. "I've got to get my personal life back together," he'd explained. "I'm okay now. They've got me on medication and I'm feeling almost normal."

"So what's wrong with you, exactly?"

"Some sort of chemical screwup in the brain, they tell me," he said, smiling wanly. "Made worse by lack of sleep and the grieving I've been going through."

"Maria must have been a wonderful woman, huh?"

"She was. Despite the fact she didn't like racing, except for The Kid. Opera and the arts were more in her line. She even got me to sit through a couple of performances at the Music Center. I enjoyed them, but getting to bed that late makes it tough to get up in the morning."

"So you were married a long time?"

"Only twelve years and the last two were tough. She had cancer and it took two years to kill her. She suffered a lot, and at the end she didn't know me, they had her so full of drugs."

Jill didn't know what to say. Nothing that could bring him comfort, that's for sure. She sniffed the aroma of the risotto with mushrooms the waiter had set down in front of her and plunged in. "Terrific," was all she said. "How's yours?"

"Great. This place serves the best Italian food in town. Maria loved it."

"You had no children, right?"

"No, Maria couldn't have any. That's why we have dogs. She loved dogs. I do, too, but not like her."

They ate in silence much of the time. Jill sensed that it embarrassed him to talk too much about his breakdown and that it was too painful to recall his married life. Like many horsemen, Jake Fontana was a quiet man who kept his emotions to himself. He was a third-generation trainer whose grandfather had won a Kentucky Derby. He was the first of his family to have come out West, his father and grandfather having trained mainly in Maryland and Florida. "My old man is still training in Florida," he told her. "He has a small string, five or six horses, but he's still out there every morning, still wins a race every now and then."

Jill told him about herself and her dream of becoming a top rider. "Only time I've ever been real happy was around horses," she said. She talked very little about her family.

"You ever hear from your brothers or your mom?" Jake asked.

"Nope. I figure they'll pop up one day, when I get famous enough."

"You don't miss them?"

"I had so little to do with 'em those last few years," she explained, "I'm not sure I'd recognize 'em now." Then she asked Jake about Bones.

"Well, you know he's been a jock's agent and a good one, but mainly he's a gambler," Jake said. "He's got the fever about horses. He's real hot now, but he has cold streaks, too. I think I kind of conned him into buying a horse with Mrs. Dinworthy."

"Was he really some kind of Mafia guy?"

"I think so, for a while. But he got out. He's never done any time either. I trust him. I don't know why."

"I think he likes me, Jake."

"You went out with him, right?"

"Only once. It was nice."

"Bones is all right."

"I like his real name better. I call him Sal."

74

"Yeah, it's a good name. It's just that everybody calls him Bones and he doesn't seem to mind."

"I can't get involved with anyone right now," she said. "I … well, I had some trouble …" She let her voice trail away into silence and averted her eyes, as if afraid to reveal too much of herself.

Jake tried to come to her rescue. "I wouldn't worry about Bones," he said. "If he could put a saddle on your back and bet on you, he might really come after you. But I think you're pretty safe. He's had girlfriends, and he's seeing somebody now off and on, but nothing lasts too long with Bones. The track is what he really cares about."

"I ain't going to date no one right now," she said. "I was married and that sure wasn't a hell of a lot of fun. Now I got my job with you and my career to think about."

"Well, Sal could really help you there, if you want him to. He knows everybody. Your marriage and all, was that why you left the Bay Area? Strikes me you'd have had an easier time getting mounts up there."

She shook her head and again looked away from him. "No, I had some other problems, personal stuff. I had to get away."

"Sure. It's none of my business, really."

"It's okay," she said. "You got a right, I guess, so long as I work for you."

"Well, we're doing real good," Jake said. "I'm not about to fire you."

CHAPTER 8

Bones stayed away from the track for the next five days, partly because the first two days were dark and the cards on the following three days were uninspiring. He would have had a hard time keeping his winning streak going, he told himself. He called Jake, however, who told him he had begun looking for a horse for Ester Gale Dinworthy. Jake also wanted assurance that Bones would come in for a piece of it, as he'd promised to do. "Yeah, yeah," Bones said to him, "though I've been asking myself what the fuck do I think I'm doing, getting back into the wrong end of the game."

"You're hooked on it, that's why," Jake said. "You aren't just a lousy gambler."

Being a Thoroughbred owner, Bones knew, was like trying to hit the lottery. It cost you nothing but money and, most of the time, the rewards were slim at best. These animals were so fragile they'd break, tear, bruise, and come down with all sorts of ailments you'd never heard of but were severe enough to knock them out of action for months, years, or often forever. If that happened and the horse you owned was a gelding or a cheap mare or a badly bred colt, well, you were stuck holding a twelve-hundred-pound sack of shit. These bums went right on eating, though, and they could run up vet bills that could keep a Beverly Hills psychiatrist's wife in sables.

You got out by selling the horse for a few bucks to the killer, who would come by the barn in a van early one morning and cart him away to be converted into dog food. Of course, if you were a softy like Jake, you didn't do that. You'd try to find a home for the bum, retire him to a riding stable, make a jumper out of him, or if he was a classy old hard knocker like Gamblin Man, you would give him to one of the racehorse retirement farms, where they would keep him standing around at considerable expense for visitors to gawk at.

After his chat with Jake, Bones lay back on his bed and again asked himself what the fuck he thought he was doing. He reasoned that he was now so far ahead for the year that he could take a flyer. What was it about these damn Thoroughbreds? They were so goddamn beautiful they dazzled you, scrambled your brains, made you believe they could carry you to the end of the rainbow. He was supposed to be a tough guy, but Jake knew his weaknesses. He had been suckered, as usual. It had happened before, and it would happen again. At least the ride could be fun, he knew that much, though having to listen to Ester Gale Dinworthy day after day might make him regret the whole deal. He began to hope Jake wouldn't be able to come up with the right horse, but he knew he would, even if it took a couple of months.

Bones enjoyed his break from the races and not having to dig through the stats in the *Racing Form* to ferret out winners. Everybody could use a little freshening, at the track and everywhere else in life. Bones wasn't the sort of guy who liked to work too hard to get along, and his needs were modest: the horses, friends, partying after winning days, the occasional broad. Or should he say lady? Yeah, why not? Broads were broads, ladies were something else, and it had nothing to do with bloodlines or money. At the track you bet on speed, but in life you look for class. Which was why he had linked up some months ago with Bingo Dupuis.

Bingo worked as a cocktail waitress at the Blue Flamingo on Little Santa Monica in west L.A. The joint was nothing special, consisting of a semicircular bar with booths lined along the opposite wall and a dining room in the rear for meat-and-potatoes guys and dolls. The owner, Marty Blenheim, was a track degenerate who poured most of his earnings back through the pari-mutuel windows, but the restaurant was popular with the track crowd and gamblers in general, so he managed to survive. Bingo had been working for him for two years and she loved the guy. "He pays great, with health insurance and all, he lets me keep all my tips, and he don't hassle me," she told Bones the night they met. "Not like those other joints I worked, where I had to go topless and put up with all kinds of shit. But what are you going to do? I got a ten-year-old kid to raise. Marty's been a godsend."

Before Bones made a move on Bingo he asked Marty if it would be okay. Marty was a skinny little guy of about sixty with a bowed neck like an old plater and a long face with sunken cheeks, big yellow teeth, a hooked nose, and soulful brown eyes; he reminded Bones of an old pushcart peddler he had known back in Jersey. But Bones had the utmost respect for him because he gave everybody a fair shake, not only his employees but also all of his customers. The food was simple but good, the drinks were generous, the atmosphere, with all the walls decorated with blowups of great horse races, comforting. "She's a nice kid," Marty told Bones. "She's been through some tough times and she's devoted to this kid of hers. So don't go messing her up, Sal, okay? Take her out, if you want to, but watch it, okay?"

"Hey, Marty," Bones said, "you know me. I'm not a saint, but I don't abuse or take advantage, you know what I'm saying?"

So that's how it started. Bones took Bingo and Tommy, her kid, out to the movies or the zoo or to ball games, and he never made a move on her. He just liked being with her. She was originally from some hick farm town in Nebraska, and she was funny as hell about growing up there. Only you could easily sense between the jokes and the funny stories that her childhood hadn't been quite such a riot and not so charming either. Her father had been a wheat farmer. He'd also been a drunk who beat her and her mother. At eighteen Bingo had fled to California, where two years later she had married a TV actor who worked in some soap opera and she had his kid. While she was pregnant, he started having sex with the script girl on his show. Six months after Tommy was born she left the actor, and she'd been on her own ever since. There had been other guys, of course—another actor, a scriptwriter, a porno film producer who tried to get her to star in some epic of his called *Babes in Chains*—but she'd dumped them all eventually. By the time Bones showed up in her life she hadn't dated anyone in more than a year. At first she wouldn't let him touch her, but he didn't mind. He liked being around her, sharing time with her, and she didn't like the horses, which was good because then he wouldn't have to worry about her losing money at the track. He quoted Pittsburgh Phil, that great horseplayer, to her one night: "A man who accepts the responsibility of escorting a woman to the racetrack, and of seeing that she is comfortably placed and agreeably entertained, cannot keep his mind on his work before him." After he'd read this maxim aloud to Bingo, she understood perfectly. "Hey, I get it," she said. "You sickos would rather lose at the track than win in life."

"Not exactly," Bones said. "If I couldn't beat this game, Bingo, I'd be doing something else."

"Like what?"

"Like maybe running for president of the United States."

"Fat chance."

"Could I do worse than this bum we got now?"

They bantered like that all the time; they could make each other laugh. So one night, after he'd taken her and Tommy home from a UCLA football game, she asked him to stay. An hour or so later, with Tommy safely asleep in his own room, she'd taken him into her bedroom and they'd gotten it on. Bones was amazed at what a terrific lay she was, uninhibited and totally into it. She was no Victoria's Secret model, but she had a tight, supple body, well proportioned, with not an ounce of fat on her. She worked out three times a week, she told him, and kept her face out of the sun so that her fair, slightly freckled complexion wouldn't become wrinkled. "You ought to work out, too, Sal," she said to him after their second or third night together. "You've got a great build, but you could lose maybe ten pounds around the middle."

"Yeah? Well, maybe," he said. "But, hey, somebody hits me there I got the fat to absorb it, know what I mean?"

She sat up in bed and looked at him. He was stretched out on his back, with his hands behind his head, and she thoughtfully ran her fingers from his neck along his chest down to his waist. "Wow, where'd you get all those muscles? You must have worked out at some time."

"I still do, just not as often," he said. "You know, I lived in a tough neighborhood, and I didn't want anybody pushing me around, you know? Then later, when I worked for the Family—"

"What family? Yours?"

"No, somebody else's. I had to collect money that was owed. I never tried to hurt anybody real bad, but I had to look like I could; know what I mean?"

She sat straight up in bed and looked at him in alarm. "Geez, Sal, don't tell me you're a Mafia guy; please don't tell me that."

"Did I say that? No, sugar—there were debts, and it was my job to collect them. I also got a little cut of the take."

"What kind of debts?"

"Mostly gambling. You know, the horses, football, basketball, base-ball, ice hockey, those kind of debts. Lots of guys don't like to pay."

"So ... so you ... so you strong-armed them—"

"Not too often. Usually I'd just show up and they'd pay me real quick, or maybe we'd make a deal where if they were tapped they could pay off in installments. You know, like you buy furniture or something."

"With interest, right?"

"Well, yeah, Bingo. Banks charge interest, credit cards charge interest. Everybody does. That's capitalism, right?"

"You didn't hurt anybody, so why do they call you Bones?"

"Well, a couple of times their guys would try to get rough with me, take me out, know what I mean? Then I'd have to defend myself. It's only natural. You hit people, sometimes bones get broken. I didn't hit a lot of people, but I can hit pretty hard, Bingo. Couple of guys I knew wanted me to turn pro, you know, become a fighter, but that wasn't for me. I don't know how to box."

"So what did you do?"

"Well, I always tried to reason with them. If that didn't work, I'd, I don't know, throw a punch or two, try to ram them up against something hard, maybe like a wall or a doorjamb. Whatever, it usually worked."

She got up from the bed and stood there, looking down at him. "Geez, Sal, I don't know," she said. "Maybe I shouldn't see you anymore. That's no way to earn a living, hurting people."

"I know, Bingo, believe me, I know," he said, sitting up and taking her hand. "That's why I got out. They were going to move me up in the ranks, and I didn't want any part of that. Prostitution, the rackets, protection, that wasn't for me. So I quit."

"They let you?"

"Yeah, I'd moved to New York by then. I was hotwalking, hanging around the backstretch. I was learning how to look at a horse and how to bet, important stuff. I think the Family figured I'd be a good source of inside info, so I strung them along for a while, gave them a few tips. Then I went to my capo, Tony Capestro, we called him Ears, and I told him I wanted out, that I was moving to California where nobody knew anything about me. Tony and I got along okay, and I'd never been busted, you know? But I figured I'd get nowhere if I had to hang around the East Coast. At some point they would ask me to set up something that could get me into trouble, so three days later I packed up and left and came out here. It took me a year to get located, get things started, but I've been doing pretty good, all legit stuff. I bet, I win, I lose some, I've been a jock's agent, I'm licensed now."

"And nobody ever bothered you?"

"Not so far and that was quite a while ago. But I know what's going on. I'm careful. I don't hear from anybody, which is good. They think I'm a hopeless loser, hooked on my own racket like my old man."

After that first night together, Bingo would come to his place, maybe once or twice a week, either after she got off work at two in the morning or on one of her two nights off. Her babysitter for

Tommy was a nice widowed and retired librarian who lived two condos down from her apartment on Fountain in west L.A. Bones lived in a studio apartment over on Laurel, only a mile or so away, so the logistics of the relationship were easy enough. And even if Bingo hung around his place until dawn, she would always leave in time to get home before Tommy had to get up for school or day camp. She was a great mother and Bones really admired her. His own mother used to lie in bed till noon, munching on Hershey bars while complaining about how life had dealt her this bum deal, a no-good husband and a fat kid who ran errands for mobsters. "She couldn't even cook a decent plate of pasta, that's the kind of Italian mother I had," Bones told Bingo one night.

"You don't hear from her?" Bingo asked.

"What's to hear? All she ever did was complain. I send her a few bucks every month, just to keep her in chocolate."

Bingo couldn't believe how Bones lived. His place consisted of one room mostly occupied by a king-size bed, a huge leather armchair, and a big flat-screen TV. The only decoration was a large movie poster of *Casablanca*, his all-time favorite flick, mounted on the far wall. His stacks of *Racing Forms* and programs going back three years were stacked in the corners. In the closet hung his one suit, six sports jackets and pairs of slacks, his two pairs of comfortable Mephisto shoes, and his athletic gear. The one bookcase, next to the bed and his reading lamp, contained mostly paperbacks of good mystery novels, *Scarne's Complete Book of Gambling*, maybe five or six of the better handicapping books, and, of course, his bible, *The Racing Maxims and Methods of Pittsburgh Phil*, still, according to Bones, the wisest book ever penned about betting on the ponies. In the kitchenette he had an espresso machine, a microwave, a small fridge containing milk and fruit juices, and an electric range to heat up the twenty or so cans of soup he kept on the shelves above the range. No woman could have loved this room because it reflected the sensibility of an obsessed loner. Which, of course, is what he was. Bones had made the choice early in life, determined not to go down the road to ruin like his old man, a victim of his illusions. He allowed himself the occasional woman in his life but never let any of them in all the way. That's what Bingo sensed immediately that first night he took her home. "Jesus Christ," she said, standing in the doorway and looking around. "It's a monk's cell. Who could live with you?"

He had to agree with her; he wasn't up to having anyone move in on him. He couldn't have put up with St. Francis himself. He would have come out of his bathroom or the kitchen one morning and found the saint standing there peaceably and he'd have said to him, "You'll have to go, pal, and take the goddamn birds with you!"

On the last night of his hiatus from the track, after Bingo had gone home, he was lying on his bed with the TV on while idly scanning the next day's entries in the *Racing Form*. On the screen was the late news and suddenly Paul Furman, the owner of Heritage Farm, appeared front and center. He was announcing his run for the Senate in the next general election. He had never run for political office before, he explained, and had kept a low profile since his daughter's tragic death the previous year, but now he felt it was time to sacrifice his private interests and personal misgivings to give the voters of this great state a chance to elect somebody to represent them in Washington who wasn't a flaming liberal, but a true middle-of-the-road candidate with the interests of the great middle class at heart. He would put his personal fortune on the line to achieve this laudable objective, and although he was, of course, a registered Republican and opposed to abortion rights, he intended to run a broadly based campaign stressing inclusion over exclusion. "Another compassionate conservative asshole," Bones mumbled to himself, ready to pop him off the air. He hesitated with the remote just long enough, however, to note what a smooth, suave, good-looking operator he was, with his ramrod posture, tanned skin, piercing gray eyes, and shock of silver-gray hair. It occurred to Bones that a lot of women had probably fallen for this guy over the years. He decided he'd ask Jill about him the next time he saw her.

Meanwhile, there was the next day's card to consider. He turned the set off and concentrated on the *Form*. Three cheap claiming races, two maiden special weights, and three meaningless allowance contests. Nothing he could immediately detect to get excited about. But there, in the fourth, was Fontana's career maiden, Princely, adding blinkers and with Jill up. Maybe he could key the whole day on him.

CHAPTER 9

I **I** adore him," Ester Gale Dinworthy said, standing next to Jake
Fontana as the groom led the three-year-old gray gelding
around in a circle. "He has a beautiful head."

"He does, Mrs. Dinworthy," the trainer agreed. "But he's kind of
skinny and maybe a little crooked behind. Looks a little like a giraffe.
I'm not sure he can run."

"Well, he's already won a race," she said, "so we know he can run
at least a little."

"That was against an easy field of claiming maidens," Fontana
said. "In other words, he didn't beat much."

"But he won by six lengths, Giacomo. That tells you something."

"Yeah, I looked at the race on tape," Fontana admitted grudgingly.
"He won pretty easy. But he might not be sound, you know. Nothing
wrong now, I had our vet check him, but you can't be sure. I—"

"Dear Giacomo," Ester Gale Dinworthy interrupted him, "all of
life is a gamble, isn't it? Look at that head, it looks like an Elgin
marble."

"They want $50,000 for him," the trainer said glumly. "That's a lot
for a crooked-legged Cal-bred."

"Offer them forty."

"They won't take it. I already have."

"I'll put up twenty. That should get us in the clear," Bones said.
"Right, babe?"

She glanced in horror at him, then turned her attention back to
Jake. "As long as no one but you has a say in what we do with the
horse," she said. "Is that understood?"

"Hey, that's fine with me," Bones interrupted. "We'll let Jake make all the decisions."

"I've known Mr. Righetti for a long time," the trainer said to Mrs. Dinworthy. "I'll make the decisions and you're the principal owner. You put up thirty; Bones here puts up twenty. But I do say it's a big gamble, Mrs. Dinworthy."

"Bones?" she asked incredulously.

"Just a nickname," Fontana hastened to assure her.

"I see," she said. "Very odd, but never mind."

She turned to confront the trainer again. "You know, Giacomo, it's a wonder you have any clients at all. Respectable ones, I mean. I want this horse. Tumultuous, that's a splendid name. Now you pay these people the money and see to it that he is moved immediately to our barn. My goodness, but you are stubborn!"

"I still say it's a big risk," Jake insisted.

"Well, that's what life is all about, isn't it? What did you say his breeding was?"

"He's by Cee's Tizzy out of an unraced mare who's dropped a couple of winners, but nothing special. You're still sure you want to do this?"

"Positive. He's magnificent." She stepped away from them, grandly sweeping her long purple shawl tightly around her. Jake walked her to her car, a blue Volvo sedan parked alongside the barn where Steve Bullion kept most of his string. After seeing her off, the trainer stepped into the entrance to Bullion's tack room. "Okay," he said, "we'll take him."

Bullion leaned back in his chair, put his hands behind his head, and grinned at his colleague. "He can run some, Jake," he said, "if you can keep him sound."

"I guess so, Steve," Fontana said. "Only, if he were really all that good, you wouldn't dump him on me."

"You asked me about him," Bullion said. "I didn't come to you, did I? Look, he's a gelding, and these guys have more horses than they know what to do with, plus stallion shares and all their broodmares.

What do they need him for? I was going to drop him in for $32,000 next week, but you'd have had to shake for him maybe."

"I know that. I'll send my groom over to pick him up in about an hour, okay? And I'll have your check deposited in your stable account this afternoon." He turned to go.

"Say, that girl of yours can ride a little, can't she?" Bullion said. "And with the weight allowance it might be worth putting her up on one of my maidens next week. Any objection?"

"No, only she won't have time to work any of them for you. I need her around my place. I'll see you, Steve."

On his way out Jake met Bones, and the two men walked back together toward the trainer's barn. The sun was high up over the track by then and the flanks of Old Baldy gleamed under a clear blue sky. The infield grass and the turf course sparkled next to the huge grandstand. From somewhere in the distance, mariachi music sounded faintly against the hum of traffic from the 210 Freeway. The two men turned the corner of the barn to find Jill sitting on a bale of hay, petting one of the dogs. She was still dressed in her working clothes, her riding helmet resting on the bale beside her. "Well, we got him," the trainer said, "only now I'm not so sure we want him. Where's Eduardo?"

"Finishing up with the Old Man."

"And what are you up to?"

"Waiting for you guys. I thought we could go get some breakfast."

"Bullion's thinking of putting you up on one of his maidens pretty soon."

"No kidding? I'll do it, but only if it's okay with you."

"Yeah, it's fine. But I told him you couldn't work any of his horses. I need you around here."

"Sure enough, boss. I'm your gal, you know that."

"Jill, what if your riding career takes off?" Bones asked. "You're going to need an agent. Namely me."

"Just riding for Jake is plenty right now," she said. "Besides, the fact I'm a woman ain't going to sit too well on this circuit, is it? Even

Julie had trouble getting mounts when she first came out here and she's in the Hall of Fame."

"Yeah, maybe. But if you keep winning—"

"It's hard here, Sal," she said. "Back East, sure, along with Julie they had Rogers, Nelson, Cooksey, a few others who did all right, but out here? Forget it. Ain't going to happen."

"Why don't you two go over to Jeannie's and I'll meet you over there," Jake said. "I've got to make a couple of phone calls first. If you get a mount from Bullion, Jill, take it. All his horses are live."

"That's what I like to hear," she said, getting up and heading for her car. "And I can use the money. You coming, Sal?"

"No, I got some studying to do. This is a tough card today. How do you feel about your horse?"

"Him?" She shrugged. "Who knows? He's got the talent, darn him. Maybe the blinkers will help."

"Say, I caught your man on television last night," Bones said. "He's running for the Senate on the keep-the-poor-down ticket."

"My man?"

"You know, Furman. You used to work for him."

"Yeah. What about it?"

"Just thought I'd mention it. Looks like a ladies' man to me. Guy's got a sick wife; he's all alone—"

Her face froze. "I wouldn't know about that," she said. "I only worked for him."

"Okay. It just struck me. Good-looking dude."

She didn't answer but hurried away toward her car.

***

Moonshine Barkley was sitting in the box when Bones showed up just before the first race that afternoon. Bones wasn't feeling quite himself, not so much because he didn't like the card but because he'd had to lay out twenty big ones on such short notice.

He'd counted on Jake maybe dragging out the process for a few weeks while he got used to the idea of being back in the game as an owner. He'd been there twice before with cheap claimers and each time had lost his whole bankroll. Owning a horse can decimate a bank account faster than a brush fire can shoot up a hillside. Bones had been telling himself that this time might be different; he'd gotten himself involved in an animal with some potential, not some broken-down bum with bandages holding him upright and painkillers flowing through his arthritic joints.

Well, he told himself, it would be his last venture of the kind; he'd only become involved because of Jake. He trusted him and knew what a good horseman he was, no flash, no PR-type wisecracks, no arrogant soundings-off about his own skills, a class act all the way. Still, Steve Bullion had let the horse go, and he wasn't known for giving anything away. A wiseguy from the sidewalks of Queens, Bullion had come up the hard way, as a bettor, then turned himself into one of the top four or five trainers in the country, despite his inability to ride a horse. Jake respected him, even trusted him up to a point, so that was good enough for Bones. Now all he had to do was forget about the twenty grand, forget about shelling it out for a skinny gray gelding with legs like a giraffe's, and just concentrate on what he did best— pick winners. The rest of the saga would take care of itself and was now beyond his control anyway.

"What's the matter with you?" Moonshine asked, as Bones slumped into the seat behind him. "You look like you just lost a tough photo."

"I'm not happy with this card," Bones said. "Maybe I should have stayed home."

"There's a winner in every race," Moonshine said. "There's a blossom on every rose. There's a—"

"Knock it off, Moonshine, you know better than to spout this bullshit at me."

"Hey, you are in a mood today. Okay, I'll keep quiet. No pick six play?"

"No. I'm making one bet, maybe."

"And what's that?"

"The fourth. Fontana's maiden."

"You're kidding! He won't hit the board. He's a common piece of shit."

"Maybe not today."

"I'm not arguing with you, Bones. Just expressing an opinion."

"Pick a horse in the race," Bones said, "any horse but Princely. I'll bet horse for horse."

Moonshine stared at him in alarm. "Hey, no way you sucker me into that kind of bet. These animals are all bums."

"So take your pick. You said Fontana's horse had no chance."

Moonshine shook his head sadly. "I've got too much respect for you, Bones. Too much respect to try to take your money." With a soulful sigh, he heaved himself out of his seat and wandered off to seek more congenial surroundings, which was just fine with Bones. All he wanted to do was sit alone and in peace to contemplate his immediate future and the possible fate of his $20,000, plus all the monthly fees that would follow while the horse was in training. He had a vivid vision of them being sucked down into a huge whirlpool accompanied by an audible flushing sound.

**

Twenty minutes before the fourth race, Charlie and his dot-com cohorts were clustered around Jake. They were all sharply dressed as usual in their Italian business suits, walking advertisements for the glamour of money. They were watching Eduardo lead their lazy colt around the ring with the other horses in the race and so didn't notice Jill until she had come up beside them. Charlie, obviously the leader of the group, spotted her first and gave her his most disarming smile. "Don't you look cute in orange and green," he said. "You going to win for us today?"

"I'm sure going to try," Jill answered, forcing herself to smile back. "Maybe the shades will help."

"Shades?"

"We decided to put blinkers on him," the trainer explained. "We thought it might help him keep his mind on business. It was Jill's idea."

"Well, I guess we had to try something, right?" Charlie said. "In business, when something doesn't work, you try something else. Only everything we've been trying lately hasn't worked." His partners all laughed nervously. Charlie focused on Jill. "So if you win, can we take you out to dinner tonight?"

"Sure," Jill said, "if Mr. Fontana will join us."

"I don't know," Jake said. "I've got a lot of work—"

"Aw, come on, Jake," Charlie said. "Lighten the load. Let's have a little fun."

"Okay," the trainer agreed grudgingly, "but only if we win." He turned to Jill. "You've seen this colt run," he said, "and you've galloped him enough, so you know about him. Give him his head when the gate opens, but don't use him too hard. If he gets an easy lead, go for it. If not, keep him as close as you can to the leaders, then ask him at the three-eighths pole. Let's hope the blinkers help him concentrate more."

Jill nodded just as the paddock judge called for the riders. Fontana gave her a leg up into the saddle, and she leaned over to pat the colt's neck as the line of horses began to move out through the gap under the stands toward the track. "You're going to run for me today, ain't you, baby," she said to the animal. "Or I'm going to know the reason why."

"You know what?" Charlie said, glancing up at the tote board where the odds showed their entry at 6-1. "I'm going to make a good bet on him today. He's going to win; I just know it." He turned to look at the trainer. "And I'm putting a hundred on him for Jill, too."

"That's nice of you, Charlie," the trainer said. "But let's just hope he runs well and comes back sound."

In the stands, as the horses galloped past, Bones kept his binoculars focused on Princely, who looked truly formidable, his neck bowed, as he headed for the starting gate.

"You still going to bet on him?" Moonshine asked, suddenly reappearing in the seat beside Bones.

"Maybe so," Bones said, his glasses still on the horse. "The price is right."

"He's got to win first. I'm going to bet Dictate, the two horse. He's the only speed in here."

"Not really, Moonshine," Bones said. "He's never gone the distance either. And his pattern is to close at six. Closing sprinters going long are not good bets."

"He'll romp in against these," Moonshine insisted, as he left his seat to head for a betting window.

"So I repeat my offer," Bones called after him. "Horse for horse. Two hundred bucks." Moonshine pretended not to hear him.

The more Bones saw of Princely as Jill maneuvered him toward the starting gate, the more he loved the way the animal looked, his neck still bowed, his body now gleaming with incipient power. He seemed tensed to spring, like a tiger on an ambush. Bones now felt certain he would win. He didn't care what the colt had done or failed to do in his previous nine tries. Today would be different. The horse was communicating with every fiber of his being that he was about to become a competitor.

When the gate opened, Princely broke alertly and went to the lead, but Jill didn't rush him, allowing two horses to sprint past him. At the turn she moved him over to the rail and tucked him in behind the leaders, a couple of nondescript sprinters that figured to tire. She kept her position all the way down the backstretch, then moved him out from the rail on the turn for home, and stung him once with a right-hand whip. Princely spurted past the leaders and turned into the stretch two lengths in front. Jill glanced back under her left armpit and saw the favorite, Dictate, coming after her with a big, wide-ranging move on the turn.

She allowed him to come up beside her, then gave her colt two more solid cracks of the whip, left and right. Princely responded. Unable to see the horse beside him or gaze out into the infield or toward the stands, the colt was forced to concentrate on the business at hand. The favorite, suddenly out of gas, spit out the bit as Princely sprinted for the finish line, four lengths in front, the easiest kind of winner.

"Shit," Moonshine said. "Did you see that pig quit on me?"

"Closing sprinters," Bones reminded him. "Bad bet, Moonshine."

Bones kept his glasses trained on the colt and rider as they galloped back toward the finish line. "One thirty-five and two," he said. "Fast time. It isn't just the blinkers either. This kid has an intangible. Horses run for her." He was talking to himself, he realized, since Moonshine had already bolted in disgust.

Jake and the dot-com plungers were waiting for Jill as she guided the colt back toward the winner's circle. The boys were giving one another high fives all around and laughing as the track photographer snapped their pictures, with Jill sitting quietly up there on the horse's back. Jake, who almost never let himself be photographed and had remained to one side while Eduardo held the horse's head, now helped Jill dismount. "Nice ride," he said. "He sure did run some today."

"The blinkers helped," Jill said, heading for the weigh-in scales. "He had to keep his mind on business."

"Hey," Charlie said, thrusting a pari-mutuel ticket into her hand as Jill started to head back toward the jockeys' room. "This is for you, honey. We'll see you and Jake later at Pinot's in Pasadena, okay? Six o'clock. We're going to celebrate!"

"Thanks," Jill said. She folded the ticket in half and stuck it into her pocket without looking at it.

"You're eight hundred dollars richer," Charlie said.

"I'll pay for the dinner."

"No way, sweetheart. You and Jake are the guests of honor. It's our first winning day since we bought this horse."

***

Bones spent the rest of that afternoon pleasantly enough, passing the rest of the card until the eighth and last race when he decided to risk a hundred dollars of his winnings on a small trifecta and lost when his selections came in one-three-four. But it didn't matter. He was another fifteen hundred dollars richer to cushion his plunge into ownership. Most of the time, between visits from Moonshine, Stats

Goldman, Sweeps O'Flaherty, and other racetrack acquaintances who wanted to bask in the glow of his winning streak, he found himself thinking about Jill. Who was she? Where had she learned to ride like that, with such ease and confidence, such an affinity for the animal under her? She was a natural, one of those rare riders who in action seemed to become one with the horse, an extension of it. She was now three for three, at the top of the jockey standings in win percentage. So what could have happened to her up north? He just couldn't help wondering about it.

CHAPTER 10

"He does look a little like a giraffe," Bones said, as Jill led Tumultuous around in a circle outside the barn a couple of days later. "You sure Jake knows what he's doing?"

"Don't worry," Jill said, patting the horse affectionately on the neck. "Sammy can run, all right."

"Who's Sammy?"

"Him. You can't call a horse Tumultuous. He's a Sammy. Anyway, that's what I call him."

"Does he know that?"

"He does now. Mrs. Dinworthy says he has this beautiful head, like an Elgin marble. What's that?"

"Some old Greek shit. Marble is a stone. You sure he can run?"

"You saw the chart on his only race, didn't you?"

"Yeah, it was a good one for the level," Bones admitted, "but nothing's come out of there to run well."

"Listen, he worked good today; went five-eighths," Jill said. "Jake caught him in fifty-eight and two, but he was just breezing."

"You rode him?"

"Yeah. He's got a nice easy stride, and he loves to run on the turns."

"Like Sunday Silence, don't I wish. That horse was a fucking ballet dancer," Bones said. "Sammy here looks like an old man in Bermuda shorts."

"Don't worry, Sal," Jill said, with a quick, staccato laugh. "Jake'll know how to get the best out of him. This sucker loves it out there on the track. He's got one fault."

"What's that?"

97

"He don't like it when horses pass him. I had to put a stranglehold on him to keep him from taking off."

"That's a fault?" Bones said, suddenly feeling better about his investment. Maybe Jake did know what he was doing and they'd get lucky. You never knew in this game. He watched her lead Tumultuous back into his stall.

"You going to the races today, Sal?" Jill asked, giving the horse one last reassuring pat.

"You're riding, so why wouldn't I? Well, I'd go anyway," he confessed.

"You got another life?"

"This is the only one that interests me."

"Weird," she said, smiling faintly.

Jake had already left for the morning, looking a little drawn and tired, so Bones asked about him. "He'll be okay," Jill said. "Some nights are worse than others, but I keep an eye on him. Dr. Barrow asked me to."

"The gambling sawbones. You know what he said to me the other day when I saw him at the track?"

"What?"

"I asked him how he was doing and he told me that exactas have killed more Jews than the Holocaust."

"What did he mean by that?"

"He has trouble cashing tickets. He's a good guy, but a bad horse-player. Too many exotics, not enough straight bets."

They were sitting now on a bench in the sun outside the tack room and looking out over the row of stalls where Jake's charges were tucked away for the morning. In the background they could hear the soft coughing, snorting, munching sounds of the horses. "So what about the Old Man today?" Bones asked. "He'll win, right?"

"He should," she said. "Same kind he just beat."

"No price, that's the only problem," Bones said. "I'll have to key him in some kind of exotic, maybe a trifecta."

"Boy, you never stop, do you?"

"No, honey, to me it's like breathing. It may not be the only game in town, but it's the best one."

"You want a cup of coffee?" she asked, getting up and going into the tack room. "We keep a pot going in here."

"No, thanks. I'm as awake as I want to be." When she returned and sat down next to him again with a container full of black coffee in her hand, he turned to look at her. "Tell me about this woman named Dulcie Clark. You know her?"

She looked startled but quickly got hold of herself. "Yeah, I knew her. She was my boss at Heritage. She pretty much ran the operation. So what about her?"

"Oh, I thought you might have heard. I guess you don't read the papers. They found her dead in a hotel room in Santa Barbara yesterday afternoon. You didn't hear anything about it?"

She turned to stare at him, her face white and drawn. "Dulcie's dead? Are you sure?"

"Yeah. I'm sorry, kid. I thought you knew. Was she a friend?"

"No, not really. I just worked for her."

"The story says she was Paul Furman's assistant, pretty much in charge of the farm, right?"

"Yeah. I rode for her at Heritage. I broke a lot of their yearlings and I'd exercise some of the two-year-olds. Dulcie ran the whole operation. What happened?"

"I don't know. They were talking about doing an autopsy. I haven't heard or seen a follow-up report."

"Jesus," she murmured, "he wouldn't."

"Wouldn't what? Who wouldn't?"

She jumped to her feet. "Nothing, Sal. Forget it," she said. "I got to go."

"What did you mean?"

"I didn't mean anything. I'll see you later at the track, okay?"

"Okay. I'm sorry if I upset you."

"You had nothing to do with it." She darted away, disappearing around the corner of the barn on her way to her car.

***

Gamblin Man won easily again that afternoon, by more than four lengths, but he went off an odds-on favorite. It also turned out to be the last race of his career. Just beyond the finish line Jill felt the horse take a bad step and quickly pulled him up. She jumped out of the saddle and stood by the animal's head until the wagon arrived. The Old Man limped inside and was driven away as Jill watched, her face a study in dismay. Jake, Rich Abernathy, and Bones were waiting for her at the winner's circle when she came walking back. "He warmed up fine," she said, "and ran just like we knew he would, but I felt him stumble just after we won. I sure hope he'll be okay."

Fontana didn't answer but looked grim. Abernathy shuffled through his wad of winning tickets. "Well, I got the exacta fifty times," he said. "That ought to pay the vet bills."

By early evening Jake knew the horse would never run again. When he arrived home, Bones and Jill were standing by the corral fence communing with The Boston Kid while they waited for him. As Jake walked up, they could tell by his face that the news was not good. "He has a broken sesamoid, and the right suspensory also looks iffy," he told them. "Now I'm going to have a problem with Abernathy."

"What kind of problem?" Bones asked.

"He'll want to put the Old Man down."

"For the insurance?"

"He isn't insured," Fontana said. "He's too cheap. But Abernathy isn't going to want to pay a lot of vet bills and upkeep on him just to keep him alive."

"You could bring him here," Jill said. "I'll take care of him."

"I haven't got room. I can't put him in with The Kid. They'd kill each other."

"So what are you going to do?"

"Get him well enough to give him to CERF."

"What's that?" Jill asked.

"The California Equine Retirement Foundation out in Temecula," Bones explained. "They take care of old racehorses."

"Like the programs they got back East?"

"Yeah."

"Will Abernathy pay the bills till then?"

"I don't know. I can't force him to," Jake said. "I'll pay them myself, if I have to." He leaned against the corral fence and stared glumly into the distance. The dogs bounded around beside him, jumping up to his casual caresses. The Boston Kid snorted angrily and suddenly moved away from them, then turned and glared at them from across the way. "He still doesn't like me," Jake said, turning to Jill, "but you—he thinks you walk on water."

Jill smiled. "He's just a crusty old codger, that's all," she said. "Don't like men and I can dig that." She turned to look at the trainer. "Let's go eat Chinese," she said. "My treat."

"Chinese, but we'll go Dutch," he said. "Okay with you, Bones?"

"No," Bones said. "Thanks to you and Jill, I had another real good day. This one's on me."

"Let me go in and wash up," Jake said. He walked into the house, followed by the dogs. The Boston Kid moved back toward Jill and thrust his muzzle toward her. She grabbed his upper lip with one hand and softly tugged it up and down, scratching between his ears with her other hand. Bones remained off to one side, as far away from The Kid's teeth as possible. Beyond the corral the lights of the valley below softly reflected a pink glow against the overcast sky off the Pacific, and overhead the moon glinted silver behind the clouds.

"It's so peaceful here," Jill said. "I'm doing what I always wanted to do and getting paid good for it. And I'm riding against the best jockeys in the whole world maybe."

"Not only that," Bones said. "You're undefeated, four for four. You're hot, babe."

"I'm real lucky."

"It's more than luck. You always need luck in this game, sure, but you've got the hands and you sit good; you look good up there. The horses run for you, Jill. It's a gift. With your talent you could make it to the end of the rainbow."

"What's there for me, Sal?"

He grinned. "A lot of gold, a big pot of it."

"I don't know. I don't know much. Horses is about it." She suddenly looked thoughtful. "You'll tell me, won't you, Sal?"

"Tell you what?"

"If you hear any more about Dulcie."

"Sure. Why wouldn't I?"

***

The Chinese restaurant was in a strip mall in Monrovia, a few miles east of the track. It was small and dark with hangings on the walls and a single plate-glass window looking out onto a parking lot. They sat in a booth at the rear of the room and ordered beers while they scanned the menu. "So is the food good?" Jill asked. "This place sure don't look like much."

"Depends on whether you like Szechwan cooking or not," Jake said. "It's spicy."

"I love spicy."

They ordered hot-and-sour soup, mu-shu pork, Mongolian beef, and sautéed garlic spinach. As they ate, they spent most of the time talking about horses, especially Jake's string. "You know, this sucker we just bought can really run some," the trainer said at one point.

"So Jill tells me," Bones said. "So, are we going to the Derby with him?"

"Yeah, sure," Jake said, grinning faintly. "But we are going to make some money with him, all right. If he stays sound."

"How's Ester Gale Looney feel about him?"

Jake laughed. "She sent him roses today, insisted they be put in a planter outside his stall."

"That broad is crazy. Think you can handle her?"

"Oh, sure. She's not heavy on brains. Heart of gold, though."

Half an hour later, as they were finishing up, Bones looked at Jake and became alarmed; the trainer's whole face seemed suddenly to have collapsed. He looked exhausted. "You getting enough sleep?" Bones asked him. "You look beat up."

"I'm trying to," Jake said. "I'm taking all these damn pills."

"Why don't you take the day off tomorrow? Eduardo and Jill can handle the horses and I can call your owners."

"Well, maybe …"

"No, no maybe. It's a deal. You show up and I'll break some bones and put you in the hospital myself. And don't think I can't do it."

"Some help you are. See, if I could just sleep through the night …"

"You must have loved your wife a lot to feel so bad," Jill said.

"I dream about her every night," Jake said. "At least the doc now has me on these pills so I can go back to sleep when I wake up. Before I couldn't, and I was going slowly crazy."

Jake recalled what it had been like the last two years. Maria had never smoked but had developed a persistent cough. A routine X-ray had revealed a tumor in her right lung so large that it had been impossible to operate. They had treated it with aggressive radiation and chemotherapy and had managed to reduce it dramatically, and for about a year Maria had been able to resume a nearly normal life, though they had had this thing hanging over them like a toxic cloud. And then the tumor had begun to grow again; the cancer had metastasized to the rest of her body. She had fought against it, but no luck. The last few weeks he'd watched her shrivel in size as the disease advanced. She didn't want to die in a hospital or a hospice, so he had brought her home. He had rented a hospital bed and set it up in their bedroom so they could still be together. He had tended to her needs, rising several times a night to help her go to the bathroom or to fetch her a glass of water. She stopped eating, lived on by sipping Ensure. Nurses came and went; pain-killing medications were prescribed. Eventually the local hospice became involved, dispatching a technician to install a shunt with a morphine drip that Maria could control by just pressing a button. Toward the end she could hardly even stay awake and Jake had had to hire round-the-clock help, someone who could be with her every minute of every day. He had turned his horses over to Eduardo's care, had lost half his clients, kept in touch with his stable mostly by phone. And then at last Maria had slipped away from him into a coma from which she never returned. "I spent all that day just talking to her," Jake said. "I know she could hear me, I know it. I guess it was more of a comfort to me than to her."

When he had finished, Jill reached out a hand and took both his folded hands in hers. "Thanks for telling me," she said. "It must have been a real hard time for you. It's got to have been like the worst. I'm real sorry, Jake."

"Everybody goes through hard times, maybe even Bones here, right?"

Bones shook his head. "Not that bad," he said.

The trainer looked at Jill. "I guess you had your share."

"Nothing like you. Nobody I know has ever been real sick. Mostly just drunk and mean."

"So exactly what did happen to you, Jill, to make you move down here?"

She hesitated a moment, still reluctant to reveal too much about herself. "A real bad relationship," she said. "I got involved with a guy who just kind of trashed me."

"Beat you up?" Bones asked.

"That, too. I don't want to talk about it, though. I'm trying to put all that behind me."

"Good idea," Jake said.

"You know, they say that people who get abused when they're kids often get into relationships later just like the ones they grew out of," Bones said. "Maybe that's what happened to you, Jill."

"Sounds plausible," the trainer said, "though I've never been much on psychiatric stuff. All I know in life is horses."

"That ain't true," Jill said. "You and Maria, that's what it was all about, right?"

"Yeah. Anyway, I didn't mean to shoot off my mouth about it. Just talking helps, I guess. That and the pills."

Bones picked up the check as agreed, and they walked out into the parking lot. "Oh, I almost forgot," Fontana said, standing by his open car door. "Bullion called me today, Jill. He's got a fast four-year-old maiden he wants to put you up on next week. I told him I'd tell you. Sorry, I forgot, what with this bad news on the Old Man. You want to ride for him? He's got a barn full of good horses one of those Arab sheikhs bought for him."

"Only if it's okay with you," Jill said. "I'm working for you."

"It's fine with me."

He climbed into his car and drove out of the lot. Jill and Bones stood there for a moment and watched him go. Overhead a sliver of a moon peeked through clouds scudding across the dark sky. The air was fresh and clean, blowing in from the ocean. Jill breathed it in and smiled, then gave Bones' arm a little pat. "Good night, Sal," she said. "You know, for a Mafia guy you're kind of nice. You wouldn't hurt nobody, would you?"

"Honey, I just go along minding my own business, you know what I mean?" he said. "Since most people in this world are assholes or fucking idiots, sometimes somebody tries to push me or steps on my toes or bothers my friends, so I try to be there for myself and for them."

"Be there?"

"That's when they remember or they find out what I'm about, see? I kind of help them understand what my name is. I could help you, too, if you ever need me."

"I'll be all right, Sal."

"Yeah, sure. But I'll be around, you understand? Count on it, sweetheart."

CHAPTER 11

Steve Bullion was standing by himself in the walking ring when Jill emerged from the jockeys' room and joined him. She was dressed in the black-and-gold silks of Crescent Farm, the trainer's top stable. Bullion seemed not particularly pleased to see her, his sullen features and his black eyes focused on her as if she were a possibly unruly kid about to commit some big social gaffe. "Something wrong?" she asked.

"Nah," he said. "What could be wrong? All you got to do is sit on this speedball and not fall off and you're a winner." The colt was a four-year-old whose debut had been delayed by a series of minor ailments. He was basically sound, however, and his only drawback was a dislike of the starting gate. There was the chance he might act up if he were kept waiting in there. Luckily, he had drawn an outside post, and Bullion had instructed the starter not to load him until the last minute. "That's it," the trainer concluded in his instruction to Jill. "The rest is up to you."

"If he doesn't break well, you want me to push him a little?" she asked. "How bad do you want to win this one?"

"Are you kidding me?" the trainer said. "When I run 'em, they're ready to run, you got that?"

He looked and sounded just like the New York hustler and horseplayer he had been before he became Steve Bullion, one of the top trainers in the world. He seemed slumped into his brown slacks, open-necked brown shirt, and black leather jacket, the sort of informal outfit he favored. His thinning black hair was combed back off his face. Jill wondered if he could even sit on a horse, though what did that matter? He trained winners; he was always in the top five in the national standings; he was already in the Hall of Fame. No one could question his competence, but she found herself wondering how he'd managed it. "Where's the owners?" she asked.

Bullion grunted. "It's better without them," he said. "They leave me alone; I win races for them."

The missing Arabs. How weird, she thought. What were they in it for anyway? Not the fun of it and not for the money. She looked at the trainer, then at the horse, who seemed calm enough as he was being led around the ring, waiting for the paddock judge's call. "So what do you need me for?" she suddenly asked. "You could have had any of your regular riders up, right?"

Bullion shrugged. "Fontana says you can ride," he said. "I thought I'd see for myself. And I like the weight allowance. The horse has never even worked seven and he might tire a little down the lane."

"I won't push him too hard early," she assured him.

"Yeah? Don't start thinking too much, you understand?" Bullion said. "Nothing worse than a jock who starts thinking. Just ride the fucking horse."

He didn't speak to her again until he gave her a leg up just before the animals headed out of the paddock toward the racing surface. "Good luck," he mumbled. "Come back safe."

"Thanks. I plan to."

It was no contest really. The colt stepped quietly into his stall, and before he began to act up, the gates opened and he popped into the clear. It took him only a few seconds to settle into a long, ground-eating stride that brought him even with the frontrunners at the three-eighths pole, at which point Jill clucked to him once and tapped him lightly with the whip. The colt accelerated, moved fluidly and steadily away, and romped home by six widening lengths. The crowd had backed him down at the last minute, and he paid off just over even-money, the price flashing on the board as Jill pulled up by the winner's circle. Smiling, she waved her stick at the crowd and vaulted easily out of the saddle. After the weigh-in and the obligatory photograph, with only the sullen trainer and a groom standing by the horse's head, she started back toward the jockeys' room, Bullion striding along beside her.

"Good ride," he said, "but you didn't have to touch him. He'd have won easy anyway."

"I just tapped him once," she said. "Help him concentrate."

The trainer growled noncommittally. "You busy tonight?"

"Why?"

"I'll take you to dinner."

"I don't think so. But thanks for asking."

"You banging Fontana?"

"What?"

"You know what I mean. You and Fontana, right?"

"Wrong. You got the wrong idea."

"Okay. Sorry I asked."

"Would you have asked me to dinner if I was a guy?"

"What do you think I am, a fucking queer? What kind of question is that?"

"Look, I'm not dating anybody," she said, "and I'm not ready right now for a relationship, all right?"

"Who said anything about a relationship?" Bullion said. "I asked you out to dinner. Big fucking deal." He walked angrily away from her toward the grandstand boxes.

"The agent offer stands," Bones said, coming up behind her. "I just came down to congratulate you. Five for five, kid. And I cashed on you again."

***

Bones took her out to a steakhouse in Arcadia because she said she needed to put on a couple of pounds. Her weight had slipped back to 104, and she wanted the added strength she thought a little more flesh would give her. They talked about the racing and her career and then Bones asked her again if he could handle her book.

"I don't think so, Sal," she said, looking a little nervous at the suggestion.

109

"Why not? I could put you up on a lot of live mounts."

She chose not to answer him directly. "So how would that sit with your owning part of a horse?"

"Well, I don't know. I'd have to check it out. Anyway, I could sort of do it for you unofficial like," he said "Maybe you owe it to yourself, Jill. You've proved you can win races and you still have your bug. That five pounds can mean something because trainers are always looking to hire a hot apprentice. Let me help you. I know my way around in this game."

"You know, a reporter from the *Form* came around this morning to interview me."

"Who was it? Jack Martin?"

"Yeah, that's him. He wants to do what he calls a background piece on me. I put him off."

"Why?"

"I was busy and Jake wasn't around," she explained. "He wasn't feeling too good, so he'd gone home after the last set. Eduardo and I were taking care of stuff and I didn't have time to talk to him."

"So find the time. Jack Martin's a good kid, straight shooter," Bones said. "He's only looking to do a nice piece about you, Jill. Jesus, it isn't every new rider who comes along and rides five straight winners. It's good publicity, kid."

"I don't need it," she said. "I'm happy doing what I'm doing and my main job is with Jake. If he says I can ride for someone else, I'll do it, but only if it don't screw up what I do for him. He's the reason I got a life down here now. I owe him plenty."

"Yeah, you do," Bones agreed, "but it doesn't mean you can't ride for some other people in the afternoons when Jake's not running one of his and you're on your own, right?"

She didn't answer but looked away from him and began to fumble with her silverware. "Let's drop it for now, Sal, okay?" she finally answered. "I sure appreciate your help and all, I really do, but I'm fine with the way things are right now, okay? Let's leave it at that."

She was damaged goods, he knew that by now, but by what or

whom he wasn't sure. Maybe just by life in general. He reached across the table and gave her a little pat on the cheek. "You're going to be all right," he said. "You're a smart kid. My old man used to spout all these old Italian sayings to explain life, you know? One of my favorites was, 'It's good to trust, but it's better not to trust.' "

Jill smiled. "Your dad was a smart guy."

"No, he was a sucker and a loser, but he knew it. Most people are suckers and losers and don't know it."

After dinner they drove back to her place. Fontana had gone to bed and the dogs began to bark inside the house. "Shit," Jill said, "they'll wake Jake up." She hurried over to the doggie door and unlatched it. The dogs bounded out to greet her and she quieted them down, then ushered them back inside and latched the door shut again. "Got to keep them inside at night," she explained, "or the coyotes will get 'em. Jake says they come down at night out of the hills. I've never seen one, but Jake has and there are several packs of them back there."

They stood by the corral, but The Boston Kid seemed uninterested in them. He remained in his open stall at the far end, immovable as a statue. "He sleeps more than any other horse I've ever known," she said.

"So tell me," Bones asked, "who else besides Bullion has made a move on you since you've been down here?"

"Oh, no one, really," she said. "Paolo Neruda likes the way I ride and he keeps telling me that and he's asked me out a couple of times. I said no. I can't be with anybody right now."

"Neruda plays the field," Bones said.

"I figured. What about you, Sal? Nobody in your life?"

"Well, yeah." He told her about Bingo.

"How's she feel about you and the horses?"

"She doesn't give a shit, basically," he said.

"You ain't going to marry her?"

"Not unless I can get her to run a mile in one thirty-four and change for me." He walked her to the short flight of stairs leading up to her room over the garage. "You going to stay here for a while yet?" Bones said, looking around.

"Maybe. I've got enough money now from my share of the purses to get my own place, but Jake needs me here."

"How's he doing?"

"Okay," she said, "but he still says he has trouble sleeping. Dr. Barrow's on top of him all the time to take it easy, but you know Jake. For him the horses come first, like for all of us."

"What else is there?" He let her go. At the top of the stairs she turned and blew him a kiss.

***

The reporter from *Trends* showed up at the barn the next morning. Eduardo was hotwalking Tumultuous between the parallel rows of stables while Jake and Bones watched. The horse had been out for a gallop and Jake was checking him out for any signs of soreness. Neither of them saw the man, who came up behind them and said, "Mr. Fontana?"

They both turned to look at him. He was in his mid-thirties, with a round ruddy face under a closely cropped mane of black curls and was dressed in khaki slacks, brown loafers, a pink button-down shirt and a brown tweed jacket. He looked, Bones thought, pure Ivy League. "I'm Fontana," Jake said.

"Wynn Messmer," the man said. "I'm doing a story for *Trends* magazine."

"Good for you," Jake said. "This here's my friend Sal Righetti." They shook hands all around. "What about?"

"I'd like to talk to Jill Aspen. I understand she works for you."

"I thought somebody would get around to doing a story about her," Jake said. "Five winning races in a row. Jack Martin from the *Form* was here yesterday."

"You're doing a racing story?" Bones asked.

"Not exactly," Wynn Messmer said. "I'm doing a piece on Paul Furman. She used to work for him."

"What kind of piece?"

112

"Sort of a profile of the man," Messmer said. "He's pretty hot nationally right now, and he's going to run for the Senate in 2006. He's also a big Republican fund-raiser, and he's a pal of a lot of people in Washington."

"What's that got to do with racing?" Fontana asked.

"Not much," Messmer admitted. "I'm just trying to get a feel for what kind of man he is. Till recently he's kept a fairly low profile, but he's in tight with Bush and his people and they're looking to pick up California. Furman may be a future star, but we don't know much about him as a person. That's why I've been assigned to write this article about him."

"I don't really see how Jill could help you," Bones said. "She just worked for him at Heritage, breaking yearlings mostly. Nothing to do with politics or personal stuff."

"Well, I've been told she knows him pretty well away from the farm," Messmer said. "I'd like to get her impression of the sort of man he is."

"Jill's out galloping one of the mares," Fontana said, "but she ought to be back any minute. And we're just about wrapped up here." He turned back to Eduardo. "He looks okay, Eduardo. Walk him another ten minutes just to be sure."

Bones gave Wynn Messmer a tour of Fontana's shed row while the trainer retreated into his tack room to make his morning telephone calls. The reporter seemed mildly interested in the horses, so Bones gave him a rundown on the status and abilities of Fontana's charges. He wasn't quite sure that Messmer's motives were as simple and straightforward as he had represented them to be and so he tried casually to probe into them. "What happened with that woman who died?" he asked, as they neared the end of their tour.

"Dulcie Clark?" replied Messmer. "That was strange. They performed an autopsy and found nothing. Her heart seemed sound, no stroke, no blood clots anywhere. It's bizarre. She just stopped breathing. No sign of foul play either."

"What do they call that? Sudden death something ..."

"Syndrome."

"Yeah. I thought that only happened to little babies."

"Right. Just goes to show though, carpe diem, right?"

"So this Dulcie broad and Furman were close?"

"Very. There were rumors about them having had an affair, but no one ever proved anything. We do know they were very close friends. She and Harvey Stone were his top people."

"Who's Harvey Stone?"

"His political consultant. He's been taken on to run Furman's political campaign and has been with him for about a year now. He's got a consulting firm in Washington. Dulcie Clark had nothing to do with any of that. She ran the stable operation. She was an expert horsewoman, and she and Furman used to ride together sometimes."

"Sounds like a movie."

"And he used to take her sometimes to public functions."

"I guess people commented about that, right?"

"Mrs. Furman is pretty much of a recluse. She hasn't left their house in several years, which is maybe why he hasn't gotten involved in politics before. Then, after their daughter died ..."

"What happened there? She drowned, right?"

"Yeah. You didn't hear about it?"

"Maybe I read about it in the *L.A. Times*."

"It was big news up in the Bay Area, I can tell you."

"So exactly when was that?"

"Early last summer. They were up at this lake where Furman has a cabin and the girl apparently just wandered off by herself to go swimming, even though it's forbidden there. The lake is a reservoir. It was strange. I mean, it happened late at night and there were all kinds of rumors. There was an investigation, of course, but nothing came of it. Mrs. Furman moved out of their house a few weeks later and went to a psychiatric clinic for several weeks, then came back. Had some kind of breakdown, apparently. Nobody's seen her since and she won't talk to the press or anybody, except maybe her psychiatrist."

"What kind of crazy is she?"

"Manic depression, probably, who knows for sure?"

As they reached the tack room, Jill returned on the mare. She jumped lightly out of the saddle and Bones walked up to her. "There's a reporter here from *Trends* magazine," he said. "He wants to interview you about Paul Furman."

Her face hardened and her gaze focused beyond him on Messmer, who had come up to join them. "I've got nothing to say," she said.

"I just want to interview you for a few minutes," the reporter insisted, fishing a pad and pen out of his pocket. "You knew Furman well, didn't you?"

"I worked for him," Jill said, "that's all. I worked at Heritage with the horses, the young ones." She began to unsaddle the mare.

"You were seen in public with Furman on a number of occasions," Messmer persisted.

"I went to some of the sales with him," Jill said. "Me and other people from Heritage."

"What's your impression of the man?" Messmer asked.

"Look, I don't want to talk to you," Jill said, concentrating on the horse. "That part of my life is over with. I live here now and I work for Mr. Fontana."

"Okay, but I'm going to write my story," Wynn Messmer said. "I thought you'd want to be interviewed."

"Why would you think that, mister?"

"Well, some people have been saying you were close to the man."

"What people? Who?"

"I have my sources," the reporter said. "Not all of them want to be quoted directly, but I have taped interviews and some documentation. But basically I'd just like to know how you feel about the guy. You agree he might make a run for the Senate?"

"Why ask me? How would I know? I don't know nothing about that," Jill said. "I don't know nothing about politics."

"There's a story you were with Furman when his daughter died."

Holding the saddle in her arms, one hand on the bridle of the mare, she stared at Messmer. "Who says so?" she asked.

"I can't reveal that right now. Do you have any comment about that?"

"No. And that's all I'm going to say." She handed the saddle to Luis, Fontana's newly hired groom, who had just finished working around the stalls, and began to hotwalk the mare. Messmer started to follow her.

"She said she's through talking to you," Bones said, taking him by the arm. "I guess you don't hear so good."

Smiling, Messmer looked at him. "You'd think she has something to hide," he said.

"Not necessarily," Bones answered. "The point is, pal, she wants to be left alone."

"I'm going to write my story, you know."

"Who's trying to stop you? Good luck with it."

Wynn Messmer glanced again at Jill, then back to Bones and shrugged. "Okay. Thanks for your help."

He stuck his reporter's pad back into his pocket and walked away toward the parking lot. Bones watched him go, wondering not for the first time, what it was about the media that pissed him off so profoundly.

CHAPTER 12

Two days later, the morning after Jack Martin's nice little puff piece on Jill appeared in the *Form*, Bones and Fontana were standing by the rail at Clockers Corner when Carl Everett showed up. He was a tall, good-looking dude in his early thirties with pale brown eyes, a thick head of dark blond hair, and the casual confident air of a man who knows where his next dividend is coming from. He was wearing a brown cashmere jacket, jodhpurs, and boots. "Mr. Fontana?" he said. "I'm Carl Everett. I own Terry's Dream. You might have heard of me."

Jake turned to look at him. "I have," he said. "You've got a nice horse there."

"Thank you. We're here to run in the Santa Anita Derby next month," he said. "Chad Bullit, my trainer, thought we'd come early, get the horse acclimated to new surroundings."

"Smart move," Jake said. "The racing surface out here is a lot different from back East."

"That's what Chad says."

"I guess you got yourself a real Derby contender," Bones said. "I mean the big one in Louisville."

"We hope."

"This here's my friend Sal Righetti," Jake said.

"How do you do," Carl Everett said, without looking at him. "Is Jill around? I was told she works for you."

"She's out on the track with one of my horses," Jake answered, then looked down the stretch for her. "She's coming back now."

Jill was up on Princely and had just breezed him a half-mile. She was coming back along the outside rail, still focused on the horse. She didn't notice Everett until she was almost up to them. When she did, her face flushed. "Carl," she said, "what are you doing here?"

"I came in with my colt. You remember my good three-year-old."

"Terry. Sure, I remember him." She pulled her animal up and stared intently at Everett. "You took him back East. You going to run him out here now?"

"In the Santa Anita Derby," Everett said. "Too much rain down in Florida this year and he's going to like the harder surface here. Anyway, I'm in town over the weekend. How about dinner tonight?"

"No way, Carl. I got to get up real early and I'm beat."

"We need to talk," Everett insisted. "I really want to see you, Jill. You know there's a reporter doing a story on Paul?"

"Yeah, I know about it," she answered. "He was by the barn a couple of days ago."

"I think I'm in it and you are, too."

"Can't help that," she said. "I wouldn't talk to him."

"He's doing the story anyway. He interviewed me. I figured it was better to talk to him than try to avoid him. Maybe you should have, too."

"Why? I got nothing to say to him."

"Somebody told him about us."

"So what? We broke up a ways back."

"Jill, you know what they're saying ..."

"I don't give a shit, Carl," she said. "I got a new life, I'm doing real good. I'm not going to let somebody, you, or nobody screw this up for me."

"Come on, Jill, have dinner with me."

"No. You and me, it's over. I'll see you, maybe." She clucked to her horse and then moved away up the track back toward the barn. Without another word to either Jake or Bones or even a gesture of farewell, Carl Everett, his face dark with anger, swiftly walked away.

"What was that all about?" Fontana asked.

"I guess he and Jill were making the beast with two backs for a while," Bones said. "He acts like he's entitled to her or something."

"He's got an attitude, all right."

"He's probably some rich kid from Marin County or San Francisco."

"Yeah, I know who he is," Jake said. "His father owns a bank and they've been in racing for several generations. Can't figure how Jill got involved with the likes of him."

"She was coming off a bad marriage," Bones explained. "The high life can be tempting."

"I've never noticed," Jake said. "Never been there, but I've had a few clients like him. I don't last long with them."

"Or they with you, right?"

"You got that right."

***

By the time they got back to the barn, Jill was hotwalking Princely. The other horses were tucked away for the day, and Jake went straight to his tack room and telephone chores. Bones strolled over to look at Sammy, who spun around the minute he sensed Bones' presence and thrust his beautiful Grecian head at him. Bones stuck a big raw carrot into his teeth and the horse bit down hard on it, crunching it up into satisfying little bits as Bones patted his neck and scratched up between his ears. "I think he likes me," he said to Jill, as she sauntered past with Princely in tow.

"Don't be too sure," she said. "He nips every now and then."

Bones fell into step with Jill. "Your ex-boyfriend is a swellhead," he said. "What did you ever see in that jerk?"

"I was real low, Sal, didn't have a job or nothing," she said. "He picked me up at the track one day and took me to all these fancy restaurants and all. He can be nice when he wants to be. And then he helped me get the job at Heritage."

"So you went out with him for quite a while, right?"

"Yeah, too long," she said. "About six months, maybe."

"And?"

"He said he wanted to marry me."

"Did he mean it?"

"At the time, maybe," she said. "I believed him for a while. Dumb, huh? But it's over. And I ain't heard from him neither, till now."

Bones left Jill still walking the horse and drove home to shower and change before heading back to the track for the afternoon card. There was a big pick-six carryover of nearly two hundred grand, and he was too busy putting together a ticket for himself and a few other players, including Moonshine, of course, even to think too much about Jill and Carl Everett, her society bully boy. The ticket got to be pretty big, over a thousand bucks, but Bones figured it looked solid and took 40 percent of it for himself, way over his usual minimum. "You don't need a lot of money at a racetrack," he liked to say, "you need winners."

***

Jill finally lost a race that afternoon. She had the ride in the second race on another one of Rich Abernathy's horses, an untalented hard knocker named Bamboozler. He was a five-year-old gelding who every year picked up enough pieces of purses to pay his expenses but who rarely won. Jill brought him in fourth in a race in which he was forced four wide on the turn. Abernathy hadn't bet on him, so he wasn't upset about losing. "The horse is a bum," he said. "I keep telling Jake to get rid of him, maybe send him up North where he can run against goats, but he won't listen. The horse pays his stable bills, that's what he says, as if I give a shit."

The trainer ignored him and kept his eyes on his horse as Eduardo led him away. "He's sound," he mumbled.

Bones looked at Abernathy's sour face and allowed himself to contemplate a small, tight jab to the mouth but quickly fought off the temptation.

Jill must have gone right home after the race because Bones didn't see her again that afternoon. He didn't think much about her or anything else because he was too busy losing money. He'd won the first four races in the pick six before going down in flames in the last two, with neither of his top selections even finishing in the money. Worse,

120

he had tried to protect his investment by betting substantially on a couple of savers, horses he hadn't used in his pick-six sequence that figured possibly to upset it. They didn't win either. Those last two contests were captured by bad favorites trained by low-percentage horsemen, the kind of guys who win maybe a race or two every six months. More than eight hundred dollars of Bones' money was sucked down the drain. "The bubble has burst," Moonshine said. "It's like the fucking stock market. I'm cleaned out."

"Easy, pal," Bones told him. "It's just one day."

"A symbolic day," Moonshine intoned. "These things run in streaks."

Maybe he had a point, Bones thought. He made a quiet resolve never again to risk that much money on a wager as chancy as a pick six. He'd been having a terrific run of luck and had become a little careless, a fatal mistake at the racetrack, which is quick and merciless in punishing overconfidence. On his way out of the grandstand his cell phone rang and he fished it out of his pocket. It was Jill. "Sal?" she said, her voice sounding tight and breathless.

"Yeah. What's up? You been running up stairs or something?"

"No, I just stepped out of the shower." But she sounded strange, as if something threatening might be happening in the background.

"So why'd you call? You alone?"

"I was, but—"

Bones could hear something pounding. "You want me to come right over?"

"Yeah. Please."

"You want me to call 911?"

"No, it's not like that."

"But you want me to come now."

"Yeah."

"I'm on my way. I'll be there in ten minutes."

When he pulled up into the yard behind Fontana's house, he could hear loud voices coming from Jill's apartment. The dogs were barking and leaping about the yard and he gathered that Fontana hadn't come home yet. He was probably delayed by having to talk to Rich Abernathy or another client or maybe he'd had to go back to the barn to check on one of his horses. Bones got out of his car, petted the dogs and tried to calm them, then called out up the stairs to Jill's place. "Hey, I'm here!" he shouted. "You okay?"

The door opened and Carl Everett appeared on the landing. His face was flushed and he glared angrily down at him. "Get out of here," he said. "This has nothing to do with you. Jill and I have got to talk."

"But maybe she doesn't want to talk to you," Bones said. Jill appeared in the doorway behind Everett. She was dressed only in a short terrycloth robe that came down to just above her knees. Her face was pale but determined. "Jill, is this guy bothering you?"

"I'm okay. I told you, I was in the shower, then Carl showed up." She came up beside Everett. "So go now, Carl."

He looked at her. "You have to talk to me, Jill," he said. "You know it's not over."

"Yeah, it is. How many times I got to tell you that? I told you over and over."

"And I'm telling you it isn't finished," he insisted. "You know it and I know it; we both know it. What we had was great. Okay, so I made a mistake. I was under a lot of pressure, you know that. But what happened doesn't matter anymore. It doesn't count."

"You're the one who ended it, Carl," she said. "You're the one who disappeared. You dumped me."

"And I've admitted I was wrong. Why can't you accept that?"

"Because I don't care about you anymore, that's why. Now please go."

Carl Everett turned to look at Bones, then back at her. "You're not going out with this guy, are you? Who is he?"

"He's just a friend. I called him when you started pounding on the door."

Everett hesitated. "Look, Jill—" he began.

But she cut him off. "Get out of here, Carl. Just get out. You don't want me to call the cops."

"You?" He laughed. "You wouldn't do that." He reached out for her and she backed away. His hand clutched at her robe and tore it open. Jill gasped and hunched over, clutching the robe around her to hide her nakedness.

Bones started up the stairs. "Hey, leave her alone," he said. "And get the fuck out of here. Didn't you hear the lady?"

Everett whirled on him. "Back off, creep!" he said. "You don't know who you're dealing with!"

"Is that right?" Bones answered, still moving toward him. "If you touch her again, pal, you'll wish you hadn't."

Everett hesitated, then suddenly started down the stairs. "Oh, get out of my way!" he said.

Bones stepped aside to let him pass, his main objective just to get him away from Jill. But as Everett passed, he suddenly took a backward swing at Bones. It was a clumsy move and Bones saw it coming. He came up under it and shoved him forward. Everett lost his footing, fell down the remaining steps and sprawled face down in the dirt at the foot of the steps. The dogs began to bound and bark around him, but Jill quickly called them off. Everett raised himself up and turned to look at Bones. "You son of a bitch, I'll sue you," he said.

"You will?" Bones turned to Jill. "Why don't you go call 911 and we'll have this guy put in the slammer on an assault charge."

Everett got to his feet, brushed himself off, and staggered to his Mercedes convertible. He opened the door and lurched inside, started the engine, and drove swiftly away.

Jill stared at Bones. "Sal, you all right?"

"Yeah, sure. He missed. I just sent him on his way."

"Thanks for coming. I saw him drive up here and that's when I thought about calling you. When he started pounding on the door ..."

"Yeah, you had a right."

"Then I got scared you'd hurt him."

"I try not to do that anymore," Bones assured her. "I broke a knuckle once on one of these assholes. So you want to have some dinner somewhere?"

"Yeah, okay. Why not? I won't be five minutes. I just got to put something on."

"What's with that rich boy anyway?" Bones asked. "Has he always been such a prick?"

"No. You can't believe how nice to me he was when we first met," she said. "I kind of fell for him, Sal. But it's long over."

"I hope so," Bones said. "He seems to have like a hearing problem, know what I mean? Doesn't get the message, even when it's loud and clear."

CHAPTER 13

"**W**hat do you say, kid? Shall we heel and toe this check?" Bones asked, as they finished up their meal with a couple of cappuccinos at the little French restaurant where they'd first had dinner together a few weeks earlier.

"Do what?" Jill asked.

"Skip out on our bill," he explained, smiling. "It's an old gambler's term for when you're down on your luck."

"You're kidding, right?"

"Yeah. I was just trying to get a laugh out of you," he said. "You've been real quiet all evening."

She had. A gloom had settled over her and nothing Bones tried had brought her out of it. He had told her a whole bunch of gambling and horse-playing stories to get her to laugh or at least to react but had only managed to elicit an occasional faint smile. Finally, she had put a hand over his across the table from her and asked him to stop. "I'm sorry, Sal," she said, "but I can't seem to come out of myself tonight."

"This guy must have cut you up pretty bad," Bones said. "What else did he do to you besides tell you he was going to marry you?"

"It's not just him," she said. "I was a jerk to believe him. You know, I guess I wanted to believe him so bad. So when he ran out on me it hurt that much more."

"So how'd you meet him? At the track, right?"

"I was riding at Pleasanton," she said. "I wasn't getting on much of anything. Mostly I was exercise riding in the mornings, scrambling around from stable to stable. It was tough going. Then Carl showed up one day. I worked a horse for him, a nice two-year-old Cal-bred filly he owned, and he came around the barn afterward and asked me out. He took me to a big party that night in San Francisco given by some friends of his, all people in racing, mostly rich owners with lots of horses. They made me feel like I was a lump of shit. Hell, I was nobody. Carl told me not to pay 'em no mind; they was just a bunch of horsey society snobs and that I was worth any ten of them. You know, Sal, I had real low confidence in myself in those days. I mean, hell, I came from nothing; my people came from nothing. My marriage had just busted up and I was at a real low point."

"And along comes Prince Charming, who's going to turn you overnight into Cinderella," Bones said. "So he began to take you out. But did you ever get to meet his family?"

"No. His mother's dead, his father owns all these banks in Frisco, Oakland, all over up there. Anyways, his type all eat pretty high up on the hog."

"When he wouldn't introduce you to his old man, had he already asked you to marry him?"

"No, that was later. He didn't want to embarrass me, he said. He said his family was all a bunch of big old right-wing Republicans or something."

"And you were white trash."

"He didn't say it quite like that," she said, smiling faintly. "Hey, Sal, you slice right down to the bone, don't you?"

"That's me, kid. Old Bones, the human shit detector."

"Anyway, he gave me things, took me places. Took me to Saratoga, in fact, though I had to stay in this motel. He'd been invited by old family friends to stay with them and he couldn't take me there."

"He'd just show up at night to tell you how much he loved you and then get down to business."

"What?" she said, looking suddenly dazed.

"Sorry, Jill, that was pretty rude. It's just that guys like Carl Everett bring out the worst in me," Bones said. "Did he at least take you to the races?"

"Oh, yeah. We sat in a box with his friends," she said. "He introduced me by saying I was an apprentice rider from California who'd worked some of his horses for him. Which wasn't too far from the truth."

"Did they buy it?"

"Who knows? I didn't even think about it, Sal. I wanted so hard to believe in him."

"And always at night he'd come by to see you, then get up, put on his pants and go back to his friends."

"Something like that." She looked at him out of big round eyes in the dim light of the restaurant. "What a dope, huh?"

"Yeah, but you were pretty easy, Jill. He counted on that and used you. When did he dump you?"

"We went back to San Francisco together, then he helped me get the job at Heritage," she said. "It was a great job for me, working with all those really nice young horses. I sure loved it. I missed the race riding, sure, but now I had some security."

"And then what happened?"

She took a minute or two before answering. "You don't want to hear this, do you?"

"Nothing you don't want to tell me."

"He just stopped calling and coming around," she said. "I didn't know why or anything, so I called him a couple of times. I mean, he was in Frisco, okay, but we was supposed to get together on my days off and he was going to come around to see me. It all just stopped happening. He kept saying he was real busy at the bank and all, and then one day I couldn't even get him on the phone. He'd have one of his secretaries put me off. And then I got this letter from him, you know the kind, right?"

"Sure. 'It's been grand, but we need to take a break from each other, find out what it all means.' Something like that?"

"Yeah." She looked away from him. He signaled for the waiter and asked for the check. "It's strange," she continued. "I was so sure he loved me. I guess I wanted real hard to believe that."

"Well, now he's had some time to think about it and he wants you

127

back," Bones said. "That's unusual, you know."

She didn't answer. He paid the check, and they walked out of the restaurant to his car parked halfway up the block. On the drive back toward Fontana's place she said nothing but stared out the window. He didn't press her for more on Everett; he figured she'd paid enough of a price just having had to talk about it. He drove into the yard as the dogs began to bark inside the house, then he got out to say good night, expecting Jill to let him kiss her on the cheek and send him away. But suddenly she looked at him and said, "Want to come up?"

He nodded and followed her up the stairs to her room. Inside it was a mess. The bed was unmade and dirty laundry had been dumped into one corner. Other clothes were piled high on the only chair, and the tiny sink was full of unwashed dishes. The only picture in the room, a large framed photograph of The Boston Kid winning the Travers at Saratoga, hung crookedly on the wall beside the bed. "I'm sorry," she said. "I ain't much of a housekeeper."

"It's okay."

They stood facing each other in the dim light seeping into the room through the drawn curtains over the one window. Bones wasn't sure what exactly was expected of him, since he'd convinced himself by then that he and Jill were going to be just pals. Without a word, however, she began to undress. First her shirt and bra, then her jeans and panties, until she stood there naked in front of him. She had a lean, muscular body with long legs and small breasts, her nipples dark and spiky. "Listen, Jill," he said softly, "I don't think this is a good idea. You're terrific, honey, but this isn't right and you know it."

"You don't want me?" she asked, not moving.

"Sure, I want you. You think I don't like you? I do. I'd take you in a minute, but ..."

"But what?"

"Look," he said, "you got to have more pride than this, babe. You're too classy a broad to take this route."

She sat down on the bed, her head slumped forward. He sat down next to her and put an arm around her. She turned into him, her face against his shirt front, and began to cry. He just held her and softly stroked the back of her neck, as if she were a little puppy or a small kid. They remained like that for nearly ten minutes, until at last she stopped sobbing, grabbed a corner of the sheet and began to dry her eyes. "I'm sorry, Sal," she said. "I guess I'm all messed up inside. I don't know what's wrong with me."

"It's okay," he answered. "This guy's pissed all over you, but you'll get over it, trust me."

She stood up, walked over to the chair, picked up her bathrobe, and quickly slipped it on. "Yeah, I'm going to be all right," she said, not looking at him. "You're a good guy, Sal. Please go now, okay?"

"You're sure you're all right?"

"Yeah. Yeah, I'm okay." She came up to him and this time gave him a quick peck on the cheek. "I want to meet Bingo," she said.

"You will," he said. "She wants to meet you. I've told her all about you."

"She like horses?"

"Can't tell one end from the other, but, like you, she's met a lot of horses' asses in her time. That kind she knows about."

"We have a lot in common, huh?"

"Yeah, you'll like each other. See you, kid." He let himself out, took a deep breath, and headed toward his car. She waited until the sound of it leaving had faded, then she lay down on the bed, cupped her hands over her breasts, and stared soundlessly up into the darkness.

***

Jack Martin's story in the *Racing Form* had brought Jill a lot of attention, and some smart bettors had finally started to follow her career with more than casual interest. It was reflected in the lower odds on the horses she rode. Except for that, however, the publicity didn't seem to have much effect on her career; riding offers didn't come piling in. Nor did Steve Bullion volunteer to put her up on any of his other horses, which made her realize he'd wanted only to get into her pants when he'd hired her to ride his first-time starter. She wasn't disappointed. She went about her chores around the barn, galloped Fontana's horses in the mornings, and rode a couple of more for him over the following week. Neither of these efforts on mediocre claimers produced another win, though she did bring one in third. Her life seemed to have settled into a routine that suited her.

On one of the track's dark days, Bones invited her to the Blue Flamingo to introduce her to Bingo, who knew they were coming. She served them drinks, then, having gotten Marty Blenheim's okay, changed into her street clothes and joined Jill and Bones for dinner. The women hit it off right away. Both had had tough childhoods, bad fathers, bad lovers, bums for husbands, and were trying to get their acts together and deal with life in a positive way—Bingo through raising a good kid, Jill through her love of the game and the animals. But Bingo, who was older, tougher, and wiser than Jill, saw the girl still had a ways to go. Bones hadn't told her about the night Jill had offered herself to him, but Bingo sensed in Jill an underlying current of desperation. "She's got problems," she told Bones later that night at his place. "I don't know, Sal, but she's pretty vulnerable," she said, leaning up on one elbow to look down at him as they lay in bed together. Bones was lying on his back, his head resting on his hands. "You didn't screw her, did you? Tell me you didn't."

"Hey, you think I'd have introduced the two of you if I had? What are you, crazy? Of course, I didn't. I just like her, and I like the way she rides. I'd like to handle her book, if she'd let me. I could put her on some winners."

"So long as she's riding horses and not you," she teased. "It'd be just like you to bang her and then make a buddy out of her."

"That's before I met you, babe. You've made an honest man out of me."

"If I catch you lying to me, you better go to sleep with one eye open or I'll have you singing soprano."

"I wouldn't do too good as a gelding," he said. "And you wouldn't like it much either. Come here." He took her in his arms and then they had one of their best nights ever together.

The next morning, another dark day at the track, Bones was hanging around the pool at his place basking like a walrus in the sun when his cell phone rang. It was Ray Weldon, a tennis coach who worked the L.A. public courts and whom Bones had helped to a few winners at the races over the years. Ray made a nice living off tennis, mostly by coaching movie actors, but until he'd met Bones five years previously he'd blown most of his earnings back on the horses. He was the kind of player who never saw an odds-on bum he didn't like, and the lower the price the more he'd bet on him. It hadn't been easy, but Bones had finally managed to get him to listen to him, and now Ray wouldn't even go to the races unless Bones had told him what to bet and how. Of course, if he won big, he'd kick back a percentage to his mentor. Nothing wrong with that, Bones maintained. "Ray, you have to pay for an education, right?" he'd told his pupil. "I mean, think of Harvard." Anyway, there was Ray Weldon on the phone, and Bones had immediately assumed that the call had to do, as usual, with his action at the races. "Listen, Ray," he said, "I haven't even bought tomorrow's *Form*. Call me tonight, or if you're coming to the track tomorrow, you know where I am."

"It's not about the track," Weldon said. "I was at my dentist's office this morning. He gets all these magazines and I picked up this one called *Trends*. It just came out today. Did you see it?"

"No, how would I have, Ray? I'm sitting on my ass by the pool wondering why I have so few normal friends. Shoot."

"Well, the cover has a big photo of this guy Paul Furman, who owns some big horse farm."

"I know who he is, Ray."

"I wouldn't have read it except the shot was framed by all these little snapshots of other people, including Jill Aspen."

"Yeah? And?"

"So I read the piece. It's quite an article."

"What does it say?"

"That there were rumors Jill was involved with him," Ray said. "Her and a slew of other women. Furman's a player, apparently. He was supposed to have had an affair with that woman who died so mysteriously. Then there's talk about other women, including your girl jockey. You better read it."

Bones thanked him, said he would, and told him he'd see him at the races the following day. Then he got dressed and went down to his corner newsstand, where he bought the magazine. He came back home, made himself a cappuccino, and read Wynn Messmer's story. It was a long one for a *Trends* profile, and at first it read like a hymn of praise for this dynamic new political figure on the national scene. Several times it hinted that Paul Furman could very well one day become a leading presidential candidate. Furman was portrayed as another of those compassionate conservatives whose political and social programs were described as enlightened, visionary, and imaginative. Furman himself, with his folksy, unpretentious public speaking style, came across as a likeable figure. Then, two-thirds of the way through the piece, Messmer slipped in the knife. Furman, many people in California hinted, was a womanizer. He had a sick wife whom people rarely saw in public; she periodically had to be treated in psychiatric clinics, especially after the tragic death of the couple's thirteen-year-old daughter, Laura Lee. The girl had drowned swimming in Lake Cachuma in the Santa Ynez Valley, where the Furmans had a small ranch they used as a weekend retreat, mainly in the warmer months.

Furman himself had often been seen in the company of glamorous women. An almost constant companion had been Dulcie Clark, who had run the Heritage Farm operation for him. Her mysterious death had left a lot of unanswered questions. Messmer had also tried to track down and verify rumors that Furman had had a relationship with a woman who worked at Heritage, an exercise rider named Jill Aspen, now working as an apprentice jockey at Santa Anita. Aspen had refused to be interviewed. No one connected closely to Furman in any way had agreed to be quoted on any of these accusations. All candidates for public office these days, Messmer had concluded, were accused of wrongdoing of one sort or another, and it was inevitable that an attractive man of Furman's stature, saddled with a sick wife, would be a subject of speculation and an object of scandalous insinuations. Furman, who had smilingly but emphatically denied all accusations while at the same time refusing to discuss his personal life, seemed likely to emerge unscathed in his attempt to unseat a vulnerable left-wing opponent in 2006. The son of a bitch, Bones thought to himself, imagining Wynn Messmer's delight at having seemed to endorse his subject while simultaneously slandering him. A clever little prick of a reporter.

Bones picked up the phone and called the barn. Eduardo answered and he asked to speak to Jill. "She no come in today, *señor*," the Mexican said. "She sick." So then Bones called Jill at home. No answer. Nor was he able to get to her later. He did finally track down Fontana, who told him Jill had called in sick but wasn't at home. He had called her earlier, when he'd gotten back from the track, then had climbed the stairs to her front door and knocked. She hadn't responded. Bones asked him to look in on her again, even to let himself into her room with his own key. "I'm worried about her, Jake," he said. "I got a reason."

Jake did so, then called him back about an hour later. "She's gone, Sal," he said. "Most of her stuff's still there, but she's up and gone. I expect maybe we'll hear from her."

"No note or anything?"

"Nope. I sure hope she's okay. What's wrong, do you know?"

Bones told Jake about the story in *Trends* and the trainer grunted his displeasure. "Goddamn, they just can't leave people alone, can they?" he said. "Where do you think she's gone?"

"I don't know, Jake. All I know is something happened to her up north. Maybe this guy Everett, maybe something else, I don't know," Bones said. "Let's just hope she'll be back in a day or two."

"Yeah," Jake said, "I got horses to worry about."

CHAPTER 14

Two days later, on Friday morning, Jill showed up at the barn. She was dressed to work, but she looked pale and distraught, as if she had returned from somebody's funeral and was still grieving. "Where the hell have you been?" Jake asked when she appeared in his tack room doorway.

"I'm real sorry, Jake," she said. "Something happened. I had to go away."

"Somebody die?"

"No, nothing like that," she answered. "It was personal. I'm sorry, but I had to go."

"And things are all right now?"

She nodded. "I hope so," she said. "I won't let you down again."

"Yeah, you could have left a message or something. Bones and I have both been wondering where you could have gone."

"I should have," she said. "I meant to."

"Have you seen Sal or spoken to him?"

"No."

"Well, I'm sure he'll be at the races this afternoon. You going to talk to him? He was more worried about you than I was."

"I sure intend to."

He looked at her sharply, seeing the pain in her eyes. "You're sure you're all right?"

"Yeah. Put me to work."

"Okay, take Sammy out for his gallop. You know he runs day after tomorrow."

"Yeah, I know. You said you was going to enter him."

"It's a non-winners of one other than claiming or maiden, and they're going seven," the trainer reminded her. "We'll find out something about him. I had to give the mount to Neruda. I didn't know whether you'd be coming back or not."

"Okay, I understand," she mumbled, turning away.

She took Tumultuous out onto the track and galloped him an easy mile and a half, feeling the latent power of the animal and his desire to shake loose from her and run. "There's something about this horse," she told Fontana afterward, as she cooled Tumultuous out. "He's like a time bomb. I could hardly hold him. My arms are sore."

"Yeah? Well, we'll see," the trainer said. "Let's hope he doesn't leave his desire on the track in the morning."

Jill dropped by Bones' box that afternoon, after the third race. The moment he saw her he left the box to join her, and together they walked down to the paddock where they could talk alone. When he asked her where she'd been and what had happened to her, she revealed no more than she had told Jake. "Don't ask me nothing else, Sal," she pleaded. "I just can't talk about it right now."

"Okay, so how about dinner tonight? There's some other things I want to talk to you about. Like your career, for instance."

"No, I can't," she said. "I'm way behind on my sleep and I got to get my act together again."

"You know you lost the mount on Sammy, don't you? Jake couldn't take the chance on you."

"I can't help that. I had to go."

"And you don't want to talk about it."

"No. I need a clear head, Sal," she said. "I can't get that if I got to account to you or anyone else for every move I make. I need some space, Sal."

"Okay." He looked closely at her. She didn't seem too anxious to return his gaze; her eyes kept looking beyond him, evading him. "Are you seeing Everett again?" he asked.

That got her attention; she stared at him in horror. "Jesus, no, never! That's over with. You got to know that, Sal."

"Hey, I'm not sure what I know, babe," he said. "I just don't want to see you piss your life away again on some bum who doesn't deserve you."

"I ain't planning on doing that."

"The story in *Trends* hinted that you and Furman—"

Her face flushed red with anger. "That fucking reporter," she said. "Writing all that crap!"

"It's not true, then."

"No, it ain't. It's not what that reporter said it was."

"Furman's a player?"

"No. He's got this sick wife and she's a bitch," Jill said. "Paul was seeing someone ..." Her voice trailed away, as if she had temporarily forgotten what she was going to say. "I don't ... I don't want to talk about it, Sal."

"Was it this Dulcie Clark broad?"

"I told you, I don't want to talk about it no more. It's over."

"What is?"

"Everything back there, it's over."

"Is that why you went back there?" he asked. "To make sure?"

She didn't answer right away. Again her gaze strayed beyond him, as if focusing on something in the distance, some vision or recollection of events so painful she wanted only to banish them from her life. "Yeah," she said at last, "to make sure it's over, that's all."

"With Everett?"

"Yeah, him, too." She looked up into his eyes now and placed a hand on his arm, but said nothing else.

"Jill, I'd like to help, if I can," he said. "You know me, right? Bones, the problem crusher?"

"There's nothing for you to do, Sal," she said. "It's stuff I got to take care of on my own. There ain't no other way out of it."

"This guy Everett racked you up pretty bad. He got you in trouble, didn't he?"

"Yeah," she said. "It's been a rough time. But it's going to be all right. Time, Sal, I need some time, you get it? I got a new life here. I ain't about to blow it."

He patted her shoulder. "And remember this, Jill. You got friends now."

***

Bones didn't see Jill again or hear from her until the day Tumultuous ran his first race for them. When he went to the barn that morning, Bones hung around with Jake at Clockers Corner while Jill galloped some of the trainer's horses. Afterward the two men walked back to the barn, where Ester Gale Dinworthy awaited them. She was dressed in another of her spectacular outfits, what looked like overlapping layers of brightly colored silks topped by a large straw hat festooned with purple plumes. Her only concession to practicality was a sturdy pair of flat-bottomed walking shoes. She was sitting in a chair by the tack-room entrance but rose majestically as they arrived. *"Buon giorno*, Giacomo," she said. "I presume our darling champion is ready to run?"

"As ready as we can get him," Jake said. "You remember Bones, Mrs. Dinworthy, don't you? He owns a piece of your horse."

"Well, of course I do," she said, staring at Bones as if he had just crawled out from under a rotting stump. "What a curious name."

"You can call me Sal, if you like," Bones said, smiling.

"Indeed," she said, with a disapproving sniff. "For Salvatore?"

"Yeah."

"That's all right, then. Salvatore it is."

"Whatever makes you happy, babe."

She ignored his reply and turned back to the trainer. "I fed him a carrot," she said. "Your groom seemed a bit upset by it. I hope I didn't do anything wicked."

Jake smiled. "Not at all, Mrs. Dinworthy," he said. "They're not supposed to eat on the mornings they run, but one carrot isn't going to make a difference."

"He looks magnificent," she said. "I expect him to win easily, don't you?"

"I don't know," the trainer said. "He may want to go longer than seven furlongs, and I haven't been pushing him for speed. He sure

138

does want to run, though. Jill has a hard time holding him in his gallops. He wants to take off."

"That's a good sign, isn't it?" Mrs. Dinworthy said. "Well, I know you have lots to do. I presume I'll see you in the paddock before the race." She then made one of her grand exits, moving toward her car in a great swirl of robes and fluttering scarves, her hat perched like a large platter on her head, its purple plumes dancing overhead.

"What a character," Bones said.

"One of a kind," Jake agreed. "Even if she is a pain in the ass at times."

Jill came riding up on the last of Fontana's horses, vaulted out of the saddle, and began to tend to her mount. She took no notice of Bones until he greeted her. She turned just long enough to flash him a quick smile. "Hi," was all she said before turning back to her animal.

"Breakfast?" Bones asked.

"Nope. I'm too busy here, Sal."

"I'll see you at the races then."

"Yeah."

Bones looked at Jake, who simply shrugged. They walked away from the barn together. "Don't feel too bad," the trainer said, as they parted. "She doesn't talk much to me either now. She just shows up, does her job, and disappears."

Bones drove back to his place and called Stats Goldman, who was busy, as usual, with his complicated calculations. Stats' real name was Herb, but everybody called him Stats. He was a numbers guy, one of those professional handicappers who couldn't tell a horse from a mule but who kept records and boiled all the statistics in racing down to specific sets of numbers on every horse in every race. This made him a useful source of information, if not the oracle he imagined himself to be. "I don't expect your horse to win today," Stats said, when Bones asked him about Tumultuous, "or do much of anything else either. He's not working to sprint, and none of the clockers have anything special to say about him."

"What do they know?" Bones replied. "All I can tell you, Stats, is that he's a handful in the mornings. He just wants to take off."

"That may be," Stats maintained in his usual dogged style, "but this race doesn't fit Fontana's pattern. He's zero for thirty-nine over the past two years with horses of his running their first race for him after a purchase or a claim. And he's almost as bad with horses coming out of maiden claiming wins for the first time."

"There's always an exception to the rule," Bones said.

"I play the percentages, Bones, and the percentages say no," the handicapper insisted. "I like your horse a race or two from now, when Fontana stretches him out around two turns. That's assuming he can run at all. That first win was against nothing."

"The speed fig was good."

"True, but the figs tend to go down when they go up against winners. There's a couple of decent horses in against you."

"So you aren't going to tout him to anyone?"

"No chance."

"That's good," Bones said, knowing that a strong endorsement from Stats could actually affect the odds on a horse. "All I'm going to tell you, Stats, is this sucker can flat-out run."

"The numbers don't lie," Stats insisted. "Not today, Bones."

"Thanks, pal," Bones said, hanging up. Knowing that none of Stats' rich clients would be hammering Tumultuous at the windows cheered Bones considerably; there's nothing like another possible killing in the offing to cast a rosy glow over a horseplayer's afternoon.

***

Tumultuous was scheduled to run in the sixth race on the card, and he was listed in the morning line, the track handicapper's estimate of the probable betting odds, at 8-1. None of the newspaper handicappers picked him and the *Racing Form* had him listed at 12-1. So Bones wasn't surprised when he arrived at the track shortly before the third race to hear from Moonshine that the private clockers in their tout sheets had nothing specific to say about him except that he might be a good play at some time in the future, presumably against an easier field and at a longer distance. As for Stats, whom Bones had come across standing under a TV monitor in the grandstand, he still seemed indifferent to Tumultuous' chances and was concentrating on putting together a pick-six ticket that didn't include the horse as one of his selections. Moonshine, as usual, was a fount of pessimism. "What a shame, Bones," he said, when he came by the box soon after Bones got there. "You sank all that dough into a claimer. What were you thinking about?"

"Making money," Bones said. "That's how I go through life, Moonshine—blundering from one hit to another."

"Well, Stats says he may not be such a bum," Moonshine conceded, "but I'm not going to pick him to do anything today. Down the line maybe, who knows? He needs a distance of ground, right? And maybe a cheaper field? There's a couple of good horses in against him today."

"Like who?" Bones asked.

"Well, there's the Arab horse, Aladdin," Moonshine said, checking his program and his notes. "He was an easy maiden winner three weeks ago, and they paid two million for him as a yearling at the Keeneland sales. There's Hot Baby, a speedball out of the Traggart barn. You know Traggart, he's got nothing but fast young horses. And then there's Sleepyhead, bred to go long, too, but a nice winner last fall at Hollywood. And a couple of others also who can run some. They'll all be out there faster than your horse."

"Maybe you and Stats are right, Moonshine. What do I know?" Bones said. "I'm only ahead over a hundred grand this meet. Anyway, he's got a beautiful head. My partner, the ditzy Mrs. Dinworthy, says he looks like an Elgin marble."

"What the fuck is that?"

"Don't worry about it, Moonshine. It just means he looks good."

"Horses run with their legs," Moonshine said. "Who cares about how they look?"

Bones let this observation pass in silence; Moonshine was beyond help. Then, as the horses for the fourth neared the starting gate, Stats showed up to ask if Bones wanted in on his pick-six ticket. "No, I'll pass," Bones said. "I'm not legally allowed to bet against my own horse, don't you know that?"

"Nobody pays attention to that shit," Stats said. "And you always bet with your head, not your heart."

"Not always, Stats, not always."

One of Stats' selections, unfortunately the favorite, won the fourth. Stats had spread the net on his pick six in the fifth, so he figured to go two for two on his ticket, but Bones didn't care. Bones was playing it cool, but by this time he was pretty hot about his own horse, so right after the fourth he left his box and went down to the receiving barn where Eduardo and Jill were tending to Sammy, who looked terrific. The horse was calm but alert, his ears cocked and his eyes taking in his surroundings with interest. He remained calm as they walked with him to the saddling area after the fifth, where Jake was waiting for them. Eduardo held the bridle and patted the horse's neck as Jake and Jill began to saddle him, after which Eduardo walked him around inside the shed row just to keep him moving. The horse showed no signs of nervousness and maintained that same air of concentrated power Bones had noted every time he'd been around him. "He sure looks good," he said to no one in particular.

"Sammy's a racehorse," Jill said. "He's a running fool."

It was at that precise moment that Bones became absolutely sure that Tumultuous was going to win. A few minutes later he spotted Stats leaning against the rail of the walking ring, but the handicapper apparently hadn't sensed any of the aura the horse exuded. Like all numbers guys, Stats never seemed to be aware of being in the presence of a gifted athlete. Some horses, not many, will convey that feeling of power and invincibility merely by their very presence. Cigar, Sunday Silence, Secretariat, all the great ones had it; they moved like gods among mortals. Bones walked over to Stats. "You better put a saver on this horse," he told him. "He's going to win."

"Not today, Bones. There's too much going against him." He grinned, the picture of the professional horseplayer, small, thin, crushed under the weight of his numbers. Bones suddenly felt sorry for him.

Out in the walking ring Mrs. Ester Gale Dinworthy, looking like a feathered Aztec goddess, surveyed the scene. "Well, Giacomo," she said, "how is our champion?"

"Doing good," Jake said. "Now let's hope he runs as good as he looks."

"Well, Giacomo, well. Not good."

"Whatever you say, Mrs. Dinworthy."

Tumultuous maintained his majestic calm in the paddock, even while a couple of the other entries were misbehaving. Hot Baby was a handful, snorting and bobbing his head up and down, and Aladdin would occasionally lash out with his hind legs, causing bystanders on the grass to stay well clear of him. None of this activity seemed to influence the tote board, which showed Hot Baby at even money and Aladdin at 5-2. Sleepyhead was the third choice, while Tumultuous seemed to be locked in at 10-1.

Jake's instructions to Paolo Neruda were concise. "I'm not sure how much pure speed he has, Paolo," he said, "but the starting gate doesn't bother him. Out there in the sixth hole the dirt won't bother him too much either. Let him run his race; he'll tell you what he wants to do."

"I expect you to emerge triumphant," Ester Gale Dinworthy said. "No horse with such a beautiful head can possibly lose."

"No, ma'am," Neruda answered, flashing her a quick smile just before Jake legged him up into the saddle.

As Bones looked back on it later, he should have known it would be no contest. Hot Baby, true to his name and Traggart's training style, bounded right to the front, with Aladdin inside of him but no more than a length back. Tumultuous came out alertly, fell back a couple of lengths, then moved up to third outside of Sleepyhead. As the field started around the turn, Aladdin spurted up to engage Hot Baby, with Tumultuous still two lengths back. Then their champion struck. Neruda clucked to him, let out the reins a notch, and the horse seemed to go into another gear. In a matter of a few yards, he swept up on the two favorites, seemed to hover there momentarily as if teasing them, then, with a tremendous burst of energy, quite simply exploded into a four-length lead at the head of the lane that became six at the eighth pole and seven, under a hand ride, at the wire. "I didn't even touch him," Neruda said, as he jumped off the horse after they had their picture taken in the winner's circle. "This is some animal. I ride him again for you any-time you want."

"You see, Giacomo, I told you so," Mrs. Dinworthy pronounced, as she graciously kissed the trainer on the cheek. "We have a champion, he of the noble Grecian head."

Stats was waiting for Bones up in the stands; he looked stunned. "Why didn't you tell me about this horse?" he asked. "He goddamn near broke the track record for the distance."

"You wouldn't listen," Bones answered. "There are intangibles in this game, Stats. It's not all numbers."

"How much did you bet on him?"

"Two hundred, and I'm feeling like a fool," Bones said. "I'd have bet more on him, if it hadn't been for your charts and stats."

"Hey, Bones, don't blame me. I didn't bet a dime and my pick six blew up."

"Look at it this way," Bones said. "Maybe you learned something, right? Two and two don't always make four."

"Too bad he's a Cal-bred," Moonshine, that walking eclipse of the sun, commented. "And he's also a gelding."

"Hey, Moonshine, let the sun in," Bones said. "Wherever you go, pal, it's always midnight."

Bones cashed his ticket, then went downstairs to look around for Jill, but she had disappeared. He felt sorry for her. Her temporary disappearance had cost her the mount on Tumultuous. Even if Jake had wanted to, the ethics of the game as played by honorable men like Jake Fontana dictated that he'd have to offer Neruda the oppor-tunity to ride the horse back in his next race. What they had in the barn now was a possible stakes winner, and the rider would bask in whatever success the horse generated. Life had dealt Jill some bad hands in the past, and all she could do now was play them out. There didn't seem to be anything Bones could do to help her either, at this point.

CHAPTER 15

After Tumultuous won his first race for them, Bones decided to spend the roughly $2,400 he'd made betting on him by treating Bingo and her son, Tommy, to a couple of days in Las Vegas. He himself was planning to spend maybe a week there, playing various tracks while getting away from the routine his life had settled into. Variety, that's what he needed, he told himself: new surroundings, different tracks, more horses. They checked into Circus Circus, the huge pink-and-white box on the Strip that featured acrobats, clowns, and other circus performers, including trapeze artists who soared fearlessly over the action on the casino floor. Tommy loved every minute of it, especially the carnival games, at which he won himself an enormous stuffed giraffe for hammering a catapult that hurtled a rubber chicken into a slowly revolving empty kettle. He lugged the giraffe around with him for the rest of the first day, while the three of them strolled the shopping malls and later basked by the indoor pool between quick dips.

Las Vegas wasn't the kind of place where most people wanted to spend much time, but Bones had always found it restful. He didn't play casino games or bet on anything but horse racing, the only action except for poker where the players, once the house has taken its cut, go up against one another. So he could have stopped in at one of the sports books to bet the horses, but he'd promised Bingo his undivided attention. He didn't find that too hard to do, even though she had her mind set on soaking up some culture, which meant stopping off at the Liberace Museum to look at old musical instruments, a rhinestone-encrusted car, and some old costumes, and the

Guinness Book of World Records Museum, which sported life-sized replicas of the world's smallest woman and tallest man. After those visits, Bones had to admit to himself that he was getting a little antsy about maybe finding a TV screen somewhere with Thoroughbreds running across it. But he resisted the impulse, and that night he got them good seats for a big magic show in which a full-grown elephant disappeared and a woman was changed into a black panther. That wowed the kid, as Bones had figured it would.

"We've really had a good time here, Tommy," Bingo said to the boy at lunch the next day, just before Bones took them to the airport.

"Aw, Mom, I wish we could have seen some more magic," Tommy said. "That was awesome. And maybe I could have won another animal."

"We'll be back again, honey. Right, Sal?"

"You bet," Bones said. "I'm sorry you have to leave, Tommy. School, right?"

"Yeah," he said, nodding miserably.

"And Mom's got to go to work, too. You understand, don't you?" Bingo asked.

Tommy nodded, and Bingo hugged him and smiled at Bones.

When they arrived at the airport for the flight back to L.A., Bones started to get out of the cab but Bingo stopped him. She leaned in the door and gave him a quick kiss. "Don't bother, Sal. We'll make the plane on our own. This was real nice." She paused. "I know you got the fever on you, right? You're a nice guy, maybe not always a good guy, but a nice one. Watch yourself."

"I'll see you in a few days," he said.

"Whenever," she answered. "You know, you don't owe me anything, Sal. I think you're a little messed up on your priorities, like where your life is going, but what the hell. I'll see you when I see you." And she quickly escorted Tommy into the terminal without a backward look.

So Bones spent the next three days playing the horses at seven or eight different tracks from morning to late afternoon. He'd moved from Circus Circus over to Treasure Island, which had comfortable, unpretentious rooms with strong reading lights and a good sports book where you could sit at a counter with your personal TV monitor and face a bank of large screens bringing in action from all over the country. It was more like an orgy for him than a gambling venture, so much action that no single entity stood out. At the end of every day he felt drained, purged, cleaned out, at least figuratively.

His usual style was to play one track at a time, fearlessly but never carelessly, with all his options accounted for and with maximum respect for the way the racetrack can strip you of your illusions in an instant—a losing photo, a disqualification, an unlucky or a dumb ride, and, worst of all, a breakdown, the sight of one of those gorgeous animals shattering a bone, tearing a tendon, pulling up lame or being carted away in the meat wagon to be put down for keeps. Horse racing was a great game, but it could be a terrifying and frustrating one as well. It was not for the weak, the sentimental, or the kings of denial. Of course, he didn't win over those three days, but he didn't lose much either and he had fun; he'd purged himself of desire. At night he'd dress up, go out to dinner in some good restaurant, drink excellent wine, and return to his room in time to handicap the next day's potential action.

Late in the afternoon of his third day, he was perched at the bar in the sports book when a woman sitting next to him said, "You ever had to deal with a thousand sellers, ten thousand kids with moms and dads, and a shitload full of toys and games?"

"You talking to me?" he asked.

"Who else?" she said. "You see anyone else here?"

"Why would you ask me that? I'm not married and I got no kids."

"That's what I figured," she said. "You look like a loner. You don't know how lucky you are."

"Yeah, I do," he said. "So what's your story?"

"I'm running this toy convention over at the Hilton," she explained. "We're hustling toys, sports equipment, furniture, games, clothes, all kinds of kiddie merchandise for tots between the ages of four and twelve. Most of it's junk; some of it's even dangerous. Luckily, that's not my concern. What I have to worry about is to make sure these hustlers sell all their crap over the three days of this convention. You ever been to one of these functions?"

"No," he said. "I'd maybe let people throw baseballs at my head rather than put up with that shit."

She threw her head back and laughed. It was a great laugh. It came up out of the bottom of her soul and turned the heads of the other customers at the bar. "I like you," she said. "You're a no bullshit guy, right? That's why I'm talking to you."

"I was wondering," he said. "Is this what you do? I thought maybe you were a working girl."

She laughed again. "I thought of doing that one time, but I got my self-respect. No, I go around putting on these shows all over, mostly here in Vegas. What do you do?"

"I play the horses, mostly. And now I own a piece of one. My name's Sal Righetti. Some people call me Bones, but for you it's Sal."

"Bones?"

"Don't ask."

"D.J. Hawkins," she said, as they shook hands.

She had a nice firm grip and he took a good look at her. She was tall, maybe five-ten or -eleven, with long dirty-blond hair she'd pulled back into a ponytail, blue eyes, a long straight nose, high forehead, a large mouth with full lips and even rows of very white teeth. She was wearing a black pants suit, but he guessed she had a good figure with long legs. "So where are you from?" he asked.

"My momma in Texas raised me to be a good girl," she said, "and now I've sunk so low in her esteem she don't even invite me for Christmas anymore. Not that I'd go. You ever been in the Texas Panhandle in December? Wind'll cut you in half and your ears will fall off."

"What part of the Panhandle?"

"A dump called Tulia. Bunch of racist bastards run the place. I left there twenty years ago when I was sixteen, and I ain't ever been back since and I ain't ever going back either."

"Your momma must miss you."

"No, she don't. She's got a nice collection of antique dolls and little glass animals to keep her happy. She doesn't need me."

"No daddy?"

"Naw, he split years ago. Smart s.o.b. Went to California and married an Argentine lap dancer. Now he's got a barbecue restaurant he opened on her money in Glendale, and he doesn't even remember he's got a daughter he abandoned a quarter of a century ago. Momma remarried, to a car mechanic with the brains of a chicken, but he takes care of her pretty good."

"Why are you telling me all this?"

She grinned. "I figured after another drink or two you'd take me out to dinner. We'll play liar's poker for the check."

"I got to shower and shave first," he said. "I stink of the *Racing Form* and the smell of uncashed tickets."

"I'll wait for you right here. And I'll pay the tab, don't worry about it."

When he came back half an hour later, dressed in gray slacks, an open-necked black sports shirt, and a light-blue sports coat, she was still there, idly dropping quarters into the video poker machine embedded in the bar in front of her. "Don't lose your money that way," he said. "Give it to charity."

She looked him up and down appraisingly. "You clean up pretty good," she said, sliding off her stool as she dropped two twenty-dollar bills on the counter for the bartender. "Let's go to Circo, over at the Bellagio," she suggested. "Good food and they keep the idiots in shorts and halters out of there."

Although the Bellagio, the super fancy casino hotel, was only a couple of blocks away, D.J. drove them there in her BMW convertible. She handed it over to valet parking, and they went straight to the restaurant, which was quiet, elegant, and expensive but served great food. They spent the first hour talking about their backgrounds, mainly hers. Bones wasn't too eager to reveal his, since he'd put those early career days well behind him and as much out of his mind as possible. D.J., on the other hand, was full of stories about the

151

horrors of life as a coordinator and troubleshooter for outfits putting on conventions and other forms of business and industrial shows. "Most of the time I'm in Vegas," she said. "That's where the business is these days."

"So you freelance?"

She nodded. "Pretty much. I've built up a good reputation in the game, so two years ago I left the agency I was with and struck out on my own. I do well. You know what my biggest hazard is?"

"What? Contagious diseases?"

"Old geezers who want to get into my panties."

He laughed. "From what I've seen of you, D.J., you can handle it."

"Some of these old coots are persistent. You have no idea. Occasionally, some nasty prick I've sent packing will send in a bad report about me, but I can't help that. People who've dealt with me before know I'm a straight shooter and pay 'em no mind."

The more they talked, the more he decided he liked her, though he wasn't quite sure why she had asked him to dinner. Maybe it was because she was basically a loner like him. When he asked her, she said, "I had to get away from the Hilton. Most of the convention people are staying in the hotel. They'd be all over me if I'd stayed put. And you looked like a guy I could talk to."

"What's the D.J. stand for?" he asked.

"Darlene Juniper," she said. "How's that for a grotesque moniker?"

"Darlene I can see, but Juniper?"

"My momma's favorite plant," she explained. "Now, Sal, you know I can't call myself Darlene Juniper, so it's D.J." She smiled and raised her wine glass. "You going with anyone?" she asked.

"Off and on," he told her. "Nothing too serious."

"Okay, so tell me more about yourself. Tell me about the horses."

He did and mentioned Jill's name as he told her about Jake, Tumultuous, and the operation of the stable.

A curious expression came over D.J.'s face. "I know about her," she said. "She used to work for Paul Furman. That the one?"

He nodded. "Yeah. She rode some on the fair circuit and the Bay

Area tracks before latching on at Heritage. She broke yearlings for them and also worked with the two-year-olds. How come you know about her?"

"Well, I lived in Frisco for a year, when I was home and not on the road somewhere," she said. "I had an off-and-on affair, mostly off, with a breeder named Busby ... Luke Busby. I used to go with him to the races and sometimes the sales. He was a friend of Furman's. I saw quite a bit of that scene for a while."

"What happened to that?"

"Oh, it was just sex, mostly. Busby and I had fun. He got serious about me after a while, but I wasn't interested, so I bailed out. I'm pretty sure I met this girl during the time I went out with old Bus."

"Ever meet a guy named Carl Everett, who's in the horse business?"

"Oh, yeah. Come to think of it, that's who Jill whatever her name is was seeing about the time I was bedding Bus. I don't think I exchanged two words with her. Everett and Busby knew each other from something at the bank. Everett's old man was a big power broker, maybe still is. Busby owed his bank money for his breeding business. I never paid much attention. I do know old Bus wasn't too high on Everett, Carl, that is, not the old man. They didn't get along at all."

"I met Everett. Shoved him down some stairs when he took a swing at me."

"No shit!" When he told D.J. the story, she threw her head back and roared. The other diners gazed at them in alarm. "Goddamn, Sal, what a great story! I love it! Then what?"

"I don't know. That's the last I saw or heard of him. His horse is still at Santa Anita. He's planning to run him in the Santa Anita Derby the first Saturday in April, but he went back to San Francisco."

"Yeah, he lives in Marin County, I think. He's also got a farm in the Santa Ynez Valley."

"Where's Heritage Farm? Near Everett's place?"

"Not far. Furman's also got a ranch on Lake Cachuma, which is just over the hills there from Santa Barbara."

"After Everett left, Jill disappeared for a few days. Maybe she went up there, I don't know why. But something happened to her, D.J., something not too good. I have no idea what it was, but it was bad enough to shake her up. It hit her pretty hard. She's been kind of quiet and remote, doesn't talk much to anyone since she got back."

"You don't have the hots for her, do you?"

"I like her looks, sure. But she's just a kid. Hell of a good rider. I'd just like to see her make it. It's a tough game, being a girl jockey in California, but she could be another Julie Krone. I could help her do that and I'd like to."

D.J. looked at him with mischief in her eyes. "Let's get out of here, honey," she said.

"To do what?"

"Let's go rumple the sheets."

"You serious, D.J.?"

"Would I kid you, Sal? You may be a sweet guy, but I got a feeling you could get a little nasty. We'll go to your place, where nobody knows me."

On the drive back to his hotel, D.J. told him some more about Furman. "He likes women and that's going to be his undoing," she predicted. "If he runs for office, like they say, the press will dig up everything they can about him. Of course there was a lot of sympathy for him when his daughter died. But there were rumors about that, too."

"What kind of rumors?"

"That he wasn't out there at the ranch with her alone," D.J. explained. "Some people were saying that he and that woman who worked for him—"

"Dulcie Clark."

"Yeah, that she was with him that night."

"At the ranch?"

"I don't know. Maybe he had her stashed away nearby and the girl was alone."

"There was an investigation, right?"

"Oh, sure, but nothing came of it. There was no woman. Dulcie

Clark said she was home."

"Was Jill ever interviewed?"

"Not so far as I know. Furman's very popular, you know. Personally, I think he's an asshole. He came on to me real strong."

"When was that?"

"When I was still dating Bus. We were at this party in Santa Ynez, lots of horse people there, and he was on me. Later he sent word to me through his assistant Harvey Stone that he'd sure like to get to know me better. Would I meet him for lunch at this private cabin he had out there."

"Where?"

"At his ranch, I think. Anyway, I turned him down. I don't mess around with married men, even hotshot politicos and celebrities."

"Did you know Dulcie Clark?"

"Met her. Bus knew her. Good-looking dame. She was supposed to have had a few flings in the hay with Furman."

"More than a few, maybe."

"Yeah, well ... Old Paul must be like Clinton. Can't keep his pecker in his pants."

"How you talk, Darlene Juniper," Bones said. "You have a mouth like a sewer."

"I'm a no-bullshit gal, Sal. Call 'em like I see 'em."

They rode up to his room in the elevator together. Once inside his room she started immediately to strip, then headed for the bathroom. "I need a shower," she said.

"I'll join you."

They soaped each other down, then rinsed and dried themselves off. By this time Bones was worked up pretty good and couldn't wait to get his hands on her. She had a terrific body, plenty of everything mounted on a pair of long legs. He tried not to think about Bingo while D.J. tugged him toward the sheets. "Wait," he said, as they tumbled over each other, "I got a—"

"Forget it, lover," she whispered fiercely. "I'm okay and so are you. I can tell."

Sex with D.J. Hawkins turned out to be much like an Olympic competition in gymnastics, a variety of amazing positions, leaps of imagination, and outstanding moves. "Did we come in first?" Bones asked, when it was all over and D.J. lay spread out on his sheets like an exhausted competitor.

"We both scored, I know that," she said. "You've got some nice moves, Sal."

"I was inspired," he said. "I think we both got the gold."

"Yeah. Now I got to get out of here," she said. "I have to get some sleep. I got two more days to go here with these goddamn salesmen and snotty kids."

CHAPTER 16

His last afternoon in Las Vegas, Bones watched Carl Everett's three-year-old Terry's Dream win the San Rafael Stakes, a one-mile prep for the Santa Anita Derby. The colt won it so easily, by a widening margin of five lengths, that Bones had to admit that Everett had himself a really good horse, maybe even a true Kentucky Derby contender. Assuming, of course, Terry's Dream first would take the Santa Anita Derby and then stay sound for the grind of the Triple Crown races. The chances of Everett's colt accomplishing this feat were slim at best, since even the top young Thoroughbreds these days didn't seem to be able to put many winning races back to back anymore. Still, winning even just one big one in the Triple Crown was accomplishment enough; you win one, you try for two, you hope for the miracle of all three.

The *Racing Form* was already touting Terry's Dream as one of the hot young colts to beat. Chad Bullit, the horse's trainer, a slick con man with an ego to match Donald Trump's and who could have sold snake oil as a cure for cancer, exuded confidence. "This colt is sound, he's fast, and I've turned him into a winner," he announced. "We're not afraid of anybody. The Eastern contenders? Bring 'em on!" He sounded like some two-bit politician at his worst.

D.J. Hawkins and Bones got together the night before they both were supposed to head out of Vegas. They ate in some small dark restaurant she knew about on a back street way off the Strip, after which she invited him up to her place at the Hilton; the convention was over and the coast was clear. As soon as they finished the romp on her king-sized bed, she kicked him out. She had to leave at seven the next morning for Detroit and another job, this one an industrial show involving car accessories. "You're a good man, Sal," she told him, as she dropped her business card into his pocket. "Whenever you're in Vegas, give me a tinkle and we'll get together."

The next morning, he called the barn and got Fontana on the phone. "How's our horse doing?" he asked.

"Real good, Bones," Jake replied. "So good we may run him in the San Felipe next week, stretch him out to a mile and a sixteenth."

"Aren't you coming back pretty quick with him and isn't that a grade II?"

"His race took nothing out of him," Jake assured him. "And he's kicking down the walls of his stall. If I don't run him, he could hurt himself. When are you coming back?"

"Pretty soon. How's Jill doing?"

"Okay," he said, "but she's still pretty quiet and I haven't seen much of her. She shows up, does her work, goes home. She rode another horse for me, one of Abernathy's, but he did nothing, finished up the track. You want me to tell her anything?"

"Just say hello. What about you, Jake? You sound a little down."

"I'm having trouble sleeping again."

"Have you called Barrow?"

"No, but I will." He paused a moment. "It's my fault. I was feeling so good there for a while I stopped taking my pills."

"Don't fuck around with this, Jake. Your condition is serious. You hear me?"

"Yeah. Thanks for reminding me."

After hanging up, Bones sat in his room staring out over the casino parking lot, then he went downstairs, climbed into a taxi, and had himself driven downtown to the Las Vegas Public Library. He presented himself at the front desk and told the young female librarian he wanted to look up some back issues of the *L.A. Times* and the *San Francisco Chronicle*. For the next three hours he sat in front of a computer screen punching up back issues and making notes. By the time he was through he had read all the major accounts of what might have happened to Paul Furman's kid, and he'd also read every account of Dulcie Clark's death, still unsolved. He'd also come across a number of pieces about Furman himself—about his horses, his political ambitions, his contributions to charity, his public pronouncements on all the issues of the day. The man was an up-and-comer, no doubt about it, good-looking, charismatic, a rising star. Bones leaned back in his chair, folded his arms, and spent twenty minutes or so thinking things over; then he got up, called a cab, and went back to his hotel to pack. He cancelled his flight back to L.A. and instead got one that afternoon for Santa Barbara, where he rented a car and immediately headed north.

It was a pleasant drive, most of it through prosperous-looking country inhabited by private homes and small ranches. The road into the Santa Ynez Valley wound over a bridge with a spectacular view of an undeveloped national forest and a large, manmade lake down below. To the right of the lake, a small village nestled up against the hills, two rows of small houses, a café, and a gas station lined up along a single two-lane street. At the far end of the road, on the outskirts of town, a blinking electric sign indicated the Village Lake Motel, a series of detached cabins built around a circular parking lot. Bones turned his rented Mustang into the lot, parked in front of the office entrance, and stepped inside the screen door.

The woman behind the counter was in her sixties, bone-thin, stooped over, with a knitted black shawl over her shoulders. She had a long narrow face with small gray eyes set close together over a hooked nose and she wore her long gray hair coiled into a tight bun at the nape of her neck. She didn't seem happy to see him. Bones smiled. "Hi," he said. "I guess you rent rooms here."

"I guess we do," she said. "How many nights?"

"I'm not sure. Probably just one."

"Cash only, no credit cards," she said, reaching up behind her for a large metal key that she dropped on the counter in front of him. "That'll be sixty dollars. You need to make calls there's a public phone out front."

"I got my own, thanks," he said, dropping three twenty-dollar bills on the counter and picking up the room key.

"Second cabin down," she said, pocketing the money. "Check out time is eleven a.m."

"How far away is the lake?"

"About two miles. You take the road opposite the gas station. Emory Blain's in charge of the dock down there, in case you want to go boating. No swimming. Lake's a reservoir. Emory can rent you the gear."

"I was just passing through. I heard the fishing's good."

"They stock it every year. Mostly bass."

"Is that where Furman goes fishing?"

She looked at him, her eyes suddenly sharp with curiosity. "He's got his own cabin on his ranch there, up the coast a ways from Emory's place, but it's private. You can't go there, mister."

"I know. But that's how I heard about this place. From a friend of mine who works for Mr. Furman. That was a terrible thing that happened there. The girl, I mean."

The woman didn't answer him but shot him one last suspicious glance before vanishing into the interior of the building.

Bones parked directly in front of his cabin, took out his two suitcases, opened the door of the cabin, and dropped them on the bed. He snapped on the light, quickly took in the furnishings, which consisted of a queen-sized bed, two armchairs, a TV set, and crudely painted landscapes, mostly depicting the lakeshore, he guessed, and then he went back to his car and drove down to the gas station. He filled up his tank, paid the attendant, a scruffy-looking youth of about eighteen, and again asked for directions. The boy pointed across the highway. "See that road there?" he said. "You take that and go about two miles to the landing. But I'm not sure it's open this time of year."

"I'll take my chances, thanks." Bones looked toward the café just up the street from the gas station. "How's the food over there?"

"Ain't bad," the boy said. "They got steak, fish, burgers, hot dogs, salads, fried chicken. You can eat pretty good, if you're real hungry."

"I'll try it. Well, thanks for your help. Oh, by the way, I hear Paul Furman has a place right on the lake, goes fishing there."

"Yeah, he does. Comes several times a year. Ain't been here since his girl drowned, though."

"That was sad. I heard about that. What do you think happened?"

"Beats me. Accident, I guess. She must have snuck down to go swimming or something."

"It was pretty late, wasn't it? I mean, what was she doing there at that time of night? Two, three a.m., wasn't it?"

"Don't really know. There was a lot of talk about it in town."

"You think she tried to kill herself?"

The boy looked suddenly alarmed. He glanced around, then shrugged. "You hear all kinds of stories," he said, "some of them pretty wild."

"Yeah? Like what?"

"You a reporter or something?"

"No, I'm just curious."

"You ain't from around here."

"No, I'm from L.A. I read about it in the papers."

"Yeah, it was a real shame. Anyway, there's not much more to it than that. There was a lot of people come from all over and the police was there, but they didn't tell us nothing. They wrote it all up in the papers and all and it was on the TV, but that's all anybody knows for sure." A pickup truck turned left off the highway and pulled up to the adjacent gas pump. "Hey, I got to go now," the boy said. "Nice talking to you." He pointed across the highway. "Over there, about two miles."

The narrow paved road ran straight between thick stands of brush and trees to an open parking lot facing the lake, which sat still and empty under a fading blue sky. To the right of the lot was a two-story wooden-frame cabin with an arm extending toward a dock thrust like a blunt finger out into the water. A sign over the wing advertised boats and fishing tackle to rent. To the left of the dock, several small outboards were drawn up on the bank, ready for departure. As Bones stepped out of the car, a man appeared on the front porch and looked at him. He was in his fifties, short, muscular, with a red face, heavy jaw, and small dark eyes that peered out from under the long bill of a blue baseball cap. He was dressed in jeans and a red plaid shirt. "Howdy," he said. "What can I do you for?"

"I thought I might rent a boat, take a little ride around the lake," Bones said. "I'm down here for a day or two, heard this was a real pretty lake. Sightseeing, that's all."

"I guess I can fix you up," the man said. "You ever driven an outboard before?"

"Yes, I have, but a long time ago. I guess you can show me how to do it. You're Mr. Blain, right?"

"That's me." He stepped off the porch in his rubber boots and stuck out his hand. "Got a driver's license or a credit card?"

"Sure thing," Bones said. He followed Blain over to the first of the outboards drawn up on the bank and helped him push it into the water. Then he handed Blain a credit card with his picture on it.

"You want to charge it on here?" Blain asked, looking at the card. "That'll be twenty-five dollars for two hours, five dollars an hour after that."

"Sure," Bones said.

Blain showed him how to start the engine, started it, and then held the boat steady for him as he climbed on board. "Can you swim?"

"Yeah. And I can float real good."

"That's good. If the engine conks out on you, which it shouldn't, there's a pair of oars in there that will get you to shore."

"Thanks. Can you tell me which way is the Furman place?"

Blain didn't seem surprised by the question. "Lots of folks wanted to go up that way after the accident," he said, "but not lately. Did a hell of a business there for a while. Folks were just naturally curious. Had some TV reporters, too, wanted to film the place. And there were the helicopters. It was hot and heavy for a while. You a reporter?"

"No, just nosy."

"You're a reporter, I can tell. You ain't from around here. But this all happened a while back. You doing a story now?"

"No, no, I'm just a tourist, up here to visit some of the horse ranches. I'm just killing time."

"Well, there ain't much new to talk about, mister. Girl just wandered away from the house and drowned, that's all. She was kind of disturbed, they say, like her mom. Maybe she wanted to kill herself, who knows? But I kind of doubt it. I knew her. She was a sad little kid, pale, kind of withdrawn and all. I don't think she knew what she was doing."

"Furman found her, didn't he?"

"That morning. Well, he didn't exactly find her. When he noticed she was missing, he called the police and they dragged the lake. That's how they found her."

"Yeah, that's what the papers said. Furman was alone in the house, right?"

"I guess. He usually came here either from Frisco or from the horse farm with a group, you know. Two, three other people. But this time he was alone. Was trying to spend time with the girl. Hadn't been paying her no mind, he said."

"A little father-daughter bonding."

"What's that?"

"He wanted to be alone with his daughter for a while, that's what I mean. Pay some attention to her. He's a busy guy."

"Sure thing. He's a fine man, you know. He's going to make a hell of a good senator. People around here really like him. By the way, don't try to go ashore when you get to his place. It's about a mile and a half up the lakeshore on your right. You can just make out his cabin through the trees and there's a small concrete dock. But there's a caretaker there, a guard, sort of. He's armed and he don't let no one come ashore. You don't want to try because he'll call the ranger and get you arrested for trespassing."

"Thanks. You've been a big help. I'll be back in an hour or two max." Bones swung the boat out into the lake, turned right, and headed up along the shore at a leisurely pace, playing the role of the casual sightseer.

He had no trouble spotting Furman's cabin. It sat up on a slope maybe a quarter-mile from the water's edge, partly hidden by tall pines. Picture windows reflected the light off the lake, making it hard to see if anyone was around. He cut the engine and drifted as he fished out a small throwaway Kodak he'd bought back in Vegas and aimed it at the site. By the time he had shot several pictures, a man appeared out of the house and walked to the dock. He was dressed in a dark-brown uniform with a trooper's wide-brimmed hat planted solidly on his head. He stood there and looked toward the boat. Bones waved cheerfully to him, then started the engine up and putt-putted away up along the shoreline. About twenty minutes later he came back. The guard was still there, as if he had expected him to return that soon. Bones ignored him this time and kept on going. Half an hour later, as Bones headed into shore, Emory Blain reappeared from inside his house and helped him disembark. "Real pretty lake," Bones said in parting.

"Sure is," Emory Blain agreed. "They don't come any prettier, and this is a good time of year to see it. Not too many folks around in the winter."

"That caretaker Furman has up at his cabin?"

"Yeah?"

"What's he so worried about?"

"You wasn't here at the height of all the fuss," Blain said. "It was a zoo, I tell you. Town full of reporters and TV folks, a regular zoo."

***

To Bones' surprise the café was almost full when he walked in the door that night after seven o'clock. There was a bar running along the wall to the right and a row of booths to the left, with a small sea of tables in between. There were TV sets mounted over each end of the bar, one of them broadcasting a hockey game, the other basketball. Country music emanated from a jukebox at the rear of the room, and drinkers were lined up along the bar. Bones sat down on a stool between two couples in their thirties who were drinking whiskies and beer and munching from the bowls of pretzels and potato chips on the wooden counter. He ordered a draft beer and smiled at the woman sitting next to him on his right, a hefty-looking blonde with her hair lacquered up into a beehive and heavy gold hoops dangling from her earlobes. She smiled back at him. "How you doing?" she asked.

"Pretty good," he said. "This sure is a popular place."

"It's a weekend," she explained. "Everybody shows up here weekend nights. You from out of town?"

"Yeah, L.A."

"Los Angeles, do tell," she said. "Hey, this here's my boyfriend, Mike, and I'm Emma. And you are?"

"Sal Righetti. I own some horses."

"That so?" Mike said. He weighed about three hundred pounds and his hands were even bigger than Bones'. He had a round baby face with red cheeks, innocent blue eyes, and a crew cut. He wore a black leather jacket, boots, and black canvas pants held up by red suspenders. "What's a horse owner from L.A. doing here? Going to buy some more horses? They got some great breeding farms here in the valley."

"Yeah, I'm going over to Heritage to look around," Bones said. "Furman's got a great operation, I hear. And he may run for senator, they say."

"Yeah, probably," Mike said. "He'd be a lot better than that Commie bitch we got now. But that little girl drowning was a damn shame, that's how people around here feel about it."

"The way I heard it he worshipped that little girl," the blonde said. "He was real close to her."

"So what about Mrs. Furman?" Bones asked. "Was she ever around?"

"I never seen her. Mike?"

"Me neither," Mike said. "Word is she's sickly."

"You know, you hear all these rumors about him," Bones said. "About how he plays around some."

"Don't they all," Emma said. "Think of Clinton."

"Wouldn't surprise me none," Mike said. "Hell, if a man's wife is sick all the time, he's got a right to some kind of life."

"So if I got sick that's what you'd do?" the blonde asked. "That's nice, real nice."

Mike shrugged. "Man's got to have some fun, don't he?" He grinned at her and gave her thigh a squeeze. "But I'd be thinking about you the whole time."

"Sure you would," she said. "Now you just take your paws off of me, Mike Stanton. I'll call the police on you."

He leaned over and kissed her on the neck, then looked at Bones again. "There used to be a gal come up here with him. Worked for him, I think. She stayed at that motel up the street here."

"You think they were together?"

"Well, there was usually a couple of guys up here, too, but they stayed at the cabin. Friend of mine, Billy Johnson, he told me he used to see Furman's car parked in the motel lot after midnight. Then the next morning the gal would be gone. Furman stayed at his cabin over the weekend then they'd go back to the farm or San Francisco. I guess he has business interests up there, too."

"And nobody knows who the woman was. Or was it different women?"

"Who knows? People don't talk about it much. One night stands, maybe."

"Could have been nothing to it," the blonde said. "Seems to me he wouldn't take a chance on something happening and him being found out and all like that. It don't make sense."

"Yeah?" Mike said. "Then what was his car doing there so late?"

"Could be Billy Johnson made a mistake," she said. "He was probably drunk, if I know Billy. And he's got a mouth on him like a trumpet. You tell Billy Johnson anything, it'll be all over the county the next day. Might as well put it up there on a billboard."

"If it was the same gal," Mike Stanton said, "it could have been a secretary or someone from his outfit. The cabin's pretty small and Furman wouldn't want her staying there, would he? Especially if his kid was with him."

"Listen, he's a good man," the blonde said. "We're all going to vote for him around here. He's helped people and he's given a lot to charity."

Mike stepped off his barstool and took Emma's arm. "Come on, honey, let's get something to eat. Nice talking to you," he said, as they moved toward the empty booth that had just come open against the far wall.

Bones sat at the bar for another hour, trying first to engage the couple on his left in conversation, then the bartender, but without much success. The experience confirmed pretty much what he'd been hearing as he'd strolled earlier in and out of the stores along Main Street, the part of the state highway that bisected the town. Nobody knew anything for sure, nobody much wanted to talk about Paul Furman and his troubles. They all felt sorry for him, they'd all grieved over the death of his daughter, they all wanted Bones to know that Paul Furman was a good man. They were proud of him; they'd vote for him if he chose to run for office, any office. He was one of their own.

The next morning Bones checked out of the motel. The woman behind the counter seemed just as surly as she had been a day earlier. "It's a real pretty lake," he said, as he dropped his key in front of her.

"I guess."

"Did a woman named Dulcie Clark ever stay here?" he asked. "She was a friend of mine and she used to come here sometimes with Paul Furman. She worked for him. I thought you might have met her."

"No, never have," she said. "Lots of people stay here when they come for the fishing."

"Any of them look like riders?"

"Riders?"

"You know, jockeys. Small people."

She shook her head vigorously. "Why would they do that? Ain't no horses to ride around here, mister. Nearest horse farm is miles away. What kind of question is that?"

"Just asking, that's all."

"I get more damn fool questions in this job than is good for me," she said, turning her back on him and shutting the door behind her.

CHAPTER 17

Eduardo was unhappy. While Luis and Tommaso, Fontana's other two grooms, were tending to the horses, he was on the telephone, talking to Jill. He did not like what he was hearing. The minute he saw Bones standing in the tack room doorway he motioned him over and thrust the receiver into his hand. "*Señor* Fontana not well," he said. "You talk to her, please."

"Jill? It's Sal. What's up?"

"Oh, you're back," she said.

"Yeah. I just got here. What's going on?"

Her voice sounded tense at the other end of the line. "It's Jake," she said. "He can't get out of bed. He's having another attack."

"Did you call Barrow?"

"Yeah. He's on his way over."

"Where are you? With Jake?"

"Yeah. He's just real low. Lies there, staring at the ceiling."

"Stay with him, Jill. Don't leave him alone, you understand me? It sounds like he's in a bad depression. Has he been taking his pills?"

"I don't know. I asked him, but he wouldn't tell me."

"I'll bet you he hasn't. Jill, it's common with people like him. They get to feeling pretty good for a while and they stop taking their meds and relapse."

"You want me to come over after the doc gets here?"

"That depends. I can handle things here, take phone calls, stuff like that. Don't worry."

"The schedule for the horses is on the chart in the tack room," she reminded him. "Eduardo can handle all that. You take care of the clients. You know Bamboozler, Abernathy's mare, she runs Wednesday."

"How's Sammy doing?"

"Like a tiger. He runs on Saturday."

"I know. Listen, call me after Barrow shows up, okay?"

"Okay."

"And how are you doing?"

"Me? Fine."

"Everything all right back up north?"

There was a fraction of a pause before she answered. "Sure," she said. "Why?"

"Just wondering. I heard a lot of rumors when I was up there. I stopped off at Santa Ynez on my way back."

"Yeah? Why?"

"To have a look around. Just curious. You hear a lot of stories."

"About what?"

"About Furman. I met someone in Vegas who knows him pretty well. Seems the guy's a real player."

"I don't know nothing about that," she said quickly. "I'll talk to you later, Sal." And she hung up.

Bones went out into the shed row to bring Eduardo up to date and calm him down. "Anybody working this morning, Eduardo?" he asked.

"No, *señor*. Just galloping. I call my friend Francisco, he work for *Señor* Logan, and he come over to gallop the horses. *Señor* Logan is very nice about it. You call *Señor* Abernathy for me, please?"

"Sure."

"Is all okay. His horse, the mare, she run Wednesday."

"I know. Who's riding? Jill?"

"*Sí*. She win, I think. She in real cheap."

"I guess even she can find a field she can beat, right?"

Eduardo nodded, then, rub rags in hand, went off to work toward the end of the row of stalls. Bones followed him partway down till he came to Tumultuous. The horse was standing with his back to him, his big gray rump a triumph of muscle and power. When Bones clucked softly to him, he first turned his head to glare at him, then swung around to thrust his soft muzzle in his direction. His ears were cocked, so Bones figured his intentions were kindly and he shoved a fat carrot into his mouth. The horse nibbled on it daintily, sucking the sugar off it, then crunched it satisfyingly between his teeth.

"Well, just look at the dear boy," Ester Gale Dinworthy said, coming up beside Bones in a flutter of brightly colored scarves and kerchiefs, like a festive Chinese junk coasting to anchor. "Isn't he a splendid beast? Look at that head! An Achilles, a Patroclus! Praxiteles himself could not have sculpted a more wondrous likeness! How can this godlike creature possibly fail to win?"

"We'll soon find out, babe," Bones said.

She sniffed her disapproval of him. "It will be no contest," she averred, as if announcing the foregone conclusion of a Third World election. "This glorious creature is a true champion. Where is Giacomo?"

Bones told her and she looked mildly preoccupied. "Oh, dear," she said. "He doesn't eat properly; I keep telling him that. The man has no conception of a balanced diet. And he comes from a race of magnificent eaters. Surely no one eats better than the Italians. Yet every time I have shared a repast with Giacomo, he settles for hamburgers or steaks, revolting American junk food."

"I know a couple of good Italian restaurants he goes to," Bones said. "And when Maria was alive she cooked some great meals, I remember."

"Ah, yes, but that was then. Oh, dear, I do so worry about him. Does he have a good doctor?"

Bones assured her that he had. Mrs. Dinworthy clucked approvingly, opened her capacious bag, fished out a lump of sugar, and proffered it to Sammy, who immediately snapped it up. "Talk about junk food," Bones said. "I just fed him a carrot."

"All my life in racing I have waited for a true champion," she said.

"And now at last I have one. I feel like the Winged Victory of Samothrace, soaring above the fray."

"Excuse me, babe, but I have some calls to make," Bones said. "By the way, I wouldn't feed him any more sugar. Not good for him."

"I know exactly what the dear creature needs," she answered. "Never fear, Mr. Boner, or whatever your name is, I know all about horses."

He chose not to argue with her but retreated to the tack room, where he called Rich Abernathy and told him his horse was definitely running. "Where's Jake?" the owner asked.

"Not feeling too good," Bones said. "He asked me to call you. But don't worry, he'll be okay."

"What's the matter with him?"

"He's feeling low, that's all. The doc told him to stay in bed for a couple of days."

There was silence at the other end; then Abernathy allowed himself a grunt. "He's going nuts, isn't he?" he said.

"I wouldn't say that," Bones replied. "He's been having trouble sleeping again. Anyway, we'll manage things here, and Matt Logan will take over the horses till Jake gets back."

"Logan? The guy's a drunk."

"He's sober in the mornings, and he's a good horseman," Bones said. "Don't worry, we'll manage okay."

"The girl riding for me?"

"Yeah."

"Good. Maybe she can get this plodder of mine across the finish line first."

By the time Bones arrived at Jake's house, Ed Barrow had already been in to see the trainer. He was standing outside, talking to Jill. "How's Jake doing?" Bones asked, as he joined them.

"I want him to stay very quiet for the rest of the week," Barrow said. "I'm sending a practical nurse over to take care of him. I want him to sleep and to take his medications. If he doesn't improve by the weekend, I'm going to hospitalize him."

"He won't go," Jill said.

"That's what he says now," Barrow answered. "If he isn't feeling better by the weekend, he'll be feeling so lousy he'll want to go. These diseases of the brain are tricky. I'm trying to stabilize him. I want somebody here to keep an eye on him, make sure he takes his pills and behaves himself. I've got this nurse coming over for the rest of the day and I've hired her for the week from eight till six." He focused intently on Jill. "I want you to spend the night in the house. Sleep on the sofa, somewhere you can hear him if he calls out. You can always call me any time of the day or night, you got that?"

"Yeah, I guess."

"You guess nothing. If you can't do that, I'll have to hospitalize him now or get someone in full time. I don't want to put him in the hospital. Those places are dangerous. You can get real sick in them." He pulled out a pack of cigarettes, lit up, and stuffed the pack back into his pocket. He took a long drag and exhaled, sending a cloud of smoke into the morning sunshine.

"What kind of doctor are you?" Jill asked. "Don't you know smoking causes cancer and all?"

Barrow grimaced. "I don't recommend it to my patients," he said, "but I believe in living my life."

"Which means cigarettes, booze, horses, and what else?" Bones asked.

"The love of a good woman," Barrow replied. "That I've got, too. So I'm a winner at life."

"Boy, you're some doctor," Jill said.

"The best," Barrow said. "I don't compromise." He fished into his pants pocket for his car keys. "Call me later," he told Jill, "after you get back from the track tonight. I want to know how he's doing." Blowing puffs of smoke behind him, he walked to his car, got in and drove away.

"So how are you doing?" Bones asked Jill.

"Better," she said. "It was rough going here this morning. Jake was trying to get out of bed, was looking for his gun. I hid it on him.

When he couldn't find it, he started for his car. I wrestled with him. The dogs was jumping all around and barking. It was really crazy. Then he hit me a couple of times." She pointed to a bruise on her cheekbone, another one on her upper left arm. "He knocked me down. I yelled at him and told him I was going to call 911 and he finally backed off of me and kind of collapsed on the sofa in the living room. He was crying and calling out for Maria. That's when I called the doc. Then I was able to get him back into bed and got him to take one of them pills. It calmed him down some until the doc got here. It was pretty wild there for a while."

"Are you hurting?"

"Naw, not bad. I've been hit harder than that. He's pretty weak. He ain't himself."

"Can you ride?"

"Hell, yes. This ain't nothing."

"I guess you and I are going to have to pretty much run the stable till Jake's okay," Bones said. "Think we can do it?"

"Yeah, we can," she said. "Only neither of us has a trainer's license. Does Eduardo?"

"I don't think so, but Eduardo called Matt Logan to get his man Francisco over to exercise the horses for you," Bones explained. "I'm sure Logan will be glad to stand in for Jake. They're old pals from way back. You know Matt?"

"Jake introduced me to him in the cafeteria," she said. "Seems like a good guy."

"One of the best. He and Ted, his brother, have been around for half a century here."

"Yeah, I know Ted, too. He's a great horseman."

"Just don't talk politics to them. They think Bill Clinton was a terrorist."

Jill grinned. "Are you sure he wasn't?"

Bones laughed and looked at her, again realizing how attractive she was. She had no makeup on and was dressed only in sandals, shorts, and a T-shirt, her small breasts pressing against the thin cotton cloth, her nipples clearly visible. Her cropped dark hair set off those big green eyes. "So how are things with you? Really?"

She looked suddenly alarmed, guarded, as if he had intruded unexpectedly into forbidden territory. "I'm all right," she said, "I'm all right, but I ain't going to talk about that right now, understand? There's some things in my life that are … well, I got some problems, Sal. There's too much going on, and I don't want to talk about it. I want to concentrate on the horses, okay?"

"Sure," he said. "We've got a stable to run."

"You going to talk to Matt Logan or you want me to?" asked Jill.

"I will. And I guess we'll have to inform the racing office and the stewards."

"I can take care of that when I get there."

"Okay. So I'll see you at the track."

"Yeah. I'm going to hang around here till the nurse comes, then I'll check with Eduardo, make sure everything's okay. Then I'll be over, maybe late afternoon."

"I'll see you at the stable."

"I can handle it, if you want."

"No, I'll come over. Want to have an early dinner?"

"I can't. Got to get back before the nurse leaves."

"Yeah, right. See you later."

***

When Bones got to the barn that afternoon, Matt Logan was in the tack room, looking over the chart. Matt was in his mid-seventies, a tall, nearly bald character with a wide gap-toothed smile. He had a large stable of mostly undistinguished claiming horses, but he was a good horseman who knew what to do with a champion if one happened to come his way; he had once won a Santa Anita Derby with a modestly bred colt and dozens of smaller stakes and handicap races in California. His older brother Ted was also a good horseman, but a more serious type with a huge store of strong opinions, mostly negative, on the state of the world and the human beings who infested it. Matt entertained no strong opinions about life but allowed it to

175

flow over him like a warm shower out of which he would inevitably emerge with a quip and a pari-mutuel ticket in his hand. He grinned when he saw Bones coming toward him. "How's Jake? Still sick?" he asked.

"Yeah, he's in bed," Bones told him, without going into any details. "And we've got that good three-year-old of mine running Saturday in the San Felipe. "Where's Jill?"

"She went home. I can manage things for Jake here. You and Eduardo will be around, too, right?"

"Yeah, of course. We need your expertise on the training end and for you to saddle the horses on racing days," Bones explained. "Luckily, Jake's got a small string."

"No problem. Who else you got going the next few days?"

Bones filled him in. Matt got up and they walked out into the shed row just as Ted showed up, his tattered cowboy hat crammed low down over his forehead so that only his beady little black eyes peered out at them, his mouth in a tight grin. He looked like a desiccated version of the Marlboro man. "Well, I'll be darned," he said, as he strolled up to them. "If it ain't the crusher himself, old Bones. Got any winners for us?"

"I like your horse on Wednesday."

"Yeah, she might run pretty good," Ted said, referring to a nice filly named Goldilocks he had entered in the feature that day, a six and a half-furlong sprint down the hillside turf course. She'd be no better than third or fourth choice, Bones figured, and she'd never run on grass before. Still, she was bred for it and Bones liked her chances. "Come down to the winner's circle if she gets it done," Ted said. "Get your picture taken."

"No pictures," Bones said.

"What are you scared of?" Matt asked. "You might wind up on a post office wall?"

"Something like that," Bones said, smiling. Before leaving the barn, Bones walked away from the Logans and called Jill on his cell phone. "How are things?" he asked.

176

"Okay," she said. "That nurse is here and she's got him calmed down. She's going to stay till eight, she says."

"Good, let her. And you keep an eye on him, too. You want me to come over?"

"No, it's okay, Sal. I can manage. Really."

"I'll see you in the morning."

CHAPTER 18

Bones spent the next several mornings sitting behind the desk in
Jake Fontana's tack room, running the trainer's racing operation.
Eduardo and Jill, with the help of the two grooms, took care of the
horses, while Bones contacted the owners and worked with Phil
Collins, Jake's accountant. Matt Logan masterminded the training
and racing schedule; horses had to be worked or galloped or tended
to and Matt knew exactly how to do all that. The practical nurse
Barrow had hired to take care of Jake during the day did a terrific job.
She was a sturdily built, tough-talking woman in her mid-fifties with
badly dyed red hair. She made sure Jake took all his medications and
spent hours talking to him and keeping him calm. He seemed to be
reassured by her presence and manner. Her name, appropriately, was
Helen Strong. She came from a small town in Missouri that periodically disappeared under the Mississippi. "I moved out to California,"
she said, "because I wanted to keep my feet dry."

The moment she settled in they felt sure Jake would be in good
hands. After the first day Helen volunteered to move in full time
because it had become obvious that Jill couldn't take responsibility
for the long nights, when Jake would wake up from time to time after
tossing and turning in the grip of his nightmares. He'd call out for
Maria and could only be calmed by somebody's soothing presence by
his bedside, holding one of his hands. It would have been too tough
on Jill to take care of him because she couldn't watch over Jake by
night, be out early in the mornings at the barn to work with the horses, and maybe have to ride in the afternoons.

On Wednesday Jill won the sixth race of her Southern California career on Bamboozler, a victory that kept her at the top of the jock-ey standings in terms of percentage. Matt Logan told her he'd put her up on a couple of his cheap claimers, but neither of them looked like possible winners to Bones. Nevertheless, her presence on a mount was now being duly noted as an asset in the *Racing Form* and by the daily handicappers; she was "the hot young apprentice" from the Bay Area. She was also nice to look at, as several of the male racing writ-ers noted. Bones had mostly stopped worrying about her. He knew there was something going on with her, something she wasn't about to discuss with him or anyone else, but he'd decided not to press her. After his visit to Santa Ynez and the lake, he'd come to some conclu-sions about what might be troubling her, but for now he kept them to himself.

After Bamboozler's win, Bones went back to his box to rejoin his racing buddies, who were, as usual, again leaning over their *Racing Forms*. Stats was trying to put together a trifecta, while Moonshine was weighing a double on the last two races of the day's card. Neither of them had bet on Bamboozler despite Bones' assurance that the mare might win, and a sullen silence had fallen over the scene. It was at this point that Sweeps O'Flaherty, looking like a whooping crane sprinting across a marsh, came up the aisle toward them with a somewhat rattled-looking blonde in tow. She was at least in her mid-thirties but dressed like a teenager: sandals, tight black low-cut tore-ador pants, and a tight pink top that left a lot of room for a deeply tanned midriff set off by a bright gold bauble embedded in her navel. "Hey, guys, I want you to meet Sarah Digby," Sweeps chirped. "Sarah, this is Stats, Moonshine, and Bones. He breaks 'em, so don't mess with him. Stats has got more tricks with numbers than you can imagine."

"No shit?" Sarah Digby said. "That's swell. I can turn 'em."

"What?" Moonshine asked.

"Tricks," she said. "My specialty is old guys."

"You're a hooker?" Stats asked.

"Naw, she's putting you on," Sweeps said. "Sarah's a dancer at this joint on Sunset, the Club Zero, strictly legit." He turned to her. "Come on, honey, take a load off. There's plenty of room."

Sarah Digby slid into a middle seat between Bones and Sweeps in the back row. "This has been exciting," she said. "I've never been to the races before."

"I invited her," Sweeps informed them. "We met at the bar after the third. I wanted her to meet you guys, so ..."

"So, sweetheart," Stats said in his kindliest, most tolerant, fatherly tone, "the first rule here is, don't ask questions. And that's also the second and the third rule."

"Really? Why not?"

"See, you've just broken the rule."

"Oh, I'm sorry. Okay, I won't talk, I promise." She jumped to her feet, however, when the bugler sounded the call to the post and clapped her hands together in excitement when the horses came out onto the track. "I think they're so cute!" she said. "And those little men all dressed up in those funny little pants and hats. Why do they wear those hats, anyway? It makes them look like dolls."

"Oh, my God," Moonshine said, heaving himself out of his chair and easing himself out of the box.

"Try not to talk, honey," Sweeps said. "You look a lot better when you don't talk."

"Gee, that's so rude. Hey, can I get you guys something to drink, maybe? Like a Coke or something?"

"That would be very nice," Bones said, handing her a ten-dollar bill. "Bring back a Coke for me."

"Me, too," Sweeps said, turning to watch her move away from them toward the nearest bar. "I love the way she moves. Pure music."

"Sweeps, what were you thinking?" Stats asked.

"What do you mean?"

"A man who wishes to be successful cannot divide his attention between horses and women," Bones declared, quoting Pittsburgh Phil.

"Aw, let's lighten up," Sweeps said. "She's just a sweet kid. And what a body! I want to see her dance. She's invited me to come."

"A kid? Some kid," Stats observed. "She could be somebody's grandmother." A few minutes later, as the horses were nearing the starting gate, Sarah Digby reappeared carrying a small cardboard tray holding their drinks. She also handed Bones his ten-dollar bill. "These are on me, guys," she said. "You're so nice to let me sit with you. And I promise to keep my trap shut."

No sooner had she delivered their drinks than they all fanned out to make their bets, returning just in time to watch Matt Logan's filly Goldilocks romp in, at odds of 9-2. Sarah was ecstatic, as Sweeps had bet fifty dollars for her on the nose. She kissed all of them and announced she had to go to her job at the Club Zero. Sweeps walked her out to the parking lot, returning to the box in time for the eighth. "Isn't she terrific?" he said.

"She's a very nice woman," Bones answered. "Don't bring her again."

"You got a death wish, Sweeps," Stats said. "What's the matter with you?"

"Aw, you guys," Sweeps protested. "I thought you'd appreciate something nice to look at."

"You know what's nice to look at?" Stats said. "Payoffs."

Bones laughed and left to cash in before heading home.

***

On Friday morning, after he'd made his phone calls and was waiting for the morning's activities to wind up, Bones poured himself a coffee, sat down again behind Jake's desk in the tack room and idly glanced through the *L.A. Times*. In the California section he came across a story about Paul Furman. There was a picture of him, this tall, good-looking dude with that thick head of silver-gray hair and wearing a conservatively cut blazer with a necktie. He was smiling broadly and waving to someone, the classical stance of a politician on the make for votes. He was in town to announce his candidacy for the Republican nomination to the U.S. Senate. He planned to deliver the news that night at a fund-raising gathering of the party bigwigs at the Biltmore Hotel in downtown L.A. He was billing himself as a social moderate but a tough fiscal conservative.

"The main issues in California," he told the *Times*, "are not abortion, terrorism, religious fundamentalism, or other such questions, but the state's disastrously mismanaged economy—the fact that people's savings and assets are being wiped out; that poverty and unemployment are on the increase, while the Democrats in the legislature do nothing or try to block every move the governor makes. We have to get behind him and his vision to restore this golden land to what it was and without raising taxes. I'm a Republican, not a Democrat, but what I promise you is an enlightened representation of the people's interests here and in Washington, working with the administration on what's right for America and against the naysayers, the terrorists, and the misguided liberals."

Some spiel, Bones thought, a skillful tissue of lies, distortions, platitudes, and oversimplifications designed to fool all of the people all of the time and to bring his fat-cat audience to its feet. Furman planned to remain in the city for a few days to confer with party leaders there.

While he was still reading the piece, Jill rode up on Princely, after having galloped him an easy two miles. "Your old boss is in town," Bones said to her, as she dismounted.

"I know."

"You going to see him?"

"No, why should I?"

"I don't know. I just thought you might."

"You think too much," she said, unsaddling the colt and allowing Luis to lead him away. Eduardo then put her up on Tumultuous for an easy jog. He was still scheduled to run in the San Felipe the next day, but Logan had begun having second thoughts about the race. Sammy had drawn the twelve hole, the extreme outside post, and seemed sure to be fanned on the first turn, perhaps on the second as well. He wanted to confer with Jake about possibly scratching the horse. "There's an easy allowance race next week for him, non-winners of two other than. Maybe we ought to think about that one for him instead."

"It's okay with me," Bones had told him. "But get Jake's okay, too. That Dinworthy babe will throw a fit."

Logan laughed at him. "Scared of that old woman, are you? Some tough guy you are, Bones."

"I can't stand women screaming."

Alone again in the tack room, Bones returned to his newspaper. The last paragraph revealed that Furman would also be staying at the Biltmore and that he hoped to have time to visit Santa Anita. "I'm in the horse business, too, you know," he had told the reporter, "and Santa Anita's one of my favorite tracks."

Bones showed up at the races that afternoon not having had time to do any handicapping, a fact he confessed to Stats and Moonshine as soon as he sank into his seat in the box. "You aren't missing much," Stats said, "I see only two races, the sixth and seventh, where there are possibilities for action. The rest of the card is ripe for takeover by the jerks who bet on odds-on favorites. I'm going to sit out most of the day."

Sweeps showed up after the first race, looking morose and with a swollen jaw. "The fucking dentist," he announced, with a grimace. "A fucking root canal. We're talking real pain here. What's going on?"

"So where's Sarah?" Stats asked.

"At the bar. She'll stay away from here."

"How long has it been since you've had a woman, Stats?" Bones asked.

"The year the Korean war ended," he said. "I can't afford the distraction and the expense."

"I don't know how you do it," Moonshine said. "All you got to do is keep the broads away from the track, that's all. See 'em during the dark days. Keep your betting life and your emotional one separate."

"Listen," Stats announced, "I'm not in shape for a woman. I mean, I look okay, right? But I'm like a nice used car. I look fine on the outside. The polish is there, the chrome gleams, the upholstery bounces, the horn works, but under the hood there are problems. I burn up oil and gas, I leak a little, the drive shaft is questionable, the plugs misfire. I'm better off just sitting in the lot minding my own business, you get it?"

So the afternoon passed pleasantly enough. Bones even cashed a nice exacta in the seventh. Sweeps showed up again after the race, excited that he, too, had managed to cash in. "Where's Sarah now?" Stats asked.

"Still at the bar, waiting for me," Sweeps said. "The kid is crazy about me."

"That'll last as long as you continue to shower her with winners," Stats pronounced.

"Cool it, Stats," Sweeps said. "I've got a good thing going there." He leaned over to glance at Stats' notations. "Anything look good in the nightcap?"

"No," Stats answered. "Strictly a pass. Neruda is on a bad favorite, and he will probably win, but it'll be 3-5, impossible to play even in the exotics. We'll watch."

What they saw wasn't good. Neruda's mount, a seven-year-old heavily bandaged gelding competing in his forty-seventh race, a $10,000 claiming affair for horses at the bottom of the racing barrel, the sort of contest Stats had once defined as the Hospital Handicap, opened up four lengths on the field by the time the animals hit the half-mile pole. Then, suddenly, he veered in toward the rail and struck it. Neruda was sent flying into the infield as the horse crumpled to the ground. The rest of the field succeeded in avoiding him, but just barely. The track ambulance, lights blinking, headed for the spot where the horse had gone down, while people dashed across the track toward the fallen jockey, who lay motionless on his side, his helmet lying on the turf beside him. The horse wagon arrived to carry away the now crippled animal, whose left foreleg seemed to dangle by a thread. He was winched up into the compartment, presumably euthanized, and carted away. They stood silently and watched Neruda being loaded onto a stretcher and driven off inside the ambulance.

"It's at times like these I really hate this game," Moonshine said. "That horse should never have been allowed to run. Where was the track vet?"

Sweeps showed up, Sarah in tow. The woman was pale and crying. "Oh, my God," she said. "Is he dead? And the poor horsey! Will he be all right?"

Sweeps turned to comfort her. "It's all right, honey. The jock'll be okay."

"But the little horsey!" she wailed.

Sweeps put his arm around her and led her away.

"There ought to be a law," Moonshine said.

"About what?" Bones asked.

"Stupidity."

Stats turned to look at Bones. "Now what?" he said.

"What do you mean?"

"Even if Neruda's not badly hurt, he's almost certainly not going to ride tomorrow. What happens with your horse?"

"He may not run. We drew a lousy post. And anyway we've got Jill."

"On a potential stakes horse?"

"You still don't think she can ride?" Bones said. "She knows the horse better than anybody. She's on him every day."

Stats didn't answer. He folded up his notebooks, slipped them into his canvas sack, and the three of them headed out of the track together. As they reached the parking lot, announcer Trevor Denman's voice boomed out over the loudspeakers. "Ladies and gentlemen," it said, "jockey Paolo Neruda is conscious and in stable condition. He is being taken to Arcadia Methodist Hospital for evaluation."

"So that's good news," Bones said.

"Yeah, a silver lining to every cloud," Moonshine observed gloomily as they parted.

***

When Bones arrived at Fontana's place, he found the trainer outside communing with The Boston Kid. Jake was talking softly to the horse while replenishing his feed bin. The mean old gelding stood aside, one malevolent eye fixed on his keeper. Helen Strong was standing in the doorway of the house, the dogs lounging happily at her feet. "You must be feeling better," Bones said, stepping out of his car. "How's The Kid doing?"

"Same old ornery self," Jake answered. "The only one who can get close to him is Jill."

"Is she here?"

"She came and left about ten minutes ago. Didn't say where she was going."

"Did she tell you about Neruda going down?"

"Yeah. He's lucky he wasn't killed."

"If he'd have hit the fence, he might have been," said Bones. He nodded to the nurse, "Hello, Helen."

"Mr. Righetti," the nurse replied, with a cheerful wave. "Isn't it nice to see Mr. Fontana feeling so much better?"

Bones agreed that it was, then he quickly brought Jake up to date on the situation of his string. "Matt's doing a good job for us," he assured him. "And Phil has taken care of the payroll and the bank accounts. Anything else you need to know?"

"No, but I want you to know I talked to Matt just before you got here," Jake said. "We're not going to run your horse tomorrow. We're going to wait till next week."

"It's fine with me. Who's going to tell Ester Gale?"

"We'll let Matt do that."

"Yeah. I don't want to be around when he does that."

Jake smiled wanly as he poured the last of the feed into the bin and watched The Boston Kid amble over to thrust his nose into it. "This horse is a doer, always was, and he loves his oats," he said. "The doc came by this afternoon."

"What'd he say?"

"That I can go back to work next week on a very limited basis, no more than a couple of hours in the late morning. I have to be sure I get enough sleep, that's all, and take these damn pills."

"No more cold turkey, right?"

He shook his head. "I learned my lesson, Bones."

"What are you on, anyway?"

"Something called Depakote. And at night another one called Seroquel. Expensive stuff, five bucks a pill. I'm in the wrong profession. I should have been a pharmacist."

Bones lingered for a while to chat some more with him, then drove back home. As he walked through the door his phone was ringing. "Hello, Sal," the female voice at the other end of the line boomed, "how are they hanging?"

"Hello, D.J.," he said. "Where are you?"

"I'm in town on a little job at the Convention Center," she said. "You doing anything tonight?"

"No. Are you?"

"No. Free as a wild turkey. I'm staying at the Biltmore, but it's a zoo down here. Some politician's hosting a fund-raiser."

"I know about it. It's Furman."

"Mr. Wonderful himself. Anyway, come on down. I'm in room 7004. We can grab a bite to eat across the street at the Pinot, next to the library, and then explore the wide open spaces of my king-sized bed afterwards."

"I'll meet you at the restaurant. I don't imagine I'll find a place to park at the Biltmore."

"You can bet on that. I'll see you in an hour. I'll get us a table."

D.J. looked terrific. She had cut her hair and it lay in tightly cropped curls against her skull, framing her face, decorated with just a splash of lipstick and a touch of mascara. She was dressed in an elegant black pants suit with a double string of pearls around her neck. She rose from the table as he joined her and planted a solid, open-mouthed kiss on his lips. "Am I glad to see you," she said, as they sat down across from each other at a corner spot overlooking the library garden. "I've been dealing with auto parts salesmen all day long, and I've heard more dirty jokes in one day than I have the last ten years. What makes guys connected to machines so fucking macho? Where'd you park?"

"In the underground public garage across from the hotel. There was plenty of room."

"That's good. So you can stay all night."

"I have to get up at five."

"What for?"

He proceeded to bring her up to date on his activities. "The last thing I ever expected to be doing with my life is running a racing stable," he said. "But you know? I'm having a good time."

They ordered drinks and dinner, and D.J. told him about her life; since he'd met her she'd been working steadily and in two days she was due back in Vegas for still another convention, this one on stereo equipment. "A three-day gig," she explained, "not too bad. After that I'm off for two weeks. Want to come out and play?"

Before Bones could answer, he saw Jill standing in the entrance to the restaurant. She was dressed better than he'd ever seen her before, in a snug black miniskirt, high heels, a long-sleeved white silk blouse, and with gold hoops dangling from her earlobes. She was scanning the room, but luckily failed to notice him. Whoever she was looking for was apparently missing, and she moved to a seat at the bar. Just as she sat down, however, a man in his mid-thirties, dressed in dark-gray slacks, a navy-blue sports jacket, and a matching tie, came in the door, took a quick look around, spotted Jill and joined her at the bar. He leaned over and spoke to her. She nodded, then got up, and together they walked toward the exit.

"What are you looking at?" D.J. asked.

He indicated the couple. "She rides for us," Bones said. "That's Jill Aspen. I don't know who the guy is, do you?"

"He looks familiar," D.J said. "I'll think of it eventually. What's up? She's not supposed to be here?"

Before Bones could answer and just as Jill and the man were leaving, Carl Everett rose up from a table across the room, where he had been dining with a large party. Angrily, he watched Jill leave and then sat back down again. "That's Carl Everett," D.J. said. "I know him. He looks pissed off."

"Yeah, I know him, too." Bones reminded her about his encounter with him at Fontana's place.

D.J. laughed raucously, causing several heads to turn in their direction. "He's such a prick," she said. "I still can't believe you did that."

"He was harassing Jill and he took a swing at me."

"What's he doing in town?"

"He's got a horse he's prepping here for the Santa Anita Derby," Bones said. "And maybe he's with Furman."

"No, those two guys hate each other," D.J. said. "And Everett is even further to the right than Furman, more like Attila the Hun about people. There were rumors he and Furman had personal stuff going on; I don't know what. When that Clark woman died, Everett was quoted in one of the local papers asking for a murder investigation. He hinted Furman could have been involved. You know she was rumored to have had a thing with old Paul."

"But nothing came of it."

"Heart failure was the coroner's eventual verdict, but the rumors, I guess, just won't die down. Even though Furman's very popular and none of his people want to admit he might have been banging her."

"How you talk, D.J. Did she have any family?"

"Just a widowed mother, pretty much out of it, and an older sister. They had nothing to say on the subject. The sister, Louise, works for the state. I think she's now assistant real estate commissioner, some bullshit job like that. And soon after Dulcie's death she got this big promotion."

"An interesting coincidence."

"Oh, she was in line for it, I guess. She's been sucking on the public tit for years."

They didn't discuss the matter again but just traded stories about their careers until, just as their cappuccinos arrived, D.J. snapped her fingers. "I know who the guy is who picked your girl jockey up," she said. "It's Harvey Stone. He works for Furman."

"Oh, I know about him. His assistant?"

"Appointments secretary, campaign manager, I don't know what all," she said, "but he's supposed to be in real tight with him. To get to Furman these days you have to go through Harvey Stone."

After dinner they walked back to the hotel together. "I'll go upstairs first," D.J. said. "I want to get myself all ready for you." She reached over and idly gave him a quick squeeze. "Give me half an hour, okay? Go in the bar, have a nightcap. I'll meet you in my room." And she walked swiftly away from him toward the elevators.

Bones liked the Biltmore. It was an old hotel that had been made over and modernized but had retained all of its charm, its basic baroque decor reflecting the rococo sensibilities of a vanished time, with high ceilings, plush furnishings, gilded ornamentation. As he stood there in the hall outside the grand ballroom, he could hear laughter and applause. Obviously, Paul Furman was in full oratorical flight. Bones walked up to the big double French doors and tried to peek inside, but a sturdy citizen in a dark gray suit blocked access to the room. "Are you an invited guest, sir?" he whispered. When Bones shook his head, the guard shut the door firmly in his face, but not before Bones caught a glimpse of a tall, well-dressed silver-haired man up on the podium acknowledging the applause and laughter of the audience seated at the tables below him. He looked just like his photographs, a career bullshitter on his way up, the image of a candidate.

Bones went into the bar just off the main lobby, sat down, and ordered a beer. The man D.J. had identified as Harvey Stone was sitting under a TV monitor watching a basketball game. Bones took his beer, walked over and sat next to him. "Who's playing?" he asked.

"The Lakers and Sacramento," the man said, without taking his eyes off the screen.

Bones took a sip of his beer. "Where's Jill?" he asked.

Harvey Stone swung around in his seat to stare at him. "What?"

"Jill, Jill Aspen, the jockey," Bones said. "You were with her at Pinot's. She's a great rider. I've won nothing but money off her."

Harvey Stone reached into his pocket, dropped a ten-dollar bill on the counter, and walked out of the room without bothering to glance back at him.

Bones spent the next twenty minutes finishing his beer, paid up, and took the elevator upstairs to D.J.'s room. "Come in, lover," D.J. called out in answer to his knock. "It's open."

He walked into an empty room. Then D.J. stuck her head out of the bathroom and smiled. "Want to hop in the shower with an old friend?"

CHAPTER 19

Bones arrived at the barn the next morning to find Eduardo looking glum. He assumed that Jill was out on the track working or galloping one of the horses, but Eduardo informed him she had failed to show up or even to call. Luckily, Matt Logan appeared and promptly sent for Francisco. "That's the trouble with women," Logan said, "you just can't count on them. You ought to know that by now, Bones. Let's have a look at the chart."

They went into the tack room to figure out which horses were scheduled for workouts, which needed to be galloped or walked, and which had appointments with the vet or the blacksmith. After sorting out Jake's horses, Logan went back to his own string. "Jake better get his ass back here pretty quick before you guys screw up the whole operation," he said in parting. "And I'm running two horses today I got to worry about."

"Thanks, pal," Bones told him. "Basically, I don't know what the fuck I'm doing here. If it wasn't for you and Eduardo, we'd be in real trouble."

"You just call the owners and feed them a little mushroom dirt," he answered. "Keep 'em smiling and dancing, and everything else takes care of itself." Again he started to leave.

"What about your horses today?" Bones asked.

"They both have a shot."

"You betting them?"

Again that wicked grin. "You know me, Bones," he said. "I bet on all my horses. It's a miracle I'm not living under a freeway overpass."

Bones went into the tack room to make his phone calls. When he emerged about an hour later, he found Carl Everett outside talking to Eduardo. "I don't know, *señor*," the groom said, pointing at Bones. "You ask him, please."

Everett looked at Bones but kept his distance.

"What do you want?" Bones asked.

"I want to talk to Jill."

"Haven't we been all through this before? She doesn't want to see you, pal."

"She's going to have to talk to me," Everett said. "And I'm sorry about last time. I was way out of line."

"Yeah, you were."

"But this is important," he said. "There's a lot at stake here. It's important that I see her."

"Well, she's not here today."

"Where is she?"

"I don't know. She hasn't called in either. Maybe she's home."

"Would you call her, please, and tell her I'm here."

Bones hesitated, and then thought why not? He was curious about her himself. He decided he wouldn't say anything to Everett about having seen both of them at Pinot's the night before. He stepped back into the tack room and called her at home. When she didn't answer, he called Fontana. Carl Everett stood in the doorway, waiting.

Helen Strong answered and put Fontana on. "No, I haven't seen her," he said. "Wait a minute." There was a long pause before he came back on the line. "And her car's gone."

Bones told Jake that she hadn't called in. He didn't tell him about seeing her the night before or about Carl Everett's presence. "Where do you think she is?" Jake asked.

"Beats me, Jake," Bones answered. "I'll call you as soon as I know something." He hung up and looked at Everett. "No one seems to know anything about her whereabouts. You have any ideas?"

"I guess maybe I ought to tell you something about Jill," Everett said, coming into the room, shutting the door behind him and sinking into a chair facing Bones. "You know we were going to get married."

"Yeah, she told me. She also told me it was over. That you dumped her."

He looked upset. "That's not exactly the way it was," he said. "Well, maybe it's partly true. I took her for granted, you see. She was such a great gal and we got along so well and ... and ..." He ran a hand over his face, as if to clear it of cobwebs. "I don't know," he continued. "It was all too easy, and I sort of lost respect for her for a while. She went to bed with me the first time I took her out. And my family, well, they just couldn't see it. She wasn't exactly a ... well, the right background, you know. My father was very adamant about it, threatened to cut me off, fire me from the bank even, if I ... if I went on with it."

"So you dumped her. You stopped calling; you didn't return her calls or her notes," Bones said calmly. "She was a redneck from nowhere, and you were this big upper class bully boy with all the right connections. How could you even think about marrying someone so far beneath you? And then what if Daddy did pull the rug out from under you, where would you have been? Have I got this right so far?"

"She told you, I guess." He looked intently at him. "How much do you know?"

"That's pretty much all of it. But now what do you want from her? You want to get her back?"

"Yes. I want to make it up to her."

"It's a little late, I'd say. And she doesn't want you. Don't you get it? She doesn't want you. Seems to me I heard her say it to you more than once."

"She doesn't know what she wants."

"And what about your daddy and mummy, what are they going to say if she's dumb enough to go back to you?"

He looked at Bones with open dislike. "You son of a bitch," he said. "Who are you to meddle around in this relationship? I suppose Jill fucked you, too, on the rebound from me and you think that gives you some sort of hold on her."

"I don't have any hold on her," Bones said. "And I didn't fuck her or lay a finger on her. All I know is somebody screwed up her life up there, probably you, and she's trying to build something new for herself here on her own. Why don't you respect that, buddy boy? Why don't you just back off and give her a chance to breathe?"

Everett suddenly stood up, turned halfway toward the door, and then paused. "You don't know anything, do you?" he said. "You don't know what happened to her after we broke up."

"Why don't you tell me."

Another pause, then Everett turned around again, a slow, nasty smile growing like a cancer over his face. "After we broke up, she got into real trouble," he said.

"What kind of trouble?"

"I warned her about it, but she laughed at me."

"That was after she went to work for Furman, wasn't it?"

"She did a little more than work for him," he said. "She was vulnerable, and he took advantage of it."

"I heard he was a player. Wasn't he involved with that Clark woman?"

"Her and others."

"That's all going to come out, if he runs for office, right?" Bones said. "He must know that."

"Hubris is Paul Furman's middle name," Everett said. "He's like Clinton. He thinks he can get away with anything. He thinks his charm will get him through anything. But I know enough about him to stop him and I will. You can count on it."

"Okay, so you think Furman was screwing Jill when she was working for him, but you're going to forgive her. Out of the greatness of your heart, you're going to take her back. Maybe you'll even make an honest woman out of her. This could be a movie. People will cry."

"Goddamn you, Bones, or Sal, or whatever your name is! Who are you to make judgments?" he said. "I'm trying to do the right thing for once in my life. I feel badly about my actions, and I feel responsible for what happened to her. Now I want to atone for them."

"The trouble is she doesn't want you anymore," Bones said. "She's told you that like maybe a hundred times, but you don't listen. You need hearing aids, maybe, or you think so highly of yourself that you think she ought to fall at your feet now that you've decided to honor your promises to her. Well, she's had it with you, pal. She's had it with the whole goddamn bunch of you back up there in fancy town. She's building a career for herself here. She's a real athlete; she's respected for what she does. Now you show up full of phony nobility and good intentions, but it's too late. So why not just back off and leave her be?"

"I'm trying to save her, don't you see?" he answered. "You don't get it. You don't know what's going on." He started out the door again, then turned back a second time. "You know, the irony of all this is that I introduced her to Furman and got him to hire her. I should have known better."

"For you it was a good way to get rid of her."

"We'd broken up. So I did a rotten thing. But I'm going to make it up to her."

"Don't count on it."

Everett ignored Bones' answer and walked out of the room. Bones got up to watch him go. As he was standing there, the telephone rang behind him. It was Helen Strong. "Mr. Righetti," she said, "I think you should know that Jill just showed up. I spoke to her, but she mumbled something and went up to her room. She doesn't look well."

"I'll be right over," Bones said and hung up.

He went straight to Jill's place without stopping by the house first to see Jake. There was no answer to his first knock, but after his second attempt to get a response she spoke to him through the door. "Go away," she said. "I can't see anyone right now."

"Come on, Jill, it's me," he said. "I have to talk to you. And I'm going to stay out here until you open the door."

There was a long pause; then at last the door opened a crack and Jill peered out at him. Her face looked drawn and frightened. "What is it?"

"Let me in, Jill," he said. "We need to talk."

"What about?"

"A lot of things. Why didn't you call in this morning? Nobody knows where you've been."

"I know; I'm sorry. I meant to, but I wasn't feeling too good."

"We've been worried about you. And that old boyfriend of yours came around this morning looking for you."

"Oh, Jesus," she said. "What do I got to do to get rid of him?"

"He says he owes you. He wants to make it up to you."

"He don't owe me nothing. I don't want to see him."

"He saw you last night."

"Where?" She looked alarmed.

"At this restaurant in downtown L.A. You were with some guy who works for Furman."

"I don't want to talk about it." She started to close the door in his face, but he put out a hand and kept it open.

"Let me in, Jill."

She turned away and retreated into the room. He pushed the door open, stepped inside, and closed it behind him. The shades were drawn and the room was in twilight. Jill was dressed only in her bathrobe, with a towel wrapped around her neck. Her hair was damp, as if she had just stepped out of the shower, and her cheeks looked flushed. Bones figured she must have been in the water for a long time. She avoided his gaze and sat down on a corner of the bed, turned partly away from him. "What do you want, Sal?" she asked.

"I'm trying to help you, Jill," he said. "You're in some kind of deep shit. I don't know for sure what it is, but why can't you trust me? I'm your friend, you must know that. You can level with me."

She shook her head. "No. No, I can't."

"Everett told me you and Furman had a thing, when you were working for him at Heritage. Is that true?"

She nodded, still avoiding his gaze. "Yeah," she whispered. "He … he took advantage …"

"How? Why?"

"I was easy, Sal. I'd just broken up with Carl. Then, when I went to work at Heritage, Paul came on to me. Not right away. He was real nice at first, real kind. More like maybe an uncle, you know? Like someone I'd never really known. Then, one afternoon, after I'd been working with the horses, he called me into his office. It was late. Everyone had gone home from the building. He ... he, well, he kind of raped me, really."

"What do you mean, kind of? Did he or didn't he?"

"I don't know how to put it. I tried to keep him off of me; I said no, but he kept on insisting and insisting," she said, her voice low and intense. "I mean, he just stood there and kept saying how much he wanted me. And then he started to take my clothes off. And ... and I couldn't stop him." She turned completely away from Bones, her eyes now focused on the wall across from him. "He took me right there, up against the desk in his office and then again on the floor. He made me do things with him I'd never done with anyone before."

"Was it just the one time or did it go on for a while?"

She didn't answer right away, and he didn't press her. He knew by this time that she'd tell him and he wanted to be her ally, not her accuser. "It went on for a while," she finally answered, almost in a whisper. "I couldn't stop it. I wanted to. I knew it was wrong, but I couldn't stop it."

"Did anybody find out about it?"

"His assistant, Harvey Stone, he knew about it."

"And Dulcie Clark, what about her? Did she know?"

Jill hesitated again before answering. "She found out about it."

"Jill, I went up there, remember? I talked to some people there. Some of them said Furman had been seeing someone. Was it the Clark woman?"

"Yeah, must have been."

"When he started with you, did he drop Dulcie Clark?" Bones asked. "Or was that already over?"

"I ain't sure. I don't know. But early on she talked to me."

"She warned you about him?"

"Yeah. She told me to get out, to go away, that that was the only way to end it. I told her I wanted to. And I did. I packed up and left."

"Without telling Furman."

"Yeah. I figured if I didn't leave, I'd never get out."

"He came after you, didn't he?" She didn't answer. "You saw him last night, didn't you?" Bones sat down on the bed next to her and put an arm around her shoulders. "What is it, Jill? What does this guy have on you?"

She shuddered and seemed to shrink inside her robe. "He told me he really loved me, you know, but that he couldn't leave his wife 'cause she's so sick."

"I figured. That's par for the course, Jill."

"He just couldn't leave her, that's what he said."

"You think maybe he told Dulcie Clark the same story? And maybe all the other women he's had?"

"I don't know." She turned her face toward him. "Dulcie was real mad about what he was doing. She said she'd do something about it, if he didn't stop with me."

"And then she died. Convenient, right?" Bones paused. "You think he killed Dulcie Clark?"

She stared at him in horror. "What? He couldn't do that! They didn't find nothing! I mean, showing that somebody did that!"

"The police investigated thoroughly, huh?"

"Yeah. They said her heart just stopped. Some kind of attack, I guess. Paul was real upset about it."

"Yeah, he must have been heartbroken," Bones said. "So, Jill, you going to see him again?"

"No. I told him last night it was over, definitely. I told him not to bother me again."

"And you think he agreed to that?"

"He has to, Sal. I'm here now, see? I got a career now. I ain't going to fuck it up."

"But you spent the night with him last night."

"Yeah. He ... he has a way of—" She couldn't seem to find the right words. Her silence filled the room.

"What does he do to you, Jill?" Bones finally asked. "What's his hold on you? Why can't you say no to this guy and make it stick?"

She shook her head and hunched over on the bed, as if in pain. The towel came loose and fell partly away. She reached up to wrap it more tightly around her neck, revealing a dark red line around her wrist. She quickly tucked her arm back inside her robe. "Please go now, Sal," she said. "I'll be at the barn tomorrow. This won't happen again, I promise."

"I'll talk to Jake," Bones said, standing up. At her door he paused long enough to look back at her. She hadn't moved an inch. "Jill, you've got a whole new life," he said. "You've established yourself as a real race rider. You can have a great career. Don't fuck it up with the likes of Paul Furman. What they did to you up there is over and done with."

"Sal, you're a good guy," she said.

"I don't know about that, Jill," he said. "I'm just a horseplayer, not a fucking psychiatrist. I should stick to handicapping and betting. That's what I do best. You're sure you're okay now?"

She nodded and looked up at him, her eyes suddenly full of tears. "I've tried, Sal, I've tried, you know? I'm good with the horses, I know that, but in my private life I can't seem to make nothing work. Maybe I ought to get a shrink, like Jake."

"I'll ask Barrow," Bones said. "Maybe he can suggest somebody." He shut the door behind him and walked down the steps toward the house. Clouds had formed up against the mountains and a gentle misty rain had begun to fall. The gloom matched his mood to perfection.

CHAPTER 20

The following Saturday Tumultuous won his second race for them, with Jill up in the saddle. It wasn't even close. Best of all, the crowd had let him go off at 4-1. A couple of the horses he beat had been considered candidates to compete in the Santa Anita Derby and had earned speed ratings five or six points higher in their previous races. The fact was, however, that Tumultuous had won his first race for them easily, running well within himself, so that his relatively low speed fig didn't mean all that much—at least not to astute bettors. The gray gelding was the sort of competitor who did what he had to do to win, and good jockeys like Paolo Neruda and Jill Aspen never asked for more from a horse than was necessary to get it done.

In this contest Jill had let Tumultuous break on his own. She had tucked him in behind the leaders around the first turn, continued to let him run easily down the backstretch, maybe five lengths behind the two leaders; then she had swung him out into the middle of the track on the final turn and tapped him lightly once with the whip at the three-eighths pole. Tumultuous had exploded with a tremendous burst of speed that swept him quickly to the lead. At the eighth pole he had been three lengths in front. Jill had tapped him twice more, then had hand-ridden him to the finish line, an easy winner, still three lengths in front.

"I'll be goddamned," Matt Logan said, as Eduardo led their champion into the winner's circle. "Why didn't somebody tell me this horse could run like that? I only bet twenty dollars on him."

"When you bet hundreds on your own bums?" Bones said. "You got to have a little more faith, Matt."

Ester Gale Dinworthy assumed her proper place beside the horse's head for the obligatory winning photograph. "Well, we are most certainly going to contest the Derby, are we not?" She pronounced rather than asked, as Eduardo led Tumultuous away.

"That might be asking a little too much of him," Bones said. "He hasn't been really tested yet."

"All the more reason to run him where he can show what he's really made of," Mrs. Dinworthy said. "Would Aristides have failed to confront the Persians at Marathon? Would Themistocles have fled in terror before Xerxes at Salamis? This horse is a great champion and now he'll prove it."

"Don't know about the Greeks, babe," Bones said. "Maybe you got something there, but it ought to be Jake who decides. You don't want to rush a good animal and spoil him."

"I am certain that when Giacomo sees the recorded race on television, he will see what is obvious to me," she said. "I have patiently waited for a real champion and now that he has arrived I will not be denied." And off she went in her usual grand flutter. The old dame was a great sight, Bones thought, like one of those old paintings you see in museums.

He fell into step with Jill as she headed back to the jockeys' room. "Sammy's really something, Sal," she said. "Some people think he looks kind of funny, I know, with those long legs and all, especially from behind, but on the turns he's like a rocket. You just push the button and off he goes. I sure hope I can keep this mount for Jake."

Neruda was temporarily out of action with a broken collarbone and two cracked ribs, so Bones told her that her chances were pretty good. "But it'll be up to Jake," he said. "I guess you know that."

She nodded. "Yeah. Whatever, I ain't going to let him down again. You can count on it," she said. "I just hope they leave me alone."

"Listen," Bones said, "I'll take care of Everett or anyone else who bothers you, you understand? I mean it, kid. All you got to do is tell me. Shit, I got an investment in you. You're riding my horse. And I'm good at protecting my investments. I used to get paid by other people to protect theirs. You understand what I'm talking about?"

She glanced up at him, put a hand on his arm, squeezed it, and disappeared into the jockeys' quarters. Bones watched her go. He was rooting for her, but he still wasn't sure about her. This guy Furman had a big hold on her. Sexual, maybe, but also something else. He'd have to keep an eye on her, all right.

***

It's funny about horse racing or any kind of gambling. No matter how sharp you are, your luck runs in streaks. Nobody can win all the time. Even the dumbest bettors, the most persistent losers will have their winning days, their little streaks of fortune. Just as the top dogs in the game will be brought down to earth for a while. The only remedy for a bad streak is to wrap up, bet less, pass on a lot of races, be patient, be tough, ride it out. But it isn't easy, and a bad losing streak can sneak up on you like a virus, infect your play, send you home every day weaker and less sure of yourself than ever.

That's what happened to Bones, beginning the day after Tumultuous' big win. Suddenly he couldn't cash a ticket, and neither could anybody else in the box. The horses that for weeks had been performing like little trained dogs now couldn't find the finish line. Stats began to spend up to ten hours a day trying to ferret out enough winners to make himself solvent again, but nothing worked. The bad favorites kept winning. The boys lost every photo, they got set down by the stewards, they finished one-three in every exacta, one-two-four or one-three-four in trifectas, blew all of their pick threes and every parlay. They began to bet horses straight again, even though the very idea of such a retreat seemed like an insult to Stats. It was beneath his dignity as a sage, he informed his friends, but only Moonshine, ever the pessimist, had the wisdom to ease himself back into the win column, which he did by cashing a couple of sizeable show bets. As for Sweeps, he spent every afternoon in a froth of frustration and rage, a behavioral crisis that all but overwhelmed poor Sarah Digby, who became convinced he had gone mad. "What's with this guy?" she asked Bones, as their losing streak stretched into its second week. "He talks crazy, like there's some kind of international conspiracy against him or something."

Bones tried to explain the facts of life to her. "All horseplayers are convinced the whole world plots against them," he said to her. "The way out is to figure an angle to get the best of the conspiracy. When they can't do it, they become paranoid. Stick around long enough during one of their bad streaks, sweetheart, and you'll find yourself fingered as the prime source of all the misery. I suggest you beat it out of here until things turn around and Sweeps comes up with a couple of winners to cool him off."

Sarah stared at him out of wide innocent eyes, her jaw slightly agape. "I don't get it," she said. "It's my fault? What did I do?"

"Nothing, nothing," he assured her. "Don't worry about it. Just get ready to disappear for a while."

That afternoon their longshot in the last race lost to an even-money bum, thus causing another losing day. Sweeps picked up his chair and slammed it to the floor of the box, causing poor Sarah, who had joined them, to leap to her feet with a squeak of alarm. "You bitch!" Sweeps screamed at her.

"What did I do?" she said, her face white with fear.

"You said it!" Sweeps shouted. "You said it! Halfway down the stretch you had to say it!"

"What did I say?"

" 'He's going to win; he's going to win!' I heard you! You dumb bitch! I heard you say it! You fucking jinxed us! You're a fucking jinx!" He stormed out of the box, flinging his program behind him in a shower of losing tickets.

"See what I mean?" Bones said. "I told you. Now it's your fault, see?"

Sarah's round little face flushed with anger. "What did I do? I didn't do nothing! The son of a bitch!"

"Forget about it," Stats said, calmly picking up his notebooks and stuffing them into his bag. "This will all pass. A few winners and the sun will shine again."

"Yeah, but he can forget about me! Nobody talks to me like that," Sarah said. "Somebody ought to slap him upside the head. How dare he talk to me like that!"

"I don't blame you, sweetheart," Moonshine observed. "Sweeps isn't a bad guy deep down—"

"Deep down? Deep shit!"

"Never mind," Moonshine said. "Losers can unhinge the brain. Sweeps maybe ought to go on Prozac for a while. This game is too tough for the paranoids."

"Oh, my God!" Sarah said. "Now what am I going to do?"

"What's wrong?" Bones asked.

"He drove me out here," she said. "I don't have my own car."

"It's okay," Bones said. "I'll drive you home. Where do you live?"

She gave him an address in West Hollywood, only about a couple of miles from his place. On the way out to his car she grumbled about Sweeps, and all the way into town she listed for Bones all the various ways in which Sweeps had humiliated her since their first meeting. "So maybe this is the end of your romance, right?" Bones said, as he eased off the freeway and began his descent into her neighborhood.

"You bet your ass!" she said. "I've been out with some nut cases in my time, but this guy takes all the medals!"

When Bones pulled up in front of her bungalow, which was on a short side street between Santa Monica Boulevard and the Strip, she invited him in. "You're so sweet, Sal," she said. "Come on in, have a Coke or something. I don't have to go to work for another couple of hours."

Bones didn't know why he accepted. Maybe because he was feeling down and saw no reason not to. Bingo was always working nights, and D.J. was back in Las Vegas. He was feeling sorry for himself, and he liked Sarah. He didn't know much about her, but she was clearly a survivor, which qualified her in his eyes as okay. That's all horse-players are, after all—survivors, victims of the gods of chance.

Sarah's little house was a one-story wooden-frame affair built generations earlier to house railroad workers. There had once been a rail line down the center of Santa Monica Boulevard. Old timers could still recall the glory days of the old Red Line, when the entire L.A. basin from Pasadena to the shores of the Pacific had been criss-crossed by trolleys that for a nickel carried passengers from one community to another. All that survived now of that vanished era were the little wooden homes built to house the workers who serviced the line; the rails themselves had long ago disappeared under boulevards and the concrete ribbons of the freeways that had led to the triumph of the automobile. "Do you own this place?" Bones asked, as he followed Sarah inside and looked around.

"No, I rent it from this real sweet gay guy who does my hair," she said. "I love it. Come on in and sit down. I'll get you something to drink. I made some fresh lemonade this morning from my own tree out in the back. How does that hit you?"

"Sounds good," he said. The decor of Sarah's quarters suited her. The colors were pink and yellow and lavender, with plump pillows piled up on the sofa and two armchairs. Through the open bedroom door he could see stuffed animals bunched up against the headboard. The walls were decorated with large posters depicting idealized countryside peppered by thatched cottages of the sort immortalized by Thomas Kinkade. It was all too cute for words, like the hostess herself, who now appeared from the tiny kitchen with a tray carrying tall glasses full of ice cubes and a large pitcher of lemonade.

"Let's go out back," she said, heading for the screen door leading into the yard.

He followed her out, and they sat down on the steps facing the back fence, a strip of grass, several scrawny-looking rose bushes, and two small lemon trees full of ripe fruit. "This is nice, kid," he said, sipping his lemonade. "Very nice, like you."

"Gee, that's sweet," she said. "Why didn't I date you instead of your friend? What a mouth he's got on him, like a sewer."

"A losing streak can do strange things to people," Bones said.

"Sweeps is okay most of the time, not a bad guy, but he was way out of line with you."

"You can say that again. And you know, like that time the poor horsey broke his leg and they had to take him away, I mean, he was so insensitive and all. I couldn't believe it."

"We've seen too many of those over the years."

"Yeah, I guess, still it don't mean he ought to shout at me and all. I didn't do anything to deserve all that abuse. He's history as far as I'm concerned. You know, I can still see the horsey. It's hard to believe he doesn't feel anything."

"The animal's in shock when that happens," Bones explained. "Then they put him out pretty quick with an injection."

"Of what? Like morphine or something?"

"Some kind of heavy drug. I'm not sure what. I should know, but I've never actually asked anyone. Must be something that stops the heart."

"I guess you could kill a person that way, too, couldn't you?"

"Yeah, sure. Funny you should mention that."

"Why funny?"

"I was thinking about that very thing the other day," he explained. "Any good vet could give a shot like that to anyone and kill him. I think a lot of condemned killers on death row now receive that kind of injection."

"No shit? Wow, I never thought of that."

"I guess I did, but I never thought about it much."

"How come you're thinking about it now?"

"Oh, no special reason," he said. "Just talking, that's all."

Sitting there with Sarah in her backyard, Bones could feel himself unwind from the stress of the past week. He also began to feel something more, a very nice buzz and a warm glow in his stomach. He turned to look at Sarah. "What's in this lemonade, kid?" he asked.

She giggled and put a hand up to cover her mouth. "You like it?"

"Yeah, but what is it?"

"Just a teeny touch of vodka. I figured it would kind of relax us, you know?"

"It's working," he said.

She put her glass down on the step beside her and leaned in close to him. "You want maybe to kiss me now?" she asked.

He took her face between his hands and gently kissed her on the cheek. "Let's not rush this," he said. "I mean, we don't even know each other, right? You're sure you and Sweeps are through?"

"Oh, yeah. That guy! He was better than some of the guys I've dated, but he's bad enough," she said. "I used to go with a guy who was into bondage. He couldn't get off unless he had me trussed up like a chicken. Why do I always get these weirdos?" She giggled again, leaned in quickly and kissed him on the mouth. "I like you, Sal," she said. "I really do."

"And I like you, Sarah, but let's get to know one another first, okay?"

"You dating someone?"

"Off and on," he said. "I'm not good at one on one."

"Okay. Why don't you come by the club one night and see my act?"

"What do you do?"

"Oh, a lot of things. But for you I'll do something special. I'll do my fertility dance."

"Maybe I will one night."

"It's not just a strip joint. We have comedians, too. Why don't you come by tomorrow night?"

"Okay, why not?" He stood up. "I guess I'd better go. Don't you have to get ready?"

"Oh, yeah. But I'm just waitressing tonight."

"No fertility dance?"

"No, I don't do that every night. Only special occasions. You'll see."

He left the rest of his lethal lemonade on her back stairs, kissed her good-bye on the forehead, and drove himself away.

***

Jake was standing outside by his shed row at nine o'clock the next morning when Bones arrived at the barn. He looked better than he had in weeks and informed Bones that Barrow had cleared him to go back to work. All he had to do was make sure that he got enough sleep and kept on taking his medications. "I've become a drug addict, Bones," he said, "but if that's what it takes to keep me sane, fine."

"Then you won't need me around anymore, right?"

"Not on a regular basis, no. But you've been a big help. Thanks."

"Where's Jill?" Bones asked, looking around.

"Out on the track galloping Abernathy's two-year-old," the trainer said. "That'll wrap it up for the morning."

"How's she doing?"

"All right, I guess. She's pretty quiet these days. Does her job, then goes home, keeps pretty much to herself. By the way, that guy Everett was here again today. She told him off, and I had to threaten to get track security to get him out of here. What's with that guy?"

"He doesn't understand rejection," Bones said. "So was Jill really upset?"

"Yeah, she was. I tried to calm her down. She kept saying they'd never leave her alone, never."

"They?"

"Yeah, they. Is there somebody else besides Everett? By the way, what's he doing around here?"

"He's got Terry's Dream, remember? He's going to be the favorite in the Derby. Everett flies in and out of here to watch his workouts."

"I think he came to see Jill."

"Yeah, probably. He's a rich boy. He's used to getting what he wants. And he wants her back. He told me all about it."

"If he keeps bugging her," Jake said, "she could get a court order to leave her alone, right?"

"Maybe I'll have a little talk with him," Bones said. "Something bad happened to her with these people and she's not over it."

"It's too bad, because she's doing real well here. She's good with the horses and she can ride, all right. I guess she's proved that."

Bones didn't stick around long enough to see Jill. Instead he went to have some breakfast. Then he sat in his car for an hour handicapping, after which he showed up at the track about an hour before post time and walked into the Turf Club. Carl Everett was sitting by himself at a small table overlooking the finish line. Without waiting to be invited, Bones sat down opposite him. Startled, Everett looked up from his program and blinked. "What do you want?" he asked.

"I want you to leave the girl alone," Bones said. "I want you to stop messing around with her head. You're making it real hard for her to live her life and to work in peace. Fontana told me you were around the barn again this morning causing trouble. It's got to stop, pal, you understand me?"

Everett leaned back in his chair and stared at him, a small, nasty smile on his face. "Who are you to tell me what to do?" he said. "You don't know anything about her, about us, about what's going on, do you? Do you?"

"I know enough to know she doesn't want to have anything to do with you, but you can't get that through your head."

"This conversation is over," Everett said. "If you don't leave this instant, I'll have you thrown out of here."

Bones stood up. "Fine. But now I'm telling you, Everett, if you don't leave her alone, I'll do whatever I have to do to put a stop to you."

"Are you threatening me? That's assault. You could get yourself arrested."

"No shit." Bones resisted the impulse to kick Everett's chair out from under him, leaning in close to him over the table. "Okay, so I am threatening you. Take it seriously, pal."

Everett pushed his chair back and rose to confront him. "I ought to take care of you right now," he said. "I should have done it the day you hit me from behind."

"I wouldn't suggest it," Bones said. "Something real bad could happen to you, like broken bones. You understand me? It's my specialty."

Everett took a step back. "Get away from me! Now!"

"My pleasure, pal. Just remember—you don't leave Jill alone, you and I will have another meeting. I'll pick the time and place and you won't enjoy it. Trust me on that."

Bones walked away from him feeling a little foolish. It wasn't really his style to threaten people. Even in the bad old days, he didn't talk much. All he'd had to do most of the time was show up. But guys like Everett, they bring out the worst in you.

CHAPTER 21

"My dear Giacomo," Ester Gale Dinworthy said, "you are not going to deny me the pleasure of watching my champion run in this race. I will not let you even consider it. We both know he will win it, don't we?"

"No, we don't, Mrs. Dinworthy," Jake said. "We don't know any such thing. You're right about the horse, he's good, but you're asking me to run him against some of the best three-year-olds in the country with just three races under his belt. It's not right. We should let him develop by running him through his conditions; then, after he's won or at least run well in all of them, at that point we'll be ready to take on the best."

"And how long would that be?"

"Several months, maybe. By the early fall we should be there, assuming he stays sound and doesn't get sick or hurt himself."

"They all get sick or hurt themselves or come down with some sort of minor ailment, don't they?" Mrs. Dinworthy asked.

"Unfortunately, yes. But maybe if we're lucky and careful we can avoid it. And by the end of the year, you'll have yourself a very good horse."

Mrs. Dinworthy sighed and gazed at the trainer with sorrow and repressed exasperation. It was eight o'clock in the morning at the barn. The sky was blue overhead and the air was chilly, with a stiff breeze blowing in from the ocean. The morning sunlight sparkled off the dew on the infield grass, the slopes of Old Baldy, and the roofs of the houses nestled among the trees on the hills surrounding the track. From the track a couple of hundred yards away they could hear the muffled sound of horses' hooves striking the soft earth as the animals worked or galloped in the cool morning air. Jake stood outside the tack room while Ester Gale Dinworthy sat on a straight-backed wooden chair facing him, a purple woolen shawl draped around her shoulders and her hands resting on a stout silver-knobbed walking stick, another of her amazing feathered hats perched on her head like a bouquet.

"By the end of the year," she repeated, nodding. "I see. Tell me, Giacomo, I don't suppose you ever met my late husband, Oliver."

"No, I'm sorry to say I didn't," Jake answered. "He must have been a fine man."

"He wasn't," she said. "He was an irresponsible, mendacious phi-landerer, an absentee father to his two worthless children, my miserable progeny, whom I refuse even to communicate with anymore, and he was also inadequate in almost every aspect of his emotional life, such as it was."

"I see," Jake mumbled, looking embarrassed. "I'm sorry to hear that, Mrs. Dinworthy."

"I'm not seeking your sympathy or your pity, Giacomo," she said. "What I'm telling you is beside the point. The point is that in the one area of his life that mattered to him, Oliver was a genius."

"What area was that, Mrs. Dinworthy?"

"Entrepreneurial capitalism," she said. "He began with nothing, not a dime. He was forced to leave school, where he failed to distinguish himself in any way. But once launched on his own into the outside world, he borrowed two thousand dollars from a cousin and went to Houston, Texas, where he began wildcatting in the oil business. Within five years of his arrival there, he had become a multi-millionaire. He invested those earnings into other ventures and prospered greatly, taking one chance after another, never pausing to consolidate or retreat or compromise or admit even the possibility of failure. At his death, Giacomo, Oliver was worth $800 million, a great deal of which my idiot sons have since squandered through ineptitude and laziness, but leaving me with enough of his earnings to indulge my passion for this sport of kings, horse racing."

"Why are you telling me this, Mrs. Dinworthy?" Jake asked.

"To prove a point," she said. "The old cliché applies, Giacomo—nothing ventured, nothing gained. Let me ask you something else. What if during the early years of the republic the country had been settled only by horse trainers, Giacomo? What do you imagine might have happened?"

"I have no idea, Mrs. Dinworthy."

"I'll tell you," she announced. "By the mid-nineteenth century the population of the United States would have consisted of an unadventurous lot crowded between the Mississippi and the Atlantic Ocean. Once a week or so the Comanche, the Kiowa, the Apache, and the Sioux would conduct raids on the settlements and towns along the border. 'Yes,' they would shout, as they pillaged, raped, and burned, 'we have oil out here and open land and gold and silver, but you can't have any of it!' Do I make myself clear, Giacomo?"

"I think so," the trainer said. "You want to take a chance."

"You're beginning to grasp my point, Giacomo," she said, pushing herself to her feet. "As you yourself have indicated, any number of things in this sport can go wrong. Why wait for them to occur? Let us, like Alexander the Great, strike now that the opportunity arises and wealth and fame await. You will agree, I'm sure, that our noble contender should contend. I consider the matter closed."

When Jake returned from having escorted Mrs. Dinworthy back to her car, he looked at Bones, who was leaning against the wall of the barn and grinning at him. "What are you laughing at?" he snapped. "The woman is a nut case. She's going to risk this horse's health and career because she thinks horse racing is like playing the stock market or drilling for oil."

"Isn't it?"

"Come on, Bones, you know better. You even own a piece of him. You ought to be worried about it."

"I don't have a vote," Bones said. "Besides, she's got a point. Anything can and does go wrong in this game. Let's go for it."

"I could quit," Jake said. "Turn the horse over to someone else."

"Who? You want to risk the horse's welfare by turning him over now to a trainer who doesn't know anything about him and could really screw him up? Come on, Jake, shoot craps."

"Son of a bitch," Jake said. "This is too good a horse to mess up."

"The old broad may have a good point there, you know," Bones said. "That stuff about the Indians—"

"Knock it off, Bones," Jake said. "I've heard enough for one morning."

"You going to ride Jill on him?"

"Probably. Neruda won't be back in time. Think I should?"

"Yeah. She knows him; she loves him. She'll ride the hair off him. If she wins, maybe her career is made out here or anywhere. She could go to the Kentucky Derby on him."

"Whoa, let's not get ahead of ourselves here. The Santa Anita Derby's tough enough."

"And Jill will be riding to beat Everett's horse, among others. That'll inspire her, right? You going to tell her or am I? You should, Jake. You're the man."

"The dummy, you mean. I let this crazy old woman ride over me."

"She could ride over anyone. If that asshole Bush had sent her to Iraq, she'd have led the troops into Baghdad in three days instead of three weeks and flushed out Saddam Hussein by herself. No wonder Oliver stayed away from her. He was so pussy-whipped that making $800 million was a snap for him compared to having to cope with her."

Jake laughed. It was a good laugh, the first one Bones had heard from him since his breakdown.

***

Bones' losing streak ended that afternoon. It wasn't a huge win, but the couple of hundred bucks he pocketed on two winning exactas gave him a small profit for the day and sent him away happy. Stats, Moonshine, and Sweeps rode along with him and so the afternoon passed pleasantly enough. Toward the end of the day Bones asked Sweeps about Sarah Digby. "You still seeing her?"

"Nah," he answered. "She won't even talk to me; I don't know why."

"Maybe after you screamed at her and trashed her in public here she might be a little tired of you."

Sweeps looked downcast. "Yeah, I was a jerk. But, hey," he said, suddenly perking up, "the world is full of dumb broads, right? Lots more where she came from."

"You've got a dismal view of the world, Sweeps," Stats said. "I'm sorry for you."

"Ah, what do you know, Stats? You're buried in your fucking numbers."

"The tone of this conversation is giving me a headache," Moonshine observed, heading out of the box. "See you guys."

Bones followed him out, drove home, and stood under a hot shower for twenty minutes. When he came out of the bathroom, his phone was ringing. It was Sarah. "Hey, Sal, sweetie, you coming by tonight?"

"Yeah, I just might do that."

"Great! I'll tell Larry—he's the manager and the emcee—that you're coming. So you'll get the V.I.P. treatment."

"I don't need that, Sarah," he said. "I'll most likely sit at the bar."

"Suit yourself but get a good seat. You don't want to miss the fertility dance."

"I'm looking forward to it."

Club Zero was a small black box on Sunset in downtown Hollywood. Bones had never noticed it before, but then he didn't frequent that part of town much. It was an area of fast-food restaurants, cheap motels, and dingy-looking shops catering mainly to people passing through. Club Zero sat there, huddled between the Crown Motel and a Denny's, its presence heralded by a revolving electric sign proclaiming live nude girls, which was better, Bones reasoned, than dead nude girls. He knew, without having to set foot in the place, that it would not be a classy joint, but he felt he owed it to Sarah Digby at least to put in an appearance. He liked her and he was lonely, because Bingo, when they finally did meet up for a drink after her work, had obviously sniffed out the fact that he'd been with someone else. You could lie and he had, but somehow women always knew. It was a mystery and he had no fallback position; D.J. was out of town, out in the Midwest again somewhere. Anyway, after Sarah's bad time with Sweeps, Bones didn't want to treat her insultingly. He promised himself he'd stay for one drink, watch her act, and ease himself out of there at the earliest opportunity.

When he walked into the club, one of the live nude girls was on display in what passed, he gathered, for an exotic dance routine. Sporting a feathered headdress, she was prancing and swooping to recorded music across a tiny stage at the back of the room and up and down a ramp that thrust itself out between packed rows of small round tables at which the customers, all men, sat as if nailed in place. Bones sat down on an empty stool at the bar immediately to the right of the entrance and ordered a beer from the bartender, a wizened gnome with a drooping handlebar mustache. "Ten dollars," the gnome said, as he set the bottle down in front of him.

"That's all?" Bones asked. "What do you charge for a real drink? Twenty?"

"Ten dollars," the bartender said. "It don't matter what you order, friend, it's always ten bucks. You're paying to look at tits and pussy."

"I got you," Bones said. "Is Larry around?"

"Yeah. He's backstage, but he'll be out in a moment."

"How about Miss Digby?"

"Who?"

"Sarah Digby."

"Oh, Sarah. She's due out next. You can catch her up close, if you sit at a table. That's another ten."

"I'm good right here."

"Suit yourself, friend."

Bones sipped his beer and watched the end of the dance, which consisted mainly of a variety of bumps and grinds that brought whoops of appreciation from a table of young dudes sitting next to the ramp. As the dancer concluded her act, a small shower of dollar bills floated toward the stage. The girl scooped up the money, bounced her breasts provocatively at the customers, and disappeared offstage.

Larry now appeared from behind the curtain and grinned at the patrons. "In a few minutes," he announced, "Club Zero will present its feature attraction, Miss Sarah Digby, in her world famous, ever popular fertility dance. Don't go away, folks. You ain't seen nothing yet!"

Larry proceeded to thread his way through the tables to the front of the house. He was a short, heavyset man of about fifty with a mass of dyed black curly hair, small dark eyes set close together under a heavy brow, and he seemed about to explode out of his gray slacks and bright crimson sports jacket. When he reached the end of the bar, Bones introduced himself. "Oh, yeah, Sarah told me about you," he said. "You got an act?"

"No, I'm not in showbiz, Larry," Bones said "And I'm sure not the right sex to take my clothes off in here. I'm just a customer, a friend of Sarah's."

"That's cool," Larry said. "But I thought maybe you told jokes or something."

"No, all I do is play the horses," Bones explained. "I've got a patter sometimes that goes with that, but it ain't funny."

"Then forget it. In here you tell jokes and they have to be good and dirty or the customers will throw their glasses at you," Larry said. "Last week we had the cops in here on account of some comedian who wasn't funny enough. They broke up the joint, and I nearly got shut down. I ain't risking that no more. Anyway, Sarah says you're a good guy to know. You a hit man or something? Or a cop?"

"No, Larry, just a concerned citizen. I'm concerned with cashing tickets."

"Horses, that's a tough racket. Anyhow, Sarah's a good kid. Not such a kid anymore, she's been around, but her heart is in the right place. Have another beer. This one's on the house."

Sarah Digby's act was amazing. She came on stage in a costume that consisted mainly of ears of corn dangling from strategic parts of her anatomy. When the music, a medley of songs from *Oklahoma* and other Rogers and Hammerstein favorites, began, she started to move around the proscenium like a tigress stalking her prey. The ears of corn bounced provocatively up and down as she moved; then, just as the music soared into a string section going all out on "The Sound of Music," she began to shed the corncobs. By the time "You'll Never Walk Alone" came on over the loudspeakers, she had lost most of the corn but retained one cob with which she proceeded to perform sim-ulated acts of such calculated lewdness that even Bones' mouth dropped open. Her audience sat transfixed, then roared its approval when she concluded. She took an encore by parading down the ramp, then lying down on her back while the audience scattered money on her naked torso.

"So what do you think?" the bartender asked. "Pretty good, huh?"

"Good is not the word," Bones answered. "Amazing, maybe."

"Yeah, she kills 'em with the corncobs. Especially where she puts that last one. I never seen nothing like it."

"Me neither, pal," Bones said. "I'm surprised the cops don't close you up."

"They would, maybe, if they ever caught her act," the bartender said, "but we make sure they don't. Larry knows 'em all and he spreads a little grease around. He also cases the joint pretty good every night. I'm glad you liked the show."

"It's not one I'm going to forget."

"I love that music," the bartender said. "Great songs."

"Who's listening?"

After Sarah's act a dozen or so of the customers began to head for the exit. Not that they were dissatisfied, it was just that they'd seen enough. After Sarah what else could they have hoped for? A live sex act on stage, sadomasochistic sex rituals, a full-scale orgy? They'd paid their money and had the satisfaction of sprinkling folding green on naked female bodies, so now, having experienced these cultural uplifts, they could get out of there and go home to their wives and children. Bones took a swallow of his second beer and suddenly found himself looking at Turk O'Hara, one of the last guys he ever expected to come across in such a joint. Turk was one of the two vets Jake used to treat his horses. He was in his mid-thirties, happily married with two young kids, and he had the innocent face of an Irish cherub, pink cheeks, bright blue eyes, a thick head of dark curls. "Hey, Turk," Bones called out, "did you enjoy the show?"

The vet did a beautiful double take, his eyes saucer wide, his mouth open in surprise. "Bones? What are you doing here?"

"I could ask you the same thing. I'm not happily married or even happily linked. You here to learn something? Maybe figure out what you've been doing wrong at home?"

Turk's face flushed bright crimson. "Oh, God, no," he said. "It's a bachelor party. My brother Jimmy's getting married, that's all. There's about ten of us in the group. Please don't tell anybody you saw me here. Angie thinks we all went bowling."

Bones laughed. "No, she doesn't," he said. "Maybe she doesn't know you're here, in this particular dump, but she knows you didn't go bowling. I've met Angie. She's too smart for you, Turk."

He grinned, looking more and more boyish. "Yeah, you're right."

"Sit down," Bones said. "Let me buy you a beer. Tomorrow's a dark day."

"I still got horses to take care of."

"So you'll get there a little later."

He nodded, said good-bye to his brother and his friends who had been waiting for him outside, then came back and sat down on the stool next to Bones. "So now it's your turn," he said. "What are you doing here?"

Bones told him about Sarah. "I like her," he said. "Nothing's going on right now, but my girlfriend's mad at me. I helped Sarah out of a jam and she wanted me to see her act, that's all. Did you like it?"

"Like it? Well, it sure was interesting. I mean, that last part ..." His voice trailed off and he looked away, blushing.

"Hey, Turk, she's okay, you know?" Bones said. "It's just showbiz.

You ever see those reality TV series where people eat worms and frogs' eyes or dive into pools full of floating turds or the equivalent or humiliate themselves in like a hundred ways just to make a buck?"

"No, but I read about them. Weird, huh?"

"Sarah's Miss Integrity compared to those morons," Bones said. "She does what she does, but nobody touches her, nobody makes a victim out of her. Just showbiz, Turk. Let's talk about horses."

So they did for the next half-hour or so. What Bones really wanted to find out was whether Turk thought Tumultuous was sound enough to turn into a star and the vet indicated he wasn't sure. "He's kind of funny behind," he said, "with those long legs of his. Could cause back problems later, maybe, but I'll keep a close eye on him for sure. And I know if there's a hint of trouble or pain, Jake will wrap up on him, no matter what you or the lady says. He's only a three-year-old; he's like a teenager, still growing." He paused, then nodded his head and smiled. "He sure can run, though. Fast son of a gun. You could make some real money off this animal."

Turk finished his beer and stood up. "I got to go, Bones," he said. "I'm beat. Got up at four this morning. It's not just the horses. My kids are two and four. That tell you something?"

"That's one reason I'm still unmarried," Bones said. "Before you go, Turk, tell me something. What is it you guys use to put a horse down? I know you inject them, but with what?"

"Usually pentobarbital sodium," he answered. "It's a narcotic, a sedative that was once used to relieve insomnia. We shoot in a massive overdose and the horse goes to sleep."

"That would work on people, too, right?"

"Oh, sure."

"What else could you use?"

"Well, potassium chloride. That would stop the heart muscle."

"These drugs leave traces?"

"Not potassium," he said. "It's a natural chemical element in the body. An overdose wouldn't show up at all. Why?"

"Just curious," Bones said. "We were talking about it after that horse went down the other day. Sarah, the fertility dancer, was there and she was pretty upset about it. I wasn't sure I knew what I was talking about. Funny, I never asked and I've seen so many of them."

A few minutes after Turk's departure, just as another dancer appeared on stage, this one attired in black leather and snapping a bull whip, Sarah appeared. She was dressed in her usual tight little miniskirt, a halter top showing her bare midriff, stiletto heels, and gold hoops dangling from earlobes. She put her arm around his neck and gave him a hug. "So what did you think?" she asked.

"I thought you were terrific," he said.

"You weren't shocked or anything?"

"Why would I be shocked? I've been to a lot of clubs in my time, kid," he said. "You're making a living, right? And you don't have to work for minimum wage in a fast-food joint or clean toilets or some-thin' like that. You're like self-employed, you're an artist, you're in showbiz. What's to be shocked about?"

"Want to come home with me, Sal?"

"You want me to?"

"Yeah, I do. You're the only good guy I've met for a while."

"This is a payoff for being a good guy?"

"Hey, you don't have to, you know."

"We could just be friends, right?"

"Yeah, right."

"Let's go that route for a bit," he said. "Not that I don't think you're terrific. I've got some unresolved problems."

"Someone else, right?"

"Two someone elses," he said. "That's one too many."

She kissed him again on the cheek, then slid off the stool and headed out of the room toward the rear and to the side of the stage, where the lady in leather was now down to a G-string. Bones paid up and left.

CHAPTER 22

Ten days before the Santa Anita Derby, Jill disappeared again. This time, however, she left a note for Jake at the house. She promised to be back within the week. "If there was some way I didn't have to go, I wouldn't," she wrote. "It's just that I'm in a bad spot with some people and I got to take care of it. Please forgive me. You've been so great to me and all and I don't want you to think I don't appreciate it. I know you might want to get another rider for Tumultuous and that's the worst part of this, but I can't help it. I told you and Sal they wasn't going to leave me alone and they won't. I thought I'd gotten out; I thought for sure I was okay, but I'm not. I got no choice, Jake, please try to understand. If you don't hear from me or I don't get back, it's because I can't. I'm sorry." She signed it but left no address or phone number.

Bones found out about Jill's disappearance and her note the morning she left. He'd showed up at the barn just before nine and found Jake still steamed about it. "I can't keep her on," he said. "I got all these horses to take care of and she just walks out on me. I had to get Matt and Ted to send over a couple of their boys to help out this morning. Luis is out with a cold. And now I got to get a jock to ride for me. Leo's back, but I can't trust him, and he's looking to get suspended anyway. The stewards gave him six months, but he says he's sober and he's appealed. Still, I don't want him. Can't take a chance."

"You won't have any trouble getting a good rider for Tumultuous," Bones said. "Anyway, you and I both know, don't we, that it's not the jock who wins the race."

"The good ones can," he said. "The bad ones can fuck you up. You remember Dinny Pearson?"

"Mr. Iron Hands, sure."

"He kept screwing up one of my horses every time he rode him."

"So why'd you keep using him?"

"I figured eventually he'd run out of mistakes."

"And?"

"He never did." He looked at Bones exasperatedly. "What the hell does she mean by 'they won't leave her alone'? Who's 'they' and why won't they let her be? Why isn't she safe here? Who's threatening her? This guy Everett?"

"Maybe. But he's not the only one, obviously."

"What do you make of it, Bones?"

"I'm not sure, Jake, but I got a pretty good idea. I'm going to get to the bottom of it."

"You think you know where she is?"

"Yeah. But I want you to promise me something."

"What?"

"Don't give up on her yet. Let me try and get her back."

"And then what? She takes off again the night before the race?"

"If I can put it all together quick enough, maybe solve the problem, you won't have anything to worry about."

Jake sank back in his chair and looked at him over his folded hands. "What are you up to, Bones? What do you know about all this?"

"I'm not going to tell," Bones said. "I could be wrong. And also I could run into a little trouble along the way, but I'm used to that. The less you know, Jake, the better. I used to handle these kinds of problems easy. I can be good at persuading people to behave, you know what I mean?"

"Listen, Bones, that was some time ago and things were different," Jake said. "This isn't New Jersey or Long Island or wherever you did what you did. You don't want to get yourself in trouble here."

"Ester Gale would understand."

"What do you mean? She'd hire a hit man or something?"

"You just sit on your hands and do nothing, you live your life without taking chances, what's the use of it? Jill's a nice kid. She's talented; she could be a top rider. She deserves the chance, right? She's done nothing but win races for you. She works her ass off every day for you. She held your hand when you didn't know which end was up, pal. You owe her, Jake. You owe her at least a few days. I'm asking you."

"Don't get yourself in trouble, Bones."

"I'll worry about that. It's what I do, if I have to. Now I play the horses, but there's other things I know how to do. I was good at them and people respected me. I earned that respect, believe me. If they didn't, well, I ..."

"Broke bones, right?"

"Not always. Just sometimes. There are a lot of shitheads around, Jake. Some of them refuse to listen to reason, even though I'm basically a reasonable guy."

"Sure, you are." Bones started to leave. "So when will I hear from you?" Jake asked.

"As soon as I have something to tell, Jake," Bones said. "Maybe in a couple of days. Here's the main thing, though: Remember the name Howard Bailey, in case anybody asks you."

"Who the hell is he?"

"Howard Bailey is a friend of yours who wants to buy some horses. Got that?"

"A real guy?"

Bones smiled. "Come on, Jake, do I have to explain everything to you? He's just some guy, understand?"

Bones skipped the races that afternoon, even though he'd done some heavy handicapping and isolated a couple of potential long-shots he really liked, but then he reasoned that a man has to make some sacrifices to accomplish anything in this life.

He went home and packed up a few belongings in an overnight suitcase, put on his fanciest outfit—dark gray slacks and a navy blue

sports blazer—and loaded up the car. Before leaving he called
Heritage Farm and got a woman named Ellen Barkas on the phone.
He told her his name was Howard Bailey.

"What can I do for you, Mr. Bailey?" she asked.

"I'm in L.A. on business," he said. "I may be moving out here per-
manently from the East in a few months and I'm interested in invest-
ing in a small racing stable. I love racing, but I've never owned horses before. My friend Jake Fontana, the trainer, told me Heritage has
the best breeding program in the state."

"He's right. We do."

"I'm coming up your way for a couple of days, and I'd like to come
by your place, have a look around, talk about horses with someone,"
he said.

"Mr. Kelsey will be happy to see you," Ellen Barkas said. "He's the
foreman here and he can show you around."

"Good. I'd also like to meet Mr. Furman, if he's available."

"I don't know about that, Mr. Bailey," she said, "but I'll ask his assistant what Mr. Furman's schedule is. I haven't seen Mr. Furman today.
He may be traveling."

"I'll take my chances," Bones said. "I should be up there by late
afternoon."

"We'll be happy to see you. I'll tell Boomer, that's Mr. Kelsey, you're
coming. If you get here after five, tomorrow morning would be a better time. You can see some of the horses on our training track and
Boomer can give you the grand tour. And, of course, if Mr. Furman
is here, I'm sure he'll be glad to meet with you."

By noon Bones was on the Ventura Freeway halfway to Santa
Barbara. He had no clear plan of action but was counting on his fine
Italian nose to sniff out what might be going on. Whatever it was that
had landed Jill in trouble, one thing he was sure of: Paul Furman and
his people were involved.

***

Heritage Farm was in the heart of the Santa Ynez Valley, about fifteen
miles from the eastern end of the lake. As Bones approached it from a

narrow road winding down an adjacent hillside, he could see it spread out over several hundred acres of meadows crisscrossed by white fences. Mares in foal stood placidly under clumps of sheltering oaks and pine trees; yearlings and two-year-olds romped beside one another in adjacent corrals; several of the farm's stallions gazed impassively at the scene from their own private pens. The stable area consisted of parallel rows of low-lying dark brown barns with slanted triangular roofs. Behind the barns lay a half-mile training track, empty at this time of day. Next to the pens holding the stallions was the breeding shed, and just inside the entrance gate, to the left, was a circular driveway leading to the farm's office. Perhaps a quarter of a mile beyond the one-story rectangular structure, partway up the slope of a hill, a large mansion with white walls and a green mansard roof peeked out over a tall hedge and a grove of orange trees and lemon trees.

Bones parked and walked in the front door to be greeted by a pleasant-looking plump woman of about fifty with closely cropped curly brown hair and large hazel eyes peering up at him through wire-rim glasses. "Yes?" she said.

He introduced himself. "I came right on over," he said. "I'm so turned on by this whole thing I couldn't wait till tomorrow morning. Any chance of having a look around today? I can always return tomorrow. But I have to be back in L.A. the day after."

"Let me see if Boomer's around," she said, picking up the phone. "By the way, I'm Ellen Barkas."

Boomer was around and he showed up ten minutes later, with a muscular calloused hand outstretched and a broad welcoming smile on his face. He was in his sixties, but very fit, with a lean horseman's body, a wrinkled wind-burned complexion, gray eyes, and a mouthful of crooked teeth. He was wearing riding boots, jeans, and a narrow blue cowboy shirt, with a soiled brown baseball cap jammed on his head. "Pleased to meet you," he said. "I got my Jeep outside. Want to have a look around?"

They spent the next hour touring the grounds while Boomer explained the operation to Bones. He also asked him if he wanted to see one of their mares bred to a stallion, an event scheduled for the following morning at six o'clock. The animals involved were stars, the mare having already dropped three stakes-winning foals in five years; the stallion was one of Heritage's best, Drumbeat, now seventeen but an established sire, a son of the great Seattle Slew and the winner in his own right of more than two million dollars in purses. Bones told Boomer he might be interested. "Will Mr. Furman be around then?" he asked.

"Could be," Boomer said. "He often shows up for the big ones. You know, Mr. Bailey, not many of these horses are ever going to amount to much and a lot of them never even get to the racetrack, but you go on breeding the best to the best, hoping for the best."

"Yeah, I know," Bones said. "Horse racing isn't exactly a sure thing like buying a U.S. Treasury Bond, but it's a hell of a lot more fun."

"There you go," Boomer said. "Here, let me show you some of the foals. They're up in the upper meadow with their mommas, next to the house. Mr. Furman likes to be able to look out his bedroom windows and see them every morning."

"Counting his chicks."

"Yeah, you could say that."

They drove up to the last pasture, where eight or nine mares with their foals snuggled close gazed at them with mild curiosity. They got out of the Jeep and leaned up along the fence while Boomer pointed to the mares and identified them for him. As he talked, Bones looked toward the house, which now loomed above the trees. A woman's pale face appeared in one of the windows. When she saw him looking at her, she quickly retreated and drew the Venetian blinds. "How's Mrs. Furman doing?" he asked.

"What?" Boomer looked startled.

"I saw a woman at the window looking at us," Bones said. "I guessed it was her. I hear she had a real hard time when her daughter died."

"Yeah, it was pretty bad," Boomer said. "She's not well, hasn't been for some time. It's been tough."

"What exactly is the matter with her?"

"Don't rightly know, Mr. Bailey," he said. "None of my business. I just run the farm."

"I don't mean to get nosy," Bones said. "It's just you hear a lot of talk, especially with Mr. Furman wanting to run for the Senate and all."

"Yeah, well, that's out of my league, too," Boomer said. "We just mostly breed and sell horses here and we also race a few. Don't know nothing about politics and all that."

"Well, it's a terrific operation you've got here," Bones said. "My friend Jake Fontana, the trainer, he told me it was and he was right. Also the gal who rides for him, that jockey, Jill Aspen? She told me she once worked here."

"Sure did," Boomer said, but he didn't pursue the topic. They got into the Jeep and headed back to the office.

"She's really a good rider," Bones said. "Told me she broke some of the yearlings for you."

"Yeah, she did," Boomer said. Again silence, this time until they reached the office and Bones got out of the car. He thanked the foreman for the tour, after which Kelsey nodded and drove quickly away.

Inside, Bones found Ellen Barkas still sitting at her desk. He told her how much he had enjoyed the tour and that he might come back the following morning in time to watch the breeding operation. "That's pretty dramatic," she said, smiling.

He was about to ask her if Paul Furman would be around, when a door opened and Harvey Stone appeared. He was dressed in a dark-gray business suit and was carrying a fat black briefcase; he seemed to be in a hurry and on his way out the door. "Oh, Mr. Stone," Ellen said. "This is Mr. Howard Bailey. I told you about him."

Harvey Stone stopped to shake his hand. "Glad to meet you," he said, looking mildly surprised. "Haven't we met before?"

"I don't think so. But maybe at the races? I've been around Santa Anita for a few days."

"Yes, maybe," Stone said, unconvinced. "I hope you saw what you needed to see here."

"Yeah, but I'd sure like to talk to Mr. Furman. I'm planning to make a sizeable investment in my stable."

"Well, he has two appointments tomorrow, both in the afternoon in Sacramento," he said. "He'll have to leave here by eleven o'clock."

"I'll be here before that," Bones said. "At the breeding shed."

"Oh, good. I'll tell him. Now please forgive me, but I'm running late. Got some papers I need signed. Nice to meet you, Mr. Bailey. Anything you need, Ellen here can take care of, I'm sure." And he was out the door.

"Where are you staying, Mr. Bailey?" Ellen asked.

"I'm not sure yet. There's a little motel near the lake. I like that little town. I might stay there."

"It's kind of grungy," she said. "There's much nicer places closer by." She wrote down a few addresses and phone numbers for him. "I could call them for you."

"No, it's okay. I can do it." He turned to go and then looked back. "By the way, I gather Mr. Furman's not at the house."

"Oh? No?"

"Well, Mr. Stone's on his way to somewhere else. The ranch, maybe?"

"Yes, Mr. Furman sometimes goes there," Ellen said. "It's quiet and close to the lake. He likes that, goes there a lot. Or used to before Laura Lee—well, you know about that, I guess. I'm not sure that's where he is, but Harvey must know. He's with him every day."

"You've been very helpful," Bones said. "I really appreciate it."

CHAPTER 23

Bones found a small wooden sign with the single word "Heritage" carved into it, posted at the corner of a narrow driveway leading down toward the lake. He cut his engine and headlights and coasted fifty yards or so to the entrance to the property, a tall iron gate in a high stone wall with shards of broken glass embedded into it. There was a control panel with a phone hanging from it on a column to the left of the gate. As quietly as he could manage, he started up the engine, turned the car around, and drove quickly back to the highway, where he turned right, went through the village, and picked up the road leading to Emory Blain's dock. Halfway there he again cut the engine and coasted the rest of the way, turning the car at the last moment into a small clearing between the trees surrounding the property. He stepped out of the car and walked the rest of the way. Though it was very dark, a sliver of a moon above the tree line provided a modicum of light. It must have been after nine by then, and Bones was hoping Blain would be asleep or inside his house with the TV on. He was pretty sure he didn't have a dog, as he hadn't heard or seen one on his previous visit.

At the edge of the parking lot, he paused and waited. There was a light on in one of the windows, and when he moved closer he could hear laughter and applause, so he was in luck; Emory had on his TV set and wouldn't be able to hear him.

Bones walked to the shoreline, detached the outboard engine from one of Blain's motorboats, then gently eased the craft into the water and drifted out into the lake. He picked up the oars and began rowing, propelling himself as quietly as possible across the calm water toward Furman's ranch.

When he spotted the lighted windows of the cabin through the trees, he stopped rowing and waited, listening for any movement from below the house or along the shoreline. Luckily it was still very dark, and unless someone was looking for an intruder, there was little chance he'd be spotted. He stood up and with a single oar paddled softly to the shore, allowing the flat-bottomed boat to scrape to a stop on the dirt. He stepped out, tugged the boat up onto the bank a few more feet, and began to move slowly toward the house. His .38 was tucked inside the belt of his jeans, but he was hoping, actually counting on not having to use it. Instead of walking up the path leading directly to the back porch, however, he came up from the side through the underbrush, again hoping there wouldn't be a dog on the premises or some sort of alarm system. The going was slow, as he had to quietly pick his way through the bushes and the undergrowth, so that it took him close to half an hour to negotiate the distance.

When he reached the corner of the clearing around the house, he crouched down in the bushes and waited. He had to be absolutely certain there would be no guard on duty like the one he'd spotted during his first visit. If what he thought might be going on inside the cabin was actually happening, he felt sure no guard would be around, but he couldn't take the chance. So he waited, checking his wristwatch from time to time, and twenty more minutes passed. He was about to move, when he heard men's voices and a door shut, then footsteps crunching away over a gravel surface. Now a car door slammed shut, an engine started, and a car drove away. He waited some more. Silence. Then lights turning off, he guessed in the front rooms. Again silence. Then the murmur of voices from the only room now with the lights on. He crept forward, eased himself around the corner of the cabin and up onto the porch. He sat with his back to the wall, just to the right of the window, and waited.

He heard voices, a man's and a woman's, speaking intensely. Suddenly, a woman's cry. The sound of a hand striking flesh, more of a slap than a punch. Bones resisted an urge to move, made himself wait. Now from inside the room he heard an angry female voice, intense, a torrent of words he couldn't make out. The man's voice, first threatening, then plaintive, even pleading, answered. That surprised Bones. It was followed by another silence, a long one this time. Then came the low, murmuring sound of the man's voice again, in it a mixture of anger, of anguish, dark and menacing, followed by the same pleading as before. Bones couldn't imagine a picture for himself that made any sense to him. There was something going on in that room he couldn't understand. In the silence that followed, something was clearly happening, but what?

The light in the window was lowered; only a soft orange glow now emanated from it. He heard movement, a soft cry, more movement, a murmuring, passionate in its intensity. Bones eased himself onto his knees and peered inside. Jill was lying on the bed, her head turned away from the man looming over her, his back to the window. He was methodically undressing her. When she was naked, he leaned over to kiss her breasts, and then he tied her by the wrists to the bedposts. He stepped back and looked down at her, speaking softly but urgently to her. Her head was still turned away from him, but she was no longer resisting him or talking back to him. Was she enjoying this or only accepting it? Bones couldn't tell. And now as he watched, the man moved over her without bothering to remove his own clothes. His head sank toward her like a bird of prey surveying an available piece of meat. As his mouth settled on her, she seemed to rise to meet him, as if prepared to let him do with her whatever he wanted, even though her head was still turned away from him, refusing to look at him.

Bones retreated from the window and sat down again. He knew who the man was, of course. He still hadn't seen his face, but he knew and it made him sick for her. He was no longer sure what he should do. He'd begun to doubt, to wonder what the hell he expected to accomplish by finding them together, Paul Furman and Jill. From what he'd observed, something in her craved him, something in her wanted to be humiliated, to be treated like available flesh. She had kept her head turned away from him, she had resisted, because he'd heard it earlier in the tone of her voice, but when she had stopped struggling against him, when she had accepted what he was doing to her, when her body had risen to yield to him, what did that mean? That Bones was being played, like Jake, for a sucker? All that anguish, all that anger, all that sorrow—phony? Maybe. He didn't know.

Now from inside the room he heard her cry out. In what? Pain? Ecstasy? Who knew? He didn't move; he just sat there, Sal "Bones" Righetti, friend, protector, fan, and sucker. He listened to Furman take her. It was quick and brutal. She cried out again, but not a sound from Furman. And then it was over and Bones heard her crying. Furman spoke to her, his voice now hard, cold, contemptuous. His footsteps crossed the floor, a door opened and closed. Bones peered again into the room. Jill was sitting now on the edge of the bed. She was alone in the room, still naked, her arms wrapped around herself, her head bowed. Was she crying? She seemed frozen in place, afraid to move. Lights went on in the front of the house; then Bones heard the sound of Furman's voice on the phone, confident, businesslike, brisk, efficient, a winner in charge of his destiny. The sound of it and the sight of Jill sitting there, her naked body cradled in her arms, forced him to action.

He walked softly around the perimeter of the cabin and climbed the three steps leading to the front door. It was too dark to see if there was a doorbell, so he simply knocked loudly. Silence from inside, then Furman's voice from behind the door: "Harvey? What is it? You should have called."

Bones said nothing and then heard Furman moving away from the door. He didn't like the sound of that, in case he had a gun, so he simply took a step back and kicked the door in. It gave way easily, probably because Furman could not have imagined an intruder at his door; he must have felt himself impregnable behind his stone walls, his iron gate, and his guards.

When Bones stepped inside, he saw Furman standing in the hallway, staring at him. He was dressed in loafers, black slacks, and an open-necked white shirt. "Don't move," Bones said, the .38 now in his right hand. "Just stay right there. Whatever you're thinking, don't try it. Now let's go into the living room. First put your hands up behind your neck, where I can see them."

"I don't know who you are or what you want," Furman said, "but you have no idea what a mistake you're making."

"Really? We'll see. Now move."

Bones followed him into a sitting room containing a large L-shaped leather sofa, two leather armchairs, a wide brick fireplace stacked full of pine logs, and in one corner a broad antique desk on which rested a phone, a stack of folders, and a laptop computer. Floor to ceiling bookshelves framed the fireplace. On the other three walls hung framed color photographs of Heritage Farm's most famous racehorses and stallions, some of them in action crossing the finish line. "Sit down," Bones said. "We're going to talk."

"Talk? What about? You want money?" Furman said, facing him, his hands still behind his neck. "My wallet's in my bedroom. I've got a few hundred dollars, that's all. Take it and get the fuck out of here."

"Didn't you hear me? Sit down," Bones said.

Furman glanced nervously behind him and then sat down facing him in one of the armchairs. Still holding the .38, Bones sat down opposite him. "Don't worry about the woman," he said. "Nothing's going to happen to her."

"What the hell is this all about? What do you want?"

"I think maybe a confession might do it," Bones said, smiling.

"A confession? Are you crazy? A confession to what?"

"Well, let's start with the death of your daughter last year," Bones said. "That's probably as good a place as any. Laura Lee, that was her name, right? Nice kid, troubled, though. Like her mother, maybe. Something of a nut case, right?"

His face flushed with anger. "I'm not going to talk to you about that, to you or to anyone."

"Oh, yes, you are," Bones said. "You're going to tell me what happened that night." He stood up, walked over to the desk and put the .38 on the corner of it next to the laptop. "There, see?" He walked away from the desk and sat down again opposite him. "No gun. Just two ordinary guys talking things over."

Furman stood up, as Bones knew he would. He obviously fancied himself in good shape, a guy who worked out several times a week and could handle himself—a boxer maybe, or a karate expert. Lots of confidence there. And Bones? Just a middle-aged fat man to him, right? No problem for him. "Get up," Furman said. "I want you out of here right now, or I'll kick the shit out of you!"

Bones sighed and looked up at him; he didn't even bother to stand up. He wanted him to act; he wanted him to shine in his chosen role of the big-time dude in charge of his destiny. Would he make a move for the gun? Not likely. He was too sure of himself. He stood over Bones now, leaning in. "Now!" he said. "Right now!"

He reached down to grab Bones' shirtfront, intending apparently to haul him to his feet, perhaps intending to slap him silly. Bones grabbed his wrist with one hand and twisted it sharply aside as he kicked out with his right leg, knocking him backward. Furman turned toward the corner of the desk where the .38 rested tempting-ly close now. Bones was right behind him, took him by the neck with his left hand and pulled him back in close to him. Furman swung out wildly and Bones ducked under it, came up inside with a short sharp jab to Furman's stomach that doubled him over. As Furman gasped for breath, Bones hit him with both hands on the back of the neck and knocked him to his knees. He waited until Furman could breathe again, then hauled him to his feet and pulled him in close. "Don't try that again, Paul," he said. "It could get painful." Then he flung him back into his chair, where he sat doubled over, still trying to get his breath in great gasping gulps of air. Bones sat down again opposite him. "Let's start all over," he said pleasantly. "Exactly what happened that night?"

Before Furman could answer, Jill appeared in the doorway behind him. She was wearing a bathrobe and was staring at Bones in amazement. "Sal? What are you doing here? What do you want?"

"Hello, Jill. The truth, I guess. I want to know what this bastard has on you."

"Please go, Sal. This isn't about you. It's … it's …"

"I think I know what it's about," Bones said. "Stay, if you want. You can tell me yourself, if you want. But I'm getting to the bottom of this right now. After which I'm taking you out of here. Where's your car? Out front?"

She nodded. "Please, Sal," she said, "this is my fault, too. Don't get mixed up in this."

"Hey, I'm already mixed up in it. And he's going to tell me all about what happened. I really don't actually need you, babe. So why don't you go and get dressed and we'll be out of here real soon, I promise you." Looking pale and distraught, she backed away and disappeared toward the bedroom. Bones hoped she wasn't going to call anyone from somewhere else in the house, but he didn't think she would. He had to believe she really did want out at this point. Still, you could never be sure. How did the old Italian proverb go? From my enemies I can protect myself, but God save me from my friends.

"There's nothing to tell you," Paul Furman said hoarsely, massaging his neck with both hands and looking up at him with hatred. "Not a goddamn thing."

"You know, Furman, if this was a police station, I'd have to read you your rights. Then I'd have to ask questions without hurting you. Then, if your lawyer showed up in time, you could just clam up and ride it out. A guy with your power and your money and your connections, shit, you'd beat the rap easy. Guys like you always beat the rap." Bones smiled. "But you know what? This isn't a police station, I don't have to read you any rights, and I don't have to let you call your lawyer. And best of all, I can hurt you as much as I like. Let me show you." He stood up, leaned over him and hit him very hard on his upper left arm. Furman yelped and grabbed it, looking up at Bones in horror. "I'm pretty good at this," Bones said. "We can sit here all night while I work you over or you can tell me what I want to hear. See, I already think I know what I want to hear, but I want you to confirm it. It would sound better, more convincing maybe, coming from you. So let me prompt you, pal, so you'll know where we're going with this. That night, the night Laura Lee drowned, you and Jill were also here. You'd come here alone with Laura Lee, but that night Jill joined you, right?"

Furman hesitated, so Bones stood up again. Furman shrank back in his chair, hands upraised to ward off a blow. "Yes," he finally whispered. "Yes."

"And then what?"

"She came here very late."

"You called her. You told her when to come. Was it after midnight, when?"

"I don't remember, exactly. Sometime after eleven."

"You thought Laura Lee was asleep. You'd maybe given her a sleeping pill, right? To sort of help it along, make sure she wouldn't wake up. Right?"

He nodded. "I—she was a very light sleeper. She—she was very … nervous."

"So you and Jill got it on, thinking she was asleep, that she wouldn't find out what was going on. And after it was over, what did you do?"

Furman stared at him with hatred and didn't answer. Bones stood up and loomed over him. "All right, all right," Furman said. "I had to get up very early to go to the farm for a couple of hours."

"Why?"

"We had a mare being bred to one of our top stallions and the owners wanted me to be there. I'd promised to show up."

"And you told Jill to stay here till you got back, right?" Bones sat down again and waited.

"I expected to get back by seven o'clock. I—I figured Laura Lee would sleep through the night till after I got back. If she didn't …" His voice trailed away, a look of genuine distress on his face.

"Jill was supposed to tell her she'd come over from the farm to stay

242

with her till you returned, right?" Bones said. "But, of course, she didn't sleep through the night, did she?"

He hesitated before answering, then shook his head. "No."

"In fact, she woke up while you and Jill were at it in the bedroom," Bones said, "and she heard you, maybe even saw you. Like I did—through the window."

Startled, Furman glanced up at him. "You ..."

"Yeah, I did. So your kid flipped out. Her wonderful, all-powerful daddy screwing one of the help. Did she leave a note?" Furman didn't answer. "If she did," Bones continued, "it must have been tough for you to read."

Bones waited for him to reply, but he didn't, seeming to shrink into his seat; his distress left Bones untouched. "And then you used your daughter's suicide to blackmail Jill," Bones said. "When you got back here, you found Jill asleep and the girl gone. You woke Jill up and you searched the grounds. At the shoreline you found footprints, I imagine. So what did you do to Jill? Scream at her that it was her fault? Abuse her? You had her now, right? It was tough till then for her to fight you off. She had a history of being abused and you knew it. She knew that what she had going with you was wrong, that it was a bad deal for her, but she also needed to be wanted. She blamed herself for everything, and now you were able to treat her like a piece of meat. The thing is, you originally came on to her as this good-looking, charismatic, power guy who was as needy in his own way as she was, a top dog with the sickly wife, the loony daughter. Two lost souls clinging to each other. Shit, what a crappy TV series this would make!"

Bones waited again for Furman to say something, but he didn't. He sat stolidly in place, his face dark with grief. "So let me bring you up to date," Bones resumed. "Despite everything, she was strong enough finally to break away from you, but you weren't about to let her do that. You continued to blame her for Laura Lee's death. You were clean of that one, because you hadn't been in the house when the girl wandered off. Tell me something, Furman, how do you live with yourself, pal? You're supposed to be one of the good guys. You're planning to run for office. People around here think you're the great-est. Yeah, you'll make a fine senator, oh yeah."

Bones stood up again and looked down at him. He could see the fear in Furman's eyes, but he had no desire anymore to hurt him. "I'm taking Jill out of here," he said quietly, "and you're never going to bother her again. Never. You know why? I'll tell you why. Because if you do, I'll be all over you. Your private guards won't be able to pro-tect you; the cops won't either. See, I know too much about you. I know how you killed Dulcie Clark."

Furman stared at him, his mouth slightly open, as if Bones had just announced the impending end of the world. "You must be crazy," he said.

"You think so? I've already written it all down and it sits in my safe-ty deposit box," Bones lied. "Hey, I knew about you and Dulcie, too. You don't need to know how I found out, but anyone could figure it out. When you dropped Dulcie and started up with Jill, she threat-ened to let the whole world know about it. That could have put a lit-tle crimp in your campaign, right? So you had Dulcie put down, as they say in the horse business. Maybe you got Kelsey to do it for you or one of your vets, but I suspect you did it yourself. Did you?"

He didn't answer; he just kept staring at him. "You can't get away with any of this," he said at last. "You can't prove anything. No one would believe you."

"No? I could get people thinking about it," Bones said. "That lethal little injection under the tongue or maybe behind the ear. Potassium, wasn't it? Almost impossible to trace. I think you lured her to that motel, told her just what she wanted to hear. Who helped you with her? Somebody must have. There was no sign of violence and you're pretty good at fooling people. Even Dulcie trusted you, up to a point. She made a bad mistake. Now that I think about it, maybe it was Harvey Stone who helped you clean up that mess. Yeah, it's true, I can't prove any of this, but hey, you know what good copy rumors can make. Not good if you're running a political campaign, trying to con the public into thinking you're one of the good guys they can trust to do the right thing. Maybe you would make a great senator, I don't know. Capitalism for the poor, socialism for the rich, right? The public's too dumb to see through it."

Bones was suddenly very tired, not physically tired, just tired of looking at Paul Furman, tired of hearing himself talk to this loser, tired of telling him what he already knew but wouldn't admit to. "Get up," he said. When Furman hesitated, Bones leaned over and pulled him to his feet. "Put your hands up behind your neck again, where I can see them."

As he did so, Bones shoved him toward the rear of the house, picking up his .38 on the way and tucking it back into his belt. Jill was standing in the doorway of the bedroom when they got there. She was dressed, but very pale, her eyes wide with fear. "You got your stuff together?" Bones asked.

She nodded. "Yeah."

"Go out and get in the car," he said. "I'll be out in a few minutes."

"Sal, don't—"

"Don't worry about it," he said. "I'm not going to hurt him."

She picked up her bag from a corner of the bed and hurried past them toward the front door. Furman turned his head to look at him. "What do you want?" he asked. "I'll pay whatever you want."

"You know what? I don't need your money. I don't need shit from you. Strip down, pal."

"What?"

"You heard me. Get 'em off."

Furman hesitated, as if considering another move, but then decided it might not be a good idea. He peeled off his shirt, dropped his pants, then kicked off his loafers and stood facing him. "All of them," Bones said, "but turn around. I'm not interested in looking at you. And after you do that, lie face down on the bed."

He tied Furman by his wrists and ankles to the bedposts with the same ropes he had used on Jill. "Please don't kill me," Furman said. "Anything you want—"

"Shut the fuck up," Bones said, glancing at his watch. "I figure it'll be about seven or eight hours before anybody comes looking for you. You'll think of something to tell them. Only it won't be about me or Jill or Dulcie, right? You'll tell them somebody you've never seen before broke in and stole your wallet. Maybe you can also tell them you got buggered, make it a headline story on the news. Or maybe it was just an ordinary burglar with a sense of humor, how about that? They'll find the wallet in the bushes, empty, of course. As for Jill, nobody knew she was here but Harvey Stone. You'll tell him what to say, I know you will. You guys are very good at lying."

Jill was sitting behind the wheel of her car, head bowed, hands clenched in her lap. Before getting in beside her, Bones took several hundred dollars out of Furman's leather wallet, wiped off the wallet carefully with his handkerchief, and tossed it into the bushes beside the driveway. "Are you okay?" he asked Jill, as he shut the car door. She nodded. "Let's get out of here," Bones told her. "When we hit the main highway, turn right. There's a couple of things I have to do before we leave."

He had Jill drop him off by the road down at the lake. "Now go home, Jill," he told her, leaning in the window. "I'll call Jake and tell him you'll be back at work in a day or two, right?" Again she nodded, but without looking at him. Shame, he wondered? Probably. She'd have to work her way through it; he couldn't help her there. Maybe Ed Barrow could. He'd ask him, but all that would come later. "Go home. Get back to your real life, kid. It'll be okay, you'll see, you'll make it. He'll leave you alone now. Jake needs you. Sammy needs you. You've got a real life there; you know that." She still didn't say anything but waited until he'd finished, then drove away.

Bones stuffed Paul Furman's money into Emory Blain's mailbox. He figured it would more than pay for having to retrieve his boat and the inconvenience of having to answer a lot of questions about how it might have gotten there. Then he walked down to his rented car, drove it back to the highway, turned right, and headed south.

CHAPTER 24

A day passed before Jill showed up for work, but she did call in to the barn to say she was sick. Bones had called her at home when he got back, but she didn't answer the phone and Jake told him he hadn't seen her around the house either. Early the next morning, however, she appeared, pale and tight-lipped. She made no attempt to speak to Jake, but it was obvious to her that he wasn't hot to talk to her either. He let Eduardo put her to work. Mostly she labored around the stalls because Jake had hired Matt Logan's boy, Francisco, to work and gallop his horses during her absence. It was well after nine, with the horses safely tucked away for the day, before the trainer decided to talk to her. He took her into the tack room, told her to shut the door behind her, and sit down. She did so, perched on the edge of the chair, her face tense with dread.

"I'm not going to fire you, Jill," Jake said. "I know you've got problems. Sal didn't tell me exactly what they were, but he made a pretty good case for keeping you on. You aren't the only one with problems, I guess you know that, and I'm sure grateful to you for what you did for me the past few weeks. That counts for something in my book. You understand what I mean, don't you?"

She nodded. "Yeah," she whispered.

"I like the way you work with the horses, and I like the way you ride," he continued. "I got a horse, that other cheap mare of Abernathy's, Sunset Ride, running day after tomorrow, but I had to put up another jock on her, Pug Simpson. He ain't much, I know, but he can get a horse out of the gate and not fall off, which is something these days. Maybe he can pick up a piece of the purse for us."

"I understand, Jake," Jill said. "I understand if you never put me up on a horse again, but I swear to God it ain't going to happen no more. I'll do whatever you want me to do. That's it, Jake, honest. I been through some bad stuff—"

"I know that," he said. "You don't need to tell me about it either. I kind of don't want to know. You got to work all that out on your own. If it's medical, call Ed Barrow. You need his number?"

"No, I got it. I already called him," she said. "I saw him yesterday."

"And?"

"He says I'll be okay. He's sending me to some other doctor. Maybe like a shrink or something. He says I need to talk to him, maybe get some pills or something."

"Sounds about right." Jake leaned back in his chair, a faint smile on his face. "So now we got a couple of nut cases running a racing stable. Maybe Eduardo ought to see a sawbones or a priest."

For the first time in weeks Jake saw Jill smile. It lit up her face like a ray of sunlight slanting in through a window. "Just being in racing, loving them horses so much is crazy enough, isn't it?" she said. "But it's all I want to do, Jake. Honest."

"I believe you," he answered. "What else keeps us here day after day, working like dogs just to keep these animals healthy and running for us? We've got to be crazy, right? Now get the hell out of here; go get yourself some breakfast, and I'll see you tomorrow. How are you feeling? You fit?"

"You bet. I can't wait. And I can't thank you enough." She hurried out the door, waved good-bye to Eduardo, and headed for her car.

Jake immediately picked up the phone and called Bones. "She just left," he said, "and she looks good. You know anything I don't know that maybe I should?"

"No, Jake, nothing you need to hear about," Bones said. "All I'll tell you is she had a real bad time with a guy who had a big hold on her."

"Everett?"

"Him, too. But listen, it's over. She went to see Doc Barrow. I think he's going to straighten her out."

Bones, however, had reservations. He'd caught up with Barrow the previous afternoon at the track, where he was standing at one of the bars in the clubhouse exhaling clouds of smoke and nursing a beer, his head bent over his *Racing Form*. "So how's our girl doing?" Bones asked. "Did she call you?"

"Yeah," he answered, without looking up from his charts. "Yeah, she called."

"You going to see her?"

"I have seen her. This morning."

"So?"

Now at last he forced himself to look up from his calculations and regarded Bones with a slightly bloodshot and weary eye. "She's my patient now," he said. "I don't talk about my patients, not even to my wife."

"All I want to know is if she's going to be okay."

He sighed, as if Bones had asked him why the jockeys all wore those funny little hats or if a horse's long tail meant he might be able to run fast, the sort of questions Sarah Digby might have asked. "I don't know," he finally answered. "I'm not sure what's wrong with her. It's not really my field."

"You got to help her, Doc. She's got some kind of identity problem."

"Is that so? An identity problem. Okay," he said. "I'm not sure I'd know what to prescribe for an identity problem."

"Don't bullshit me, Doc," Bones said. "I like this kid. I'm worried about her and I'm trying to help her."

Another sigh and a shrug of the shoulders. "I'm sending her to someone who can help, okay?" he said. "And that's all I'm going to tell you. But I'll stay on top of it, Bones. And now let me ask you something."

"Sure."

"Who do you like in the third here? I'm trying to put together a trifecta, but I've got five horses and I can't isolate the key one."

"Lost in trifecta land, eh, Doc? Sometimes it's a trap."

"Tell me about it. So who do you like in here?"

"I'd key the two horse," Bones told him. "He's got some speed, maybe the jock can rate him, bring him in at least second."

Barrow grunted and made a notation on his program. "Thanks," he mumbled. "I thought he might be the one."

"How about exactas?" Bones suggested. "They're not quite as dangerous to your health as trifectas. And then, of course, you could try betting straight. This horse should be four to one or better."

"Only one horse?" The doctor regarded Bones with horror, as if he had suggested he jump into a pile of steaming manure. "Are you insulting me, Bones? One horse? The straight bet is for sissies."

"How about for tortoises?"

"Tortoises?"

"Like in the old fable of the tortoise and the hare. Remember who won that race? It's a much safer bet."

"Safe? You think I come to the racetrack to play safe?" he said. "All day long I'm dealing with dead and dying and sick people and you want me to come to the racetrack and play safe? I'm here for shots of ecstasy, for liberation."

"What's liberating about losing?"

Barrow made a grotesque attempt at a smile, at least that's what Bones thought it might be. "The joy of possibilities, the anticipation of the big score," he said. "Safe? I can't do bungee jumping at my age or climb Everest. I can go to the racetrack."

"Okay, Doc," Bones said, patting him on the shoulder. "Key the two horse and good luck."

"You always need luck," Barrow mumbled, turning back to his *Form*. "Don't worry about the girl. She's in good hands."

So that was all Bones had been able to find out, and it wasn't as reassuring as he'd hoped it would be. He was still too worried about Jill, not that she'd relapse and go running back to Furman, but that she'd been so damaged by what had happened to her that she'd be unable to put her life back together. Bones promised himself to keep an eye on her, to intervene for her with anyone who might endanger her. He was no expert on the sort of emotional and mental problems of people who had become used to being abused physically or mentally, so all he could fall back on now was to trust in Ed Barrow. And in Jill herself, of course. How close would she allow herself, however, to be to him? He'd witnessed her being humiliated and sexually exploited and that recollection, he reasoned, might make her want to distance herself from him. Whatever happened, he'd be rooting for her, he told himself, backing and protecting her even from a distance, if that was how she'd want to play it. What would save her, he felt sure, was the horses, the only living beings who had never failed her or used her or betrayed her or hurt her. Her truest, happiest moments had come from being around them, from caring for and about them and, above all, from riding them. Horses had a way of insinuating themselves into your soul. In them, perhaps, would lie her salvation. Bones knew that, just as surely as he knew Paul Furman would eventually make one last try to reclaim her. In his own way he was as vulnerable as she was.

***

Meanwhile Bones had to embark on his own reclamation project. Since getting back from Santa Ynez, he had tried calling Bingo several times but had never gotten through to her, and she didn't return his calls. So he decided to drop in on her at the Blue Flamingo, where he persuaded Marty Blenheim, the owner, to seat him at one of her tables. "She's pissed off at you," he said, as Bones hovered just inside the front entrance.

"How do you know? She tell you that?"

"Not in so many words," Marty said. "But when I ask about you and why you haven't been in here for a few weeks, she gives me one of those looks, you know? Like maybe you're infected with some fatal disease or something. What'd you do, fuck around on her?"

"I was alone for a few days in Las Vegas," Bones explained. "This nice-looking gal came on to me."

"Some hooker? What's the matter with you, Bones? Ain't you got no respect for yourself?"

"She wasn't a hooker, Marty," Bones said. "She was kind of terrific, actually. I really like her."

251

"So you expect Bingo to accept that?"

"No, I don't. That's what I'm doing here. So cut the sermon, Marty."

He shook his head sadly. "You know, when the women's lib shit started and you heard all about how a woman's sex drive is just like a man's, I had to laugh," he said. "I mean, shit, if that was true, I'd sell the restaurant and buy a motel, rent rooms to couples by the hour. I never knew a guy who can go through a whole day without seeing some chick he'd like to hammer for twenty minutes or so regardless of his great marriage to someone who looks like Sharon Stone and has got a fistful of great kids. No wonder women are pissed off at us. We're fucking hopeless."

"Okay, Marty, I fucked up," Bones said. "Now help me out."

Marty led him into the dining room to a table in the far corner. Bingo wasn't around, probably picking up an order in the kitchen, so she didn't spot him until she came sweeping out through the swinging doors and set plates down in front of an older couple across the room from him. When she turned and saw him smiling at her, her face froze. She hesitated a moment, then headed toward the bar to talk to Marty. Bones got up and quickly followed her, catching up to her just before she reached her boss. "Hey, Bingo," he said, gently taking her arm. "It's only me, your old pal Sal the idiot, Sal the swine, Sal the sorry guy who makes mistakes but still cares about you."

She turned to look at him, disengaging herself as she did so. "I don't think I want to talk to you," she said. "And I sure don't want to wait on you. Where's your girlfriend?"

"What girlfriend? I thought you were my girlfriend."

"You thought wrong. You don't have girlfriends, Sal; you got dumb chicks who think you're a good guy and they put up with you. Only eventually we all get tired of putting up with your shit, you know what I'm saying?"

"I can't pretend to be something I'm not, kid," he said. "I try to be honest with you, at least. But you got to know I care about you. And Tommy."

"I got to get back to work," she said, brushing past him on her way back toward the dining room.

Marty, who had witnessed this little scene, grimaced and shrugged his shoulders. "Dames," he muttered. "What can you do?"

Again Bones caught up to her, this time near the kitchen doors. "Hey," he said, "I got three tickets to the Lakers game Sunday night. Two are for you and Tommy, the third one is for me. Here." He dropped them into her apron pocket, where she kept her checks. "You want me to go with you, call and I'll meet you just before the game. If not, tell Tommy to invite a pal along, okay? I'll understand."

Their conversation was attracting the attention of some of the other diners, but Bones didn't care. Bingo did. "I can't talk to you now, Sal," she said. "You're hopeless, you know that?"

"Yeah, but I'm not so terrible, right?"

She went back into the kitchen without answering him, but she kept the Lakers tickets. Bones decided he ought to take some of the pressure off her, so he left the room. Marty saw him heading out. "Bad, huh?" he said. "She won't talk to you, right?"

"She'll get over it," Bones said.

"Maybe," Marty answered. "Women never forget and they never forgive. It's not in their nature, Bones. Guys, shit, we're all patsies. Hate each other one day, buy each other drinks the next."

"Not if you're Italian and from the south, Marty," Bones assured him. "There it's a question of honor."

"That so? I'm glad I'm Jewish."

"Well, you guys aren't so good on forgiving either," Bones said. "You been to the Middle East recently?"

"That's just racial crap," Marty answered. "Mankind in action."

"Yeah, we like all that killing and torture. Nothing like religion to bring it all on. Sometimes I think the whole world stinks."

"The horses don't stink," Marty said, "though some of the people in the game do. Hey, what's with this Pug Simpson riding for Jake? What's up? You ever seen Pug Simpson arm a horse? He could keep an elephant away from a bale of hay."

"Don't worry, he'll ride for Jake. Only the mare ain't much. She'll maybe pick up a piece of the purse."

"Where's the girl? She can ride and she tries every time."

"She's been sick, but she's back."

"You handling her book?"

"Not officially, Marty. Advice, that's all. I'll see you."

"Yeah. You want me to say something nice about you to Bingo?"

"No, she'll get there on her own. She'll just think I put you up to it."

He gave Marty's shoulder a light pat and left.

***

He grabbed a bite to eat at a deli a few blocks from his place, then drove home. It was about ten o'clock when he nosed the car down Laurel toward the building's underground parking structure. A black Acura sedan was parked a few yards away down the street, the hood facing toward him. There was a man sitting behind the wheel whose features Bones couldn't quite make out, but he wasn't about to take any chances. Ever since leaving New Jersey he had made it a point every waking moment of never taking anything even slightly out of the usual for granted, especially at night. He'd left no unfinished business behind, no debts, no obligations, and he'd been cleared by his capo, all that was true, but there were threads that still linked him to his past and always would. Every year he'd heard from Tony Ears from time to time, sometimes directly, sometimes through intermediaries. In that world, you were out but never quite out. You kept your eyes and ears open, your mouth shut. That way you stood a chance. Now it occurred to him that he hadn't heard from Tony Ears in months. He'd heard that Tony had been sent up for a while. Who had taken his place? He hadn't asked; he didn't know. He'd used silence as a shield. But now here was some guy seated behind the wheel of a car down the block from his apartment. It could be nothing; it could be everything. Being careful had become second nature to Bones, an automatic reflex, like breathing, like the beating of his heart.

So instead of turning into his parking space, he drove quickly past the structure, turned right onto a side street, then right again and parked on the street. He waited about ten minutes, then got out, walked back to the corner of Laurel and stood under the shelter of a small carrotwood tree. The Acura was still parked there, the man still sitting behind the wheel. Bones waited another few minutes, until two cars came slowly up Laurel, their headlights shining into the Acura's rear window. Bones was at least ten pounds overweight, but he could move very fast over a short distance of ground. He ran up the sidewalk and reached the Acura just after the cars had gone past it. He had planned to kick the window in, if he had to, but he was in luck. The passenger door was unlocked, so he was able to slide quickly into the seat beside the driver. Startled, the man turned just as Bones grabbed his right arm with his left hand and his neck with his right one. The man's eyes began to bulge as he gasped for air. It occurred to Bones that maybe Harvey Stone hadn't been waiting to try and kill him, so he now let him go, but told him to keep both hands on the steering wheel where he could see them. Harvey Stone was still gulping for air as Bones finished patting him down. "Jesus, man," he said hoarsely, "I just wanted to talk to you."

"At this time of night, pal? I got a phone."

"I wasn't sure you'd see me. And the phone's no good."

"So what was the plan?"

"I was waiting for you to get home so we could talk one on one."

"Yeah? About what?"

"Can I move my hands?"

"Keep them right where they are."

"Okay, so reach into my inside jacket pocket. You'll find an envelope." Bones reached in and pulled it out; it was a fat one. "Open it," Harvey Stone said.

Bones glanced inside and saw a stack of crisp new bills, which he didn't bother to count. "How much?" he asked.

"Fifty thousand dollars," Harvey Stone said. "It's for you."

"No shit. What am I, a charity? A good cause? What's the payoff for, Harvey?"

"Mr. Furman would appreciate your discretion in certain matters."

"He would, huh?"

"Do you have any photographs?"

"Sure," Bones lied. "Several very good ones."

"Let's consider this a payment for the negatives," Stone said. "As well as for your discretion."

"Paul Furman is a great human being," Bones said. "What's to be so discreet about? He's going to run for the Senate, right? He may even win. He'll make a shitty senator, but that would put him in good company. The people get what they deserve, right, pal? You can fool them all of the time; we know that. So what's Furman so worried about? A little gossip, a few snapshots? Keep your fucking money." He stuffed the envelope back into Harvey Stone's pocket.

"Don't be a fool, Righetti," Stone said. "We know all about you, where you come from, your connections. We can make it unpleasant for you. You don't want that."

"You won't do shit," Bones said, "but I'll tell you what. I want to read in the papers, especially the *Racing Form*, in the next few days that Paul Furman, out of the generosity of his great heart, has made a fifty-thousand-dollar contribution to the jockeys' retirement fund. You know, the one that takes care of crippled old riders too broke to care for themselves. Think you can arrange that, Harvey?"

Harvey Stone didn't answer. Bones got out of the car, then looked back inside. Stone was still sitting there, frozen into position, his hands still gripping the top of the steering wheel. "Think of the good publicity for the senatorial campaign," Bones said. "Fewer babies to kiss, fewer photo ops, fewer outright lies. Just a simple vote-generating gesture. I'm surprised you didn't think of it yourself. After all, the guy is in the horse business."

Bones stepped away from the car and slammed the passenger door as hard as he could; then he stood there and watched Stone drive away.

CHAPTER 25

"I thought you were a smart guy," Steve Bullion said. "You can't be serious about running that plater of yours in the Derby. I just heard about it in the racing office."

Jake turned to look at him. He and Bones had been standing at the rail at Clockers Corner, watching Jill gallop Abernathy's good two-year-old, and so they hadn't seen Bullion come up. But there he was, dressed in one of his usual outfits—black jeans, a black leather windbreaker, a Yankees baseball cap jammed low over his eyes—and with a cynical smile on his lips. "Well you're probably right, Steve," Jake said. "It wasn't so much my idea as my owner's. She kind of insisted, and she's used to getting her way."

"Since when are you letting your owners decide where to run your horses?" he asked. "Any owner does that to me I tell him to take his horses out of my barn."

"Sure you do," Bones said. "If Prince Baboom al Shitabunch, or whoever it is who puts up the dough for your operation, decided to tell you where to run them, you'd jump through a hoop for him like a little trained dog."

"I ain't talking to you," Bullion said. "I'm talking to a good horse-man here. He knows better."

"I tried to talk her out of it," Jake admitted. "Yeah, I'd have waited, sure, run him through his conditions. But Ester Gale, she makes up her mind, it's hard to move her."

"See, Steve, we don't have forty horses here," Bones said. "We've got this one kind of funny-looking gelding we bought off a trainer who didn't think he could run much, but it turns out the horse can run like the fucking wind. You got a horse in the race?"

"You know I don't, Bones," Bullion said. "I don't give a shit if you run or not. I'm just telling you what I think. I don't rush my horses."

"Yeah, you're a good trainer," Bones said. "Only it was you who got rid of this little horse. Well, actually, he ain't so little. Great big long stride, especially on the turns. Looks like a fucking ballet dancer out there, right? Whirls right past you on the way home. It would sort of make you look bad if he won the race, right?"

"Fuck you, Bones."

"Easy, Steve," Bones said, smiling.

"We're just talking horses here," Jake said. "Back off, both of you."

Bullion shrugged and walked away. "Good luck," he called back. "You'll need it to get a piece of that pie."

Who's to say he's wrong, Bones thought to himself. Thanks to that crazy old broad's insistence that they run Tumultuous in the Santa Anita Derby, they'd had to cough up fifteen thousand dollars to enter and then, if he actually ran, another fifteen grand before post time. Thirty thousand bucks for the privilege of maybe getting their brains beat out. Of course, if he did win, they'd pick up the winner's share of $450,000 from the total purse of $750,000, not chump change, right? Still, it was a big risk. Bones found himself wishing that Jake had tried harder to talk Ester Gale Dinworthy out of this move, to let their horse develop facing softer competition. There were other stakes races further down the line for their champion. The idea would have been to build up his confidence in a series of easier contests before throwing him into the arena with the top contenders. Screw the Triple Crown; there were all those big races in the late summer and fall to shoot for.

From what Bones had gleaned from reading the *Racing Form*, the field for this Derby figured to be a real tough one, boasting several seasoned contenders in addition to the overwhelming favorite in the race, Carl Everett's Terry's Dream, undefeated through his first five races and by widening margins. He had all of the makings of a true classic colt—pedigree, speed, style, temperament, and adaptability to the shape of the race. After Bullion's departure, Bones shut his eyes and tried to envision exactly how Tumultuous could possibly compete at this level and he couldn't. If somebody had come up to him that morning and offered to buy him out of what he'd already put into the animal, he'd have accepted like a shot.

Just then Jill came riding up to them on High Jinks, Abernathy's feisty little colt. "Wow, Jake," she said, "I couldn't hardly hold him. But he's so green. Every time some horse comes near him, he just wants to take off. He's moving good, though."

Jake nodded. "We'll back off him a little," he said. "We're a couple of months away, and I don't want him to hurt himself. Just slow gallops till we get to Hollywood. Maybe we can get him fit by Del Mar."

"Mr. Abernathy may have himself a real nice little colt," she said.

"That'll make his day," Bones said. "If you can hide his workouts and let Abernathy bet a bundle on him first time out."

"I don't know about that," Jake said. "My job is to get the horse fit and ready. The betting doesn't interest me."

"Don't you want to keep your owners happy?"

Jake ignored him. "Take him back to the barn, Jill," he said. "Tell Luis to walk him and you get on Sammy. We're going to breeze him three, and Eduardo ought to have him ready by now."

"Sure thing." She flashed him a quick smile and turned the colt back toward the barn.

In these couple of weeks since Jill had come back to work, she'd only won one more race out of five mounts, that one on a mediocre claimer of Matt Logan's. Not that she'd ridden badly in any of her efforts; it was just that the California scene still didn't have room for a woman rider, even an apprentice with an attractive weight allowance. Not even Julie Krone's success on the local scene had made much of a difference. Jill had the highest percentage of winners at the meet, but the mounts were not coming her way. If she'd have let Bones handle her book, it might have made a difference, but all she wanted to do now was work for Jake, maybe ride the occasional horse for the Logans. She had begun to think about eventually moving east to the Maryland or New York circuits, where her gender wouldn't prejudice anyone against her, but that possibility lay in the future. For now she had Jake and, above all, Tumultuous to worry about.

It angered Bones, though, to think about it. What did these good old boys expect of the kid? All she did was ride the hair off their horses, in a sport where one mistake can cost you your life or cripple you. That was why out of the starting gate an ambulance tracked the field toward the finish line. This kid was a race rider, no doubt about it, and Bones could have helped her, badgered trainers and owners into hiring her, but so far she had resisted him. She seemed to be happy at last and safe in her new life and that obviously mattered more to her at this point than recognition and success. In the unlikely event, of course, that she could pick up at least a piece of the Derby purse with Tumultuous, all that could change. It would be hard to overlook talent when it loomed before your eyes in terms of wins and dollars earned.

Tumultuous breezed the easiest kind of three-furlong workout that morning, with Jill never even clucking to him or asking him for any speed. "What'd you catch him in?" Bones asked.

"Thirty-five and two," the trainer said. "About what I expected."

Bones turned his back to the track and leaned up against the rail. A cheerful hum of conversation arose from the hundred or so fans at Clockers Corner having breakfast or sipping coffee as they watched the workouts. He shut his eyes and turned his face toward the sun, thinking to himself that this had to be the best of all possible ways to spend an early morning—him, Jake, the horse people, and the animals themselves. Maybe what was wrong with the world was a lack of racing emporiums around the globe. Maybe they should open racetracks in the Gaza Strip, all over Africa, in Iraq and Iran and Syria and China. Yeah, even in the DMZ between the two Koreas. Weapons of mass destruction? Nah. Who do you like in the double?

***

Paul Furman's move on Jill coincided with his announcement a few days before the Derby that he was planning to donate fifty thousand dollars to the Don MacBeth Memorial Jockey Fund. The gift would be made through his newly created foundation that would, over the course of years, donate regularly to a bunch of charities connected to horse racing. If he were to be elected to the U.S. Senate, Furman also stated to the press, he'd push hard in Congress for measures designed to protect other workers, like grooms, hotwalkers, exercise riders, mutuel clerks, and racing employees in general. The announcement made the front page of the *Daily Racing Form* and was praised by one and all. As for the pure gambling aspect of racing, Furman reassured the bigwigs in his party that he would be against putting slot machines onto the grounds of the tracks themselves and he'd oppose the spread of other forms of gambling in the state, though he had nothing to say about the Indian gaming casinos, whose financial support, Bones knew, he needed for his campaign. To celebrate his gift, Furman was going to be asked to award the trophy to the winner of the Santa Anita Derby that Saturday. "You'll have a friend of racing in Congress," Furman declared at the end of his press conference.

Bones sighed, got up from the table in his breakfast nook, and made himself a second cappuccino. He sat back down, opened the *Form* to the day's past-performance charts, and began handicapping.

That was the morning Harvey Stone followed Jill home from the racetrack. He parked below Jake's spread and called her from his cell phone. "Mr. Furman would like very much to see you," he told her. "It's very important to him. He wants you to know how sorry he is for some of the things that have happened."

She didn't answer right away but sat on the edge of the bed, holding the receiver in her hand. She could hear Harvey Stone's voice as if from a great distance, a tinny plaintive sound, a call from a now distant past.

"Jill?" the voice called out. "Jill? You there?"

She put the phone to her ear. "There ain't nothing he can say to me that matters a damn," she said.

"You'll want to hear what he has to say," Harvey Stone insisted and then gave her an address a few miles away in Sierra Madre. "He'll be there this evening around seven. He'll wait for you."

She hesitated again, shut her eyes, and heard herself answering, "Yeah, I'll go. But I'm telling a friend of mine where I'm going to be."

"Mr. Furman would like to see you alone."

"Yeah, I figured," she said, "but I want this friend of mine to know where I'm at. Otherwise, forget it."

"Okay," Harvey Stone said. "He'll be expecting you."

No sooner had he hung up than Jill called Bones, who had been sipping his second cappuccino and working the *Form*. "Don't go," was his first reaction. "Not a good idea."

"I got to go, Sal," she said. "I got to put an end to it."

"We did that already; it's over."

"No, it ain't. I ain't done it; you did," she said. "It's kind of up to me, don't you get it? I got to do this for myself."

"You want this guy to knock you around again?"

"He ain't going to hurt me now, Sal," she said. "I'm a lot stronger than I was. You got to trust me."

"He's got a hold on you, Jill—"

"I been dealing with it, Sal. This doctor I been seeing, she's really helped a lot. She'd tell me I got to do this."

"You sure? Why don't you ask her?"

"I ain't got time. I know she's out of town a couple of days, some conference or other back East. But I can do this, Sal. You got to trust me."

"You, maybe. Him, no."

"I'm going to see him, Sal."

"Tell me where you're going to be."

She gave him the address in Sierra Madre and he wrote it down. "Don't worry, Sal," she said, "I'll be okay."

"Why don't you wait for me after the races and I'll take you there?"

"No, Sal, no way."

"Okay, but if I don't hear from you within a couple of hours, I'm coming after you."

She didn't answer him right away but let her silence speak for her. "I'm going to handle this, Sal," she said. "It's up to me. You got to know that, don't you?"

Bones didn't know any such thing. All he could think about was what had happened to her, how she'd been taken advantage of, lied to, sexually abused, practically blackmailed into giving herself up to this sick, ambitious, ruthless guy. The fact that in his own way Paul Furman was as vulnerable as she was and tortured by his unhappy marriage, the death of his neurotic traumatized kid, his abnormal sexual appetites, just didn't matter to Bones. What mattered was Jill, whom he valued, as much for her courage as for her grace and talent as an athlete. And he was afraid for her, because of what had happened to Dulcie Clark. Furman might not have killed her, she might have died of natural causes, they'd probably never know, but Bones didn't think so. He could take care of himself, but Jill?

The address Stone had given her was that of a small two-story brick house set behind a row of tall cypresses at the end of a short driveway leading up into a canyon at the foot of the hills that cradled the village of Sierra Madre directly below. Jill drove up to the front entrance, parked, got out and rang the doorbell. She was dressed in her working clothes—jeans, boots, a plaid long-sleeved shirt open at the collar. She wore no makeup, no jewelry, not even earrings, nothing to even hint to Paul Furman that she might be available to him.

He opened the door for her and she walked in, passing him without acknowledging his presence. When he shut the door behind her, she turned to confront him. He smiled and offered her a drink. She turned him down. "What do you want, Paul?" she asked.

"Come on in here where we can talk," he said, leading the way into the living room, which was small, rustic-looking, with low-lying masculine leather armchairs and a big sofa facing a huge TV screen. The walls were decorated with racing prints and hunting trophies; a large bearskin rug covered the floor under a glass-topped rectangular coffee table. Nothing suggested to Jill the possible presence of a woman. "Please sit down," he said.

She shook her head. "No, this ain't going to take long," she said. "Let's get it over with. What do you want?"

"Oh, Jill, this is hard on both of us, I know that," he said. "I took a lot of my frustrations, my unhappiness out on you. I was wrong. I even blamed you for Laura Lee's death. I don't know now how I could have done that."

"But you did."

"I did a lot of wrong things, I admit that," he said. "But let me ask you, Jill, how was it at first? How did I treat you when you first came to work for me?"

"You was real nice, Paul; you was good to me."

"Yes, and when I realized what Carl had done to you, how did I treat you then?"

She looked at him. He stood across the room from her, his back to the fireplace. He seemed almost to be dancing in the dim light, his shape in its open-necked white shirt and dark slacks poised to move, his sunburned face tight with anticipation, his eyes nearly invisible under his heavy brow. "You was always good to me, Paul," she said softly.

"You see?" He held out a hand toward her.

"But you changed," she said quickly. "Stay away from me now."

"It's because I fell in love with you," he said.

"No, that ain't right," she said. "It's because you wanted me, that's all. You saw how I was after Carl dumped me and you took advantage of it."

"You didn't want me to?"

"No."

He began to move around the room like an animal in a cage, talking as much to himself as to her. "Those looks you gave me, the little smiles, the little hints you dropped about handsome older men, all the teasing, the way you brushed up against me once when we were standing by the fence looking at the yearlings, the way you touched me, your hand on mine that day. Admit it, Jill, you came on to me and you know it. I was alone, with a sick wife who didn't want to have anything to do with me and I fell for you. Come on now, admit it."

"No," she said, shaking her head, "no. You took advantage … I was pretty desperate, I couldn't see no way out. All I had was this job with the horses, and I wanted you to like me, that's all, to make myself really needed, so I'd be able to go on working for you, to get a life. And then you kicked it all apart cause you wanted to fuck me. That's the way it was."

"And you didn't want me to."

"No. I tried to fight you off."

"At first. But then you gave in, didn't you? Didn't you? You wanted me, Jill."

"No, I just couldn't fight you off. That's how you ought to put it. You and your dirty talk. The way you came on and whispered to me, the way you tore my clothes off, the way you took me right there in your office that day. I did my best, goddamn you, but it wasn't enough! You ruined everything!"

"But you went along with it, Jill, didn't you? You wanted me, too, didn't you? You liked what we had together. Don't lie to me, Jill. Don't lie to yourself. We had something there for a while and it was great, it was tremendous. And it can be that way again."

"No, it can't. It's over," she said. "It's taken me a while to get a grip on all this. Yeah, sure, I gave in to you, I always gave in to you. But no more. It's over." She turned away from him as if to leave, but he came up behind her, grabbed her by the shoulders and turned her toward him. She put both hands on his chest to push him away, but he leaned in to kiss her neck. She fought free of him and retreated behind one of the chairs. "You stay away from me!" she shouted.

"Jill, please, I need you," he said. "We're really alike, you know that. We need each other." Again he made a move toward her, but she managed to stay away from him.

"And what about Dulcie?" she said. "What about her? Did she need you, too? What did you do to her?"

He stopped and stared at her. "Nothing," he said. "You know that. Nothing. It was a tragic event. I had nothing to do with it."

"Dulcie knew about us. She was going to go public with it. You knew that."

"We had talked," he said. "I told her how I felt about you."

"And she said great."

"Yes, she accepted it."

"You're lying, Paul. She told you that if we didn't stop, she'd tell people about us."

"She'd never do that."

"You made sure she wouldn't."

He didn't answer her right away this time. He just stood there and stared at her. "My God, look at you," he said. "Look at the two of us. You say you don't want me, you don't need me, and I know you don't mean it. And me? I'm trying to do something important, something big with my life and my career, and I look at you standing there, your eyes so full of hatred for me, and I still want you." He took a step toward her. "Jill, please …"

"If you touch me," she hissed, "I swear to God I'll tell the whole goddamn world about you. About Dulcie and about us, all about us, Paul, and where I was and why when Laura Lee drowned. You hear me? I don't give a shit no more. It's over for you, everything. You're history. And now I'm getting out of here and you ain't never going to bother me again. Never. You got that? Never."

She headed quickly for the front door. As she opened it, she cast one backward glance before stepping out into the night. Paul Furman was standing in the doorway to the living room, immobile, his face frozen in grief.

CHAPTER 26

O n the day of the race, Bones showed up at the barn just after seven to find Ester Gale Dinworthy already on the scene, her hair a bright shade of purple under one of her broad-brimmed straw hats, her large body all but invisible under an overflow of pink and orange shawls. She was wielding her silver-knobbed walking stick like a baton, her usual torrent of observations overwhelming the scene. Jake looked slightly dazed by it all, managing every now and then to slip a word or two past her to Eduardo about what needed to be done. Bones lingered by the corner of the barn long enough to stretch and enjoy the feel of the early morning sun on his back. It was one of those spectacular Southern California spring days, the sky overhead already a bright blue and a soft breeze blowing gently through the barn area. He looked in vain for Jill but figured she must be out on the track with one of the horses.

"You're not paying attention to me, Giacomo," Ester Gale was saying as Bones joined them. "I'm trying to explain to you what needs to be done to assure our triumph this afternoon. You must relay my instructions to this young woman you have seen fit to put up on our champion and about whose skill and trustworthiness I harbor distinct reservations. Am I making myself clear, Giacomo?"

"You sure are, Mrs. Dinworthy," Jake said. "But if you'll excuse me now, I have things I have to take care of this morning."

"What could possibly be more important than making certain no mistakes are being made with our magnificent animal?" she replied. "Tell one of your subordinates to concern himself with the trivial matters. We must discuss the strategy of the race. I insist upon having your full attention."

"I can't do that, Mrs. Dinworthy," Jake explained. "I'm personally responsible for the care of all these horses, not just Sammy."

"Sammy?" Her eyebrows shot upward in horror. "Sammy?"

"That's what we call him around the barn," Jake said. "It's his nickname."

"This is not acceptable," Ester Gale Dinworthy said. "The horse's name is Tumultuous, a splendid, poetic appellation."

"Hey, I know a guy who went to St. Peter's in Rome once to see that statue by Mike Angelo," Bones said. "He called it 'Jesus under glass.' And for him the Statue of Liberty was always 'that broad out in the harbor with the torch.' "

"Outrageous!" Ester Gale said, turning furiously on him. "You, Mr. Boner, are clearly a vulgarian. I'm ashamed to be associated with you."

"Tough shit," Bones said. "And that's also the way the cookie crumbles. But I'll tell you what, babe—"

"Hey, Bones, knock it off!" Jake interrupted.

But something in Bones had snapped. Jill had hardly spoken two words to him since her meeting with Furman. What had she done? He needed to know; he deserved better. What the hell was wrong with women anyway? And now here was this stupid, spoiled old phony lecturing everybody. He leaned in on her. "Here's what, babe," he said. "After the race, no matter what happens, you can buy out my share of Sammy for what I paid for him plus whatever share of the purse he might win, okay? How does that strike you, kiddo?"

"Kiddo? Your command of the English language is greatly to be deplored," she said. "I shall never speak to you again."

"Terrific news," Bones said. "Now why don't you take your fat ass out of here so the man can take care of his horses and we'll all get together for a happy time later in the paddock."

Ester Gale Dinworthy whirled in fury on Jake. "I'm going this instant," she announced. "I'm deeply disturbed, Giacomo, that you have seen fit to plunge me into a financial arrangement with a gang-ster and a philistine. As far as I am concerned, I shall forever ignore his existence, and I expect you to extricate me from all future contact with him. Failing that, I shall have to take drastic measures to assure my own position in the future. I'm deeply disappointed in you, Giacomo." She proceeded to stage an exit worthy of a queen, a great swishing and flouncing of garments, a rat-a-tat-tat with the walking stick, a bobbing up and down of her feathered headdress as she moved toward her limousine. As the door slammed behind her and her chauffeur nosed the car out toward the exit, Jake stared at Bones. "What the hell were you thinking of, Bones?" he asked. "You trying to lose me a client?"

"No," Bones answered, "I was trying to make your job a little easi-er. You ought to thank me."

"Horse shit," Jake said, stepping past him to talk to Eduardo, who had retreated to the end of the shed row to get away from the friction.

Bones went into the tack room, poured himself a cup of coffee, then walked down the row of stalls to where Tumultuous stood qui-etly in place, his head thrust out into the morning air. And suddenly Bones had this overwhelming feeling of joy, as if he'd just hit the lot-tery jackpot. He stuck a fat carrot into the horse's mouth and listened to him chew it into satisfying little chunks; then he patted his neck and whispered to him. "One time, baby," he heard himself say, "just this one time. Show the unbelieving bastards what you're made of. Stick it to 'em!"

You've got to be nuts to be in the horse business, he thought. You find yourself talking to animals, you find yourself trusting in destiny, you find yourself believing in glory, you feel yourself close to the secret of immortality. You shut your eyes and one vision dominates—that huge conquering move that sweeps you to the finish line in a thunder of pounding hooves. You've been swept to rainbow's end.

***

He spent the next part of the morning wondering what to do with himself. When Jill had finished galloping the last of Jake's horses and was finishing up her chores, he asked her to have breakfast with him. She accepted but glanced toward the tack room. "Want to ask Jake?"

"He's still talking to his clients. Anyway, he's pissed off at me."

"What about?"

"Ask him."

"Okay, go on over to the kitchen and wait for me."

"Want me to order you something?"

"Couple of eggs, sunny side up, toast, no butter, and low-fat milk."

"That ain't enough. You got to be strong."

"I am strong, but I still got to watch my weight. Go on, Sal. I'll be right over."

When she got there about ten minutes later, Bones was sitting at a corner table in the low rectangular room, paper towels draped over her plate to keep it warm. He was nursing another cup of coffee, the fingers of his left hand drumming a soft tattoo on the Formica surface of the table. She slid into the seat opposite him and reached across the table to put her hand over his. "What's wrong, Sal?" she asked. "Never seen you so edgy before, like an old cat in heat."

"I never had a horse in a race this big before," he mumbled. "Maybe I'll wash out on my way to the paddock." He made an effort to smile, but failed. "Anyway, it's you who ought to be nervous, right?"

She shook her head. "No," she said, "it's up to Sammy. I'll be okay." She peeled the paper towels off her breakfast and took a bite of her eggs.

"So what's going on with you, Jill?" he asked. "You okay? I hardly heard from you since the other night."

She went on eating, cramming the food into her mouth, head bent low over the plate. "It's okay," she said at last, her mouth full of eggs and dry toast. "Yeah, it's okay. I took care of it. Told you I would."

"You sure?"

She nodded vigorously. "It's over." Now she quickly finished up the last of her breakfast and looked seriously at him. "So it's true? You sold your share of Sammy to Mrs. Dinworthy?"

"Oh, so Jake told you. Yeah. I don't want to have to go through this every fucking time. See, it's not me, kid. It's not only I don't want to put up with that old broad, though she's bad enough. Somebody ought to put her in a cage with a gag in her mouth, you know what I'm saying? She's going to drive Jake off his rocker again. There ain't enough pills in the world to protect you from goofs like her."

"And if Sammy wins?"

"Ups the price on my share, know what I mean? It's a good deal. I got to get back to my life. So maybe you'll let me handle your book, right?"

"Yeah, I might. If Sammy wins. Maybe people will want to hire me then, right?"

"I could help persuade them, but you got to get your strength up."

"I'm working on it," she said. "I drink a lot of power stuff."

He stared at her, amazed at her quiet confidence. "How are you going to ride this race?" he asked. "You thought about it?"

"I'll let Sammy tell me what to do."

"That's no answer. Every good jock ought to know what the other horses in the race might do. You have to look at form and speed. You don't do that?"

"No. Jake tells me what to do and then the horse tells me out on the track."

Bones leaned back in his seat, folded his arms and looked at her. "Maybe you're right," he said. "Most jockeys think too much. Their brains are too small to handle it." He smiled as he said this.

She giggled. "Thanks a bunch, Sal." She stood up. "Hey, I got to go. I need to catch a little shuteye. I'll see you in the paddock."

"How come you're so fucking cool and I'm tied up in knots?"

"I'm a pro, Sal," she said. "I don't know much about a lot of stuff, I guess you know that, but this is who I am, see? It's up to me and Sammy now to get it done."

After she'd gone, Bones lingered behind. He spread the *Form* out before him and again burrowed into the numbers on his charts. He'd already worked them and reworked them and tried to account for every possible scenario, and nothing he'd come up with reassured him. Tumultuous had drawn the three hole in a six-horse field. Inside of him were two late closers from the East, Balding and Go Lad. Just to his outside, in post four, was Terry's Dream, who had some speed but, as a long-striding horse, preferred to come from just off the pace, two or three lengths back. The two outside horses, Lavishly and Watchagonnado, were the speed; they'd go out on the lead, hopefully kill each other off to set it up for the closers. It was impossible to figure out where Tumultuous fit into this picture. If he went out of the gate after the leaders, he could be cooked by the pace; if he waited, he'd have Terry's Dream to his outside, possibly boxing him in along the rail. Bones told himself he really shouldn't risk a dime on the race and wouldn't. But then, as he was wondering what to do, it struck him with the force of a hammer blow that he didn't have to do anything. They were chasing a huge pot of three-quarters of a million bucks; even a third or a fourth would enrich him. Bones felt as if someone had just pricked a big balloon in his guts, and he relaxed into a weird sort of glacial calm. He folded up his *Form* and strolled out of the cafeteria to the parking lot, where he got into his car, partly lowered the windows, leaned way back and snoozed for half an hour. Then, at eleven o'clock, he walked into the track and sat down on a bench under a tree beside the paddock railing. He thought about his life.

It had become a lot simpler in the past few days. Bingo and Tommy had allowed him to show up and join them at the Lakers game, after which Bingo had let him come back to her place for a drink. After Tommy went to bed, though, she hadn't let him stay or even kiss her on his way out. "We'll see, Sal," she said, keeping a hand on his arm as he stood at the door. "It's too soon. We got a way to go here. You still seeing someone else?"

"That's over with, Bingo. Done. There's no one else."

She didn't press him but just looked at him as he stepped out into the hallway. "Thanks, Sal. Tommy had a real good time. It was nice of you. I'll see you, all right?"

"Yeah. Sure." And he knew as he walked out of there that maybe they'd be all right. It would take time; it always did with dames, at least the best ones. And then the day after they decided to run Sammy in the Derby, he called and left a message on her voice mail that he'd leave two tickets for her at the clubhouse will-call window that Saturday. He gave her his box number and said there'd be two seats for her and Tommy. "I know you don't give a shit about the races," he ended, "but this is a big deal for me. I'd sure like to have you there."

That was also the day D.J. called him from Las Vegas saying she had the weekend free and did he want to meet up with her somewhere. He told her she was a great gal, but that he'd made a commitment to someone else and they'd just have to be friends from now on. "Hey," she said, "that's all we've ever been, right? I don't commit, you know that. Just a little friendly romance. Not up to it, huh?"

"No, D.J. It don't feel right. I really like this lady."

"Your loss, honey. But it's been fun." And she hung up. A nice gal, he thought, no doubt about it, but what the hell, you can't go through life slashing and burning the people who really care about you.

He left his seat by the paddock before the first race and went up to his box, where he found Moonshine and Stats waiting for him. Sweeps, for some reason, was missing, but Bones preferred it that way. Actually, he'd have been happier being alone just then, even though Stats was excited to see him. "I've been looking at the numbers," he announced. "I think your horse has got a good chance. Providing the girl don't fuck up."

"How do you figure?" Bones asked, not really caring but knowing that Stats would want to explain it to him anyway.

Which he did. His analysis of the race had Tumultuous being pinned along the rail and getting clear in time to make his one big move. Stats, being a numbers guy, couldn't actually envision how the race might be run; all he could do was juggle his figs as if they were bowling pins. "See?" he concluded. "Your horse makes his move on the turn, opens up on the others, and holds off the favorite."

"So why don't we just go and cash our tickets on him now?" Moonshine asked sarcastically. "Who needs to see the fucking race? It's all decided, right?"

Bones let them argue it out while he went in search of a sandwich and a root beer. Instead of going back to his box, he lingered at a table in the clubhouse, just sweating it out. The Derby was the fifth race on the card, early enough so it could be televised nationally back East, which luckily meant that Bones wouldn't have to worry through seven other contests. Maybe for the only time in his life he was wearing a jacket and a tie to the track and only the air-conditioning was keeping him from washing out like a crazy two-year-old. He couldn't get his head cleared either and had forgotten all about Bingo and Tommy. When they didn't make the first race, however, he figured they'd decided not to show up, but when he headed for the paddock twenty minutes before the Derby there they were, standing by the railing outside the enclosure. Bingo was all dressed up in a cute little pink-and-green mini-skirted outfit she'd sewn herself and Tommy was wearing his only pair of long pants, a pair of dark-gray slacks, a white shirt open at the collar, and a navy-blue blazer with gold buttons. They waved to him and he hurried over.

"Hey," he said, "come on in here!" And he led them around to the entrance so they could join him on the grass.

"You must be hot," Bingo said, dabbing at the sweat on his forehead with a tiny silk handkerchief.

"I'm washing out in the post parade," he said. "Luckily, it ain't me who's doing the running."

Just then the horses came filing into the walking ring from under the saddling shed. A silent crowd of beady-eyed fans lined up four deep along the rail to eye them. "Is that ours?" Tommy asked, pointing at Tumultuous, as Eduardo led him into the circle.

"Yeah, that's him," Bones said. "He looks good, huh?"

"Yeah," Tommy said. "He's going to win, isn't he?"

"I don't know, Tommy. There's some tough horses in here, but he's going to do his best. That's all you can ask for, you know?"

"Wow, he's awesome!" Tommy said. "I want to bet on him!"

Bones glanced at the tote board. Terry's Dream was the clear favorite at 8-5, with the two Eastern invaders, Balding and Go Lad, at 3-1 and

9-2, respectively. Tumultuous, Lavishly, and Watchagonnado were the outsiders in the betting, with Tumultuous hovering around 12-1. Bones decided he wouldn't look at the odds again. What was the point? For once he didn't have to risk a dime on his horse; all he had to do was root him home. It made him a little dizzy just to stand there and think about it.

He decided it might be a good idea to avoid Ester Gale Dinworthy for as long as possible, so he didn't join Jake and her around their horse until the last few minutes, when Jill appeared with the other riders from the jockeys' room. He introduced Bingo and Tommy to her, but ignored Ester Gale, who was glaring at him from about four feet away. As usual, she looked like a ship under sail. "Who's that?" Tommy asked.

"That's Mrs. Dinworthy," Bones said. "She owns the horse."

"I thought you did."

"I own part of him. She owns most of him."

"What part? Like the legs?"

"Yeah, the best part."

"Boy, she's weird," Tommy said.

"Outrageous!" Ester Gale Dinworthy exclaimed. "Appalling!"

Jake and Jill ignored this exchange. All Jake said to Jill now was, "Okay, it's you and the horse, Jill. You know him better than anyone, but I wouldn't rush him."

"I ain't going to, Jake." She patted Tumultuous' neck just as the paddock judge called the riders up.

As the horses began to file out toward the track, Jill again leaned over Tumultuous' neck and gave him a reassuring pat. The horse responded by shaking his head up and down, while bouncing lightly on his feet like a dancer warming up. "He's on the muscle," Bones murmured. "He's going to run real good."

"On the muscle?" Tommy asked. "What's that mean?"

"It means he's ready to run, right?" Bingo said, looking at Bones.

"Yeah, that's right." Bones was watching Everett's horse in line directly behind theirs and he felt a sudden stab of pure panic. Terry's

Dream looked every bit as tremendous, even more so, than Tumultuous.

The champions, the monsters in this game, look it. They dominate by their very presence, as if they're sending a message to their opponents. Look at me, their looks say, look at me in wonder, I'm the best, I'm all muscle and breeding and speed and courage and desire and I'm going to beat your brains out, I'm going to humiliate you, I'm going to leave you in my wake with shattered confidence and broken dreams. The way Secretariat dominated Sham and broke his heart, the way Affirmed looked Alydar in the eye and wore him down race after race, the way Seabiscuit took on War Admiral and left him lumbering in the dust of his flying hooves. Thoroughbreds aren't competitive? They wouldn't run if people didn't force them to? They'd just stand around under trees all day between playful romps in open pastures? What a crock of shit, Bones thought. These are trained athletes, they want to win, they love the challenge, they know how good they are. Bones wasn't at all sure Tumultuous could handle this kind of pressure, mainly because he'd never had to before, whereas Terry's Dream and Balding and Go Lad were all coming into the race off stakes wins in important contests. Tumultuous was suddenly being matched against the best and it was scary, even to Bones, tough guy that he was supposed to be.

As they left the paddock Bones found himself walking alongside Carl Everett, who was with a group of slickly dressed Bay Area aristocrats, the men in dark business suits, the women in elegant fashions from the Guccis, Armanis, and Versaces of the style scene. Everett looked at Bones pityingly. "I suppose I should wish you and Jill good luck," he said, with the hint of a sneer around his mouth. "But I hope your cheap little nag eats my dust, so long as Jill doesn't get hurt."

"Your horse has got a lot of class," Bones said. "You don't." He quickly steered Tommy past him, with Bingo right behind them as they made for the escalator up to the grandstand.

"Why did that man say that?" Tommy asked. "What did he mean?"

"You know, Tommy," Bones said, "some people are real jerks, you know what I'm saying?"

"Yeah? If he says anything else to us," Bingo piped up right behind him, "I'll kick him in the balls."

Tommy giggled and Bones turned his head to grin at her. "He's nothing, Bingo," he said. "Just a rich daddy's boy with no manners, that's all. Let's go watch the race."

When they got to the box, Bones introduced Bingo and Tommy to Stats and Moonshine, who proceeded to move into the back row. Bones picked up his binoculars and focused briefly on Tumultuous, who was moving in a slow canter toward the starting gate like a real pro, his neck bowed, Jill standing up in the stirrups and leaning over him, probably talking to him, he figured. Then he passed the glasses over to Tommy, explained to him what he was looking at and all about what might be going to happen. Bingo told Tommy to give the glasses back to him as the horses neared the starting gate, but Bones told the boy to keep them. "I can see real good," he said, thinking to himself that maybe it would be better if he didn't have to watch the race up close. Tumultuous was the only gray in the field, and it would be easy to pick him out all the way around the mile and one-eighth of the contest. Besides, Bones was sweating rivers and Bingo kept dabbing at him with her handkerchief. He stole a quick look at the tote board and noted, to his surprise, that the odds on Tumultuous had plunged to 8-1. Somebody knew something, or maybe Stats wasn't the only numbers guy in the stands who'd figured that the gelding could run and had the style to do well in this race. Terry's Dream was still very much the established favorite at 6-5, while the others were about where they had been all along.

Bones was so nervous that when the gate opened, with thirty thousand fans roaring in excitement around them, he looked away, afraid Tumultuous might have stumbled or broken sideways or had his head turned and been left lengths behind. But Stats' voice rang in his ears. "He broke good," he said. "Go ahead, baby, tuck him in there!"

Bones looked up. The speed horses went out in front on the first turn contending the pace, Terry's Dream had settled back into a comfortable third with Tumultuous to the inside of him, a neck back and running along the rail. Go Lad and Balding were content to trail, running fifth and sixth. On the backstretch Watchagonnado edged away to grab the lead, and as they neared the turn for home, he opened up three lengths in a fast time, with Lavishly now dropping back. Bones was wondering what Jill was going to do, wait and wait or go when Terry's Dream moved. Whatever she did, he could no longer picture her winning the race.

And now Terry's Dream, with top jockey Carl Fuentes up, began to lengthen stride and eat up ground. Jill let him go. Bones looked at the two Eastern horses, who were now also moving, threatening to come up outside her and pin her on the rail again. But just as they were about to draw even with her, Jill asked Tumultuous to make his run. Three lengths ahead of her, Terry's Dream had hooked Watchagonnado and it was clear he had that one beaten and would pull away in the stretch. Bones was just hoping they wouldn't be disgraced, that they might pick up a minor piece of the purse.

But Tumultuous was running now on his favorite part of the track. He accelerated like a frenzied dancer leaping across a stage. He swooped down on the leaders, then past them, running, Bones found out later, one of the fastest quarter-miles in the history of the race. Later that day, in a TV close-up of the rerun, Bones saw Fuentes look in disbelief at Jill as she and Tumultuous zipped past him, opening up more than two lengths by the eighth pole. With the whole of the stretch now in front of her, Jill flattened out along her horse's neck, blending into him, at one with him, every fiber of her taut, lithe body becoming part of the animal beneath her. Not once did she touch him with the whip, Tumultuous already giving her his all, as they sped toward the finish line.

Terry's Dream, however, wasn't done and neither were the closers. All three took off after Tumultuous, with Terry's Dream's long stride eating up the ground as he came relentlessly on. Fifty feet from the finish line he caught up and the two animals lunged for the wire together, Tumultuous and Jill refusing to yield another inch. In the box they were all up out of their seats screaming, poor Tommy, being too short, unable now to see what was happening. Bones grabbed the binoculars and focused on the action just in time to see them nearing the finish, with Go Lad and Balding also there, a neck and a half-length away. Both the leaders' heads were down as they hit the wire, with Terry's Dream suddenly coming over just afterward to slam Tumultuous into the fence. Jill was barely able to hang on, but her colt lurched away, limping badly. Go Lad and Balding skirted Tumultuous, as Jill desperately pulled him up next to the rail.

Jill sprang from the saddle, grabbed the bridle, and held him still as the other horses swept past.

The photo sign went up as Stats began pounding Bones' shoulder. "You won!" he shouted. "You won! His nose was down on the wire first! I saw it!"

Bones didn't answer, but kept his glasses glued to Jill and Sammy, standing there, still, fearful. "What happened, honey?" Bingo asked.

"I don't know," Bones said. "He got slammed after the finish. He's hurt." He handed her the glasses. "I'm going down there. You and Tommy wait here, okay?" She nodded, and Bones turned to make his way down to the winner's circle.

"I'm telling you he won," Stats insisted to Bones on his way out of the box. "But, hey, we'll settle for the dead heat, right? It's still a real nice win, and sometimes the best you can hope for in this life is a dead heat."

Bones didn't respond as he walked off.

"I hope the horse isn't hurt," Bingo said, her arm around Tommy's shoulders.

"It's definitely a dead heat. You know what a dead heat is?" Moonshine said. "It's life. First you got heat; then you're dead."

"You're fucking pathetic," Stats said. "Oh, sorry." He grimaced at Bingo.

"He's heard them words before," she said. "It's okay." She had the glasses focused now on where Jill was still standing beside her horse. The rider was crying.

It took over five minutes for the cameras to confirm Moonshine's assessment; it was a dead heat. "Well, that ain't too bad," Moonshine said. "You split the purse and it's a biggie."

"I could have sworn we had it by a lip," Stats said. "Bad camera angle for sure."

Bingo didn't answer. She had the glasses focused now on Jill and her mount, standing there so patiently, as if nothing were wrong. Jill, however, was still in tears.

By the time Bones got down there, Jake and Eduardo had joined Jill just as the horse ambulance arrived. Tumultuous limped badly, favoring his left front leg, as he moved up the ramp to be taken away, Eduardo in the wagon with him. Jake and Jill walked back to the winner's circle, where Bones was waiting for them. "So, how bad is it?" he asked.

"It's bad," Jake said. "How bad we won't know till X-rays, but he tore or broke something."

"He just come over on me right after the finish," Jill said. "He was trying to savage Sammy."

Her analysis was confirmed later, when Carl Fuentes walked over to apologize to Jake after the ceremony in the winner's circle. "I got no idea he'd do that," he said. "I'm real sorry, man. Maybe we should put blinkers on him next time. I sure hope your horse is okay. He ran a hell of a race."

Only Ester Gale Dinworthy consented to have her picture taken in the winner's circle, holding the trophy—presented to her by Paul Furman—unsmilingly in her arms, after which she confronted Everett. "Your horse is a criminal," she informed him. "If he were a human being, he'd be in jail."

Bones looked at the swarm of people around Paul Furman as the cameras clicked and he smiled and waved to a scattering of applause and boos. When Bones looked around for Jill, she had already gone.

CHAPTER 27

Two days after the race Tony Ears called Bones up on his cell phone. Bones was sitting in his breakfast nook nursing a second cappuccino while idly scanning the sports pages of the *L.A. Times*. He was planning to leave in about twenty minutes to meet with a lawyer about finalizing his deal with Ester Gale Dinworthy, and he wasn't really in the mood to talk to anyone about Tumultuous, much less Tony "Ears" Capestro. Still, there wasn't much he could do about it; you don't hang up on guys like Tony Ears. "So, Bones, we hear you own a piece of a nice horse," the familiar grating voice murmured in his ear. "That so?"

"Yeah, that's so, Tony," Bones answered. "How are you, Tony? Long time no hear."

"I was away for a while. You didn't know about it?"

"I'm out of the loop, Tony."

"Yeah. Well, they got me on a bullshit concealed weapons charge," he said. "Two and a half to four they give me, but I'm out in twenty months. I've been a good boy."

"Glad to hear it, Tony. So what can I do for you?"

"We was thinking maybe you could cut us in on this one."

"In what way?"

"You know, sell us a piece of the action."

"There's no action, Tony. And anyway it's too late."

"It's never too late, Bones; you ought to know that. And what do you mean there's no action?"

"The horse is hurt real bad, Tony. It'll be at least a year, maybe more to bring him back, and it's only fifty-fifty he'll make it back at all.

281

Right now the horse is worth nothing. And besides I sold my share in him."

Tony thought that one over before answering, then said, "You're kidding me, right?"

"Why would I kid you, Tony? I know better than that. This old Dinworthy broad, she already owned two-thirds of him. Before the race I told her I'd sell her my third back. Now my third ain't worth much, but a deal's a deal."

"How come? What made you do that?"

"It's not my scene, Tony," Bones explained. "I got another life out here now. And it's got nothing to do with owning horses. One more race like this one and I could have a fucking heart attack."

"You don't want that to happen, right?"

"No."

"Still, you did all right with this one."

"Yeah, I did."

"How good?"

"Maybe about seventy-five big ones net."

"Chump change, Bones. You want me to believe that?"

"Let me explain something to you, Tony," Bones said, slowly and carefully, so there'd be no misunderstanding on the point. "This is a nice horse, Tony, but even if he does get back to the races, he ain't going to be what he was before. The injury is too serious. He's got a hairline fracture of the cannon bone and a slightly torn left suspensory. They don't come all the way back from them kinds of injuries. Point two, Tony, this horse is a gelding. He's got no value as a stud, which is where the big bucks are. I'm getting out while the getting is good. I triple my investment, see, and I'm out of all the future shit that can go wrong, plus all the vet and stable bills over the next year or more."

"You ain't shitting me, Bones?"

"Tony, these animals are as fragile as glass. A thousand things big and small can go wrong with them and usually do. The vet bills are huge and all the time they keep on eating good. It costs a minimum of two, three grand a month to keep 'em in training, maybe a little less to lay 'em up and then maybe they never come back and then you're stuck with twelve hundred pounds of worthless flesh. You get what I'm saying? I'm a horseplayer, Tony, not a fucking charity. I don't need the aggravation. I got a good life out here, I've made some dough, I got a nice girlfriend, I'm going to go back to being a jocks' agent, if I can find the right client. And that's about it, Tony."

There was a long pause at the other end and Bones waited, then Tony said, "Well, Bones, I got to talk this over with the Family. Maybe you could toss a few bucks our way, right?"

"Find me a good charity, Tony, and I'll make a contribution."

Another pause. "Okay, how about Father Caminetti's church in Trenton. Know the one I mean?"

"Yeah, I do. He runs a sports program for the neighborhood kids, right?"

"Yeah. And he's my cousin, remember? Silvio?"

"Sure."

"He'll see to it the money gets to the right people."

"Yeah, I'm sure he will. I hope the kids get some of it."

"We'll take care of it, Bones. Say twenty-five big ones?"

"That's pretty steep, Tony."

"You'll get some papers to sign, get a nice tax deduction."

"Okay, but that's it, Tony. Is that a deal?"

"It ain't written in stone like Moses," he said, "but yeah, count on it."

"You've always been straight with me, Tony, and me with you. Let's keep it that way. No more phone calls."

He didn't answer but hung up. Bones figured what the hell, what was twenty-five thou to him now? He was out of everything; he was back to his life. A good deal, he figured.

The lawyer he went to see in downtown Pasadena later that morning had all the right papers for him to sign, which he did, but only after a close reading of the fine print that took him over an hour. These fucking lawyers had mastered a way of writing absolutely dedicated to masking simple truths. But this document was fairly straightforward; it simply assigned his share of the horse over to Ester Gale Dinworthy for twenty thousand, exactly what he'd paid originally. It was a hell of a good deal, all things considered, and he was out of the game for good.

***

Not much went right for Jake's barn the rest of that meet and well into the first month of Hollywood Park. Abernathy's good two-year-old came down with a bad cough that developed into a lung infection and had to be taken out of training, and none of Jake's other horses won a race. Strangest of all, despite her great effort on Tumultuous in the Santa Anita Derby, Jill failed to get many more mounts to ride. Even the Logans, who liked her despite being basically old California hands, put her up only on their worst animals. And from Steve Bullion nothing came her way. Bones had been trying to help her out by unofficially hustling mounts for her, but except for Julie Krone no woman rider seemed to be acceptable to the good old boys on the Southern California circuit. Still, Bones kept trying and eventually did get her put up on a winner, for a good young trainer named Ike Levine, newly moved out to California from the Maryland tracks. He promised he'd use Jill again, but he didn't have a big string, maybe eight or nine horses, none of them potential champions.

Jill and Bones got to talking about her situation one night over dinner at the Italian joint in Pasadena. She told him she was basically happy with her life and grateful to both Jake and him for what they'd done for her. She was still going to therapy sessions and she felt she'd really learned a lot about herself; she was sure now that she had a good solid grip on her personal needs and desires. Neither Everett nor Furman had tried to contact her, but she was certain she could have dealt with it if they had. What she didn't have, she said, was the kind of career she wanted. "And what's that?" Bones asked her.

"I'm a race rider," she said. "It's what I need to do more than anything. Nothing else matters as much to me, Sal. You know what I'm talking about?"

"Yeah, I guess," he said. "You're an athlete; you're a competitor.

It doesn't go away, does it?"

"No, it don't. See, I get up on a horse's back and it's like I'm a whole different person. All that power, all that desire under me, the feeling you get when this animal moves, makes his run. It's … it's better than anything, Sal. Maybe I can't explain it to you. I ain't got the words."

"Yeah, you do. You just did explain it." He leaned back in his chair and looked at her in the dim candlelight of the small room, almost empty now of other diners. "So why don't you get the hell out of here and go back East? The fact you're a woman won't count as bad against you back there. Gets you away from all the trouble you've been through back here. And when High Jinks comes back and maybe Sammy, you know Jake'll call for you."

"Yeah, he said he would."

"You talked this over with him?"

"Yeah, he agrees. He says he'll send me to Mort Jones. He's a top agent in New York."

"I know Mort. He's good, very good. He said he'd take you on?"

She nodded, then looked away from him. "I hate to go," she said, "but I got to. If I stay here, nothing's going to happen." She looked back at him, her eyes suddenly full of tears.

"Hey," he said, "knock it off, kid. You're an athlete, remember? You're a pro."

She leaned across the table and kissed him on the cheek. "Yeah, Sal, I'll be back for High Jinks, maybe for Sammy."

***

Jill never did come back, and that was the last time she and Bones ever spoke to one another. Jake would hear from her and keep Bones posted, and her name kept cropping up in the *Racing Form* as well. Thanks to Mort Jones she was getting a lot of mounts at Aqueduct, then at Belmont, and was winning her share of races for a number of different trainers. By the time the horses went to Saratoga she had moved into the top ten in the jockey standings at Belmont. She was planning to come to Del Mar for High Jinks' first race, but at the last moment the colt came down with another ailment and had to be taken out of training again. So she went on riding at Saratoga, finished that meet ninth in the standings, and went on to the Belmont fall meet. Jake continued to hear regularly from her, maybe once a week, and would pass her news along to Bones. She had been accepted by her peers, she had fans who wrote her letters and e-mails, she was reported to have begun dating a young computer guy who was part-owner of one of the horses she'd won with. She had made it; everything was going right for her.

Which was why it was such a shock to everyone when she went down. The horse she was riding, a cheap claimer breaking from the one hole on a track slick and treacherous from three days of cold rain, fell on the turn for home, his left front leg shattered. Jill was hurled to the ground, her head striking the inner rail, her helmet knocked away. She'd been making a move on the inside at the time and was in mid-pack, so that when she fell the horse directly in back of her couldn't avoid her. A hoof struck her on the right side of her skull and she was killed instantly. Three horses also died; it was the worst spill in New York racing history.

Jake spent the next few days moving like a ghost around his barn, not speaking to anyone except Eduardo and refusing even to call his clients. When the work around his string was over every morning, he'd shut himself inside his tack room, sit at his desk, and stare at the walls. Then he'd go home, feed his dogs and The Boston Kid, spend every evening inside his house or standing outside, looking at the old gelding Maria had loved so much. His only consolation during this period was the continued good news about Tumultuous, who apparently was doing well on the farm, putting on weight and giving every sign of one day being able to come back to the track. He tried not to think too much about Jill, but it was as much her image as Maria's that now haunted his sleep.

As for Bones, he'd never been a religious guy. He'd been baptized and raised a Catholic, of course, but had never gone to church and basically doubted very much there was any kind of god. If there had been, he reasoned, he wouldn't have let shit like this happen. But one night after Jill's death he went to a small church in West Hollywood. He sat in a back pew for maybe an hour trying to get his mind around what had happened to Jill. He even lit a candle for her. Like most dedicated athletes, she had burned, he realized, with a quiet, true flame of desire. And she'd paid for it, but by doing at last what she loved best. That was more than most people could claim. So maybe she was lucky, he told himself.

He went to the races at Santa Anita the next day but sat by himself in a seat high up in the grandstand, away from everybody, and picked five winners. Go figure. Maybe Stats had it right: The best you could hope for in life was a dead heat.

The End

ABOUT THE AUTHOR

Villiam Murray enjoyed a distinguished career as a novelist, journalist, and playwright. He wrote for thirty years for *The New Yorker*, mainly as a contributor of "Letters from Italy." Two of his books on Italy—*Italy: The Fatal Gift* and *The Last Italian: Portrait of a People*—were selected by *The New York Times* and the American Library Association as Notable Books of the Year. His translations of the plays of Luigi Pirandello continue to be produced all over the United States.

Photo by Alice B. Murray

He wrote four nonfiction books and nine novels about the world of horse racing in addition to *Dead Heat*. Among them are *Tip on a Dead Crab*, *When the Fat Man Sings*, *The King of the Nightcap*, *The Getaway Blues*, and *A Fine Italian Hand*. Several of these were also Notable Books of the Year. Two novels, *The Sweet Ride* and *Malibu*, were produced for a feature film and a TV miniseries, respectively. Several of his articles have appeared in best-of-the-year collections, and he was awarded the LOLA (Local Author Lifetime Achievement) award in 2002 by the San Diego Library Association.

Mr. Murray died in March 2005 before publication of *Dead Heat*.